Ian Wedde was born in 1946. He is the author of five
novels, a dozen collections of poetry and two collections
of essays, as well as edited anthologies and art catalogues.
His work has been praised for the vigour of its language
and the wide scope of its ideas. His first novel, *Dick
Seddon's Great Dive*, was awarded a National Book
Award for fiction in 1976 and was briefly notorious
when a sex scene in it was discussed in the House of
Representatives. In 1986, *Symmes Hole* established him
as a major voice in Pacific fiction; the novel was hailed in
the *NZ Listener* as 'a remarkable and even triumphant
achievement'. His recent satirical novel, *The Viewing
Platform* (2006), was described as 'satire with bite, but
also cunning narrative' (*Dominion Post* picks for 2006).
Chinese Opera is Wedde's fifth novel; the book's central
character, the gangster Little Frank, is his most complex
and disturbing creation to date.

CHINESE OPERA

Ian Wedde

Victoria University Press

TE WHARE WĀNANGA O TE ŪPOKO O TE IKA A MĀUI

VICTORIA
UNIVERSITY OF WELLINGTON

VICTORIA UNIVERSITY PRESS
Victoria University of Wellington
PO Box 600 Wellington
vuw.ac.nz/vup

National Library of New Zealand Cataloguing-in-Publication Data

Wedde, Ian.
Chinese opera / Ian Wedde.
ISBN 978-0-86473-5850
I. Title.
NZ823.2—dc 22

Published with the assistance of a grant from

creative
nz
ARTS COUNCIL OF NEW ZEALAND *TOI AOTEAROA*

Printed by Astra Print

If the rich could hire other people to die for them, the poor could make a wonderful living.

Yiddish proverb

Quanti ho visto morire per me!

Princess Turandot,
in *Turandot* by Giacomo Puccini,
libretto Adami & Simoni,
Act 3 Scene 1

Though the tortoise blessed with magic powers lives long,
Its days have their allotted span;

Though winged serpents ride high on the mist,
They turn to dust and ashes at the last

Cao Cao (Emperor Wu) (155–220),
'Though the Tortoise Lives Long'

Part One

THE PLACE

I, 'Little Frank' with a capital 'L', was born of circumstances that we'll get back to shortly. Little baby Frank with a little 'l' was delivered by his teenage mother under the routinely professional care of Wellington Public Hospital on 11 September 1971. Thirty years later this would be a momentous day. It would be Little Frank's thirtieth birthday. It would be the day Hokkaido left me. It would also be the start of the Thirty Year Terror. But the momentous day I was thinking about was another one. It was the day my mother left me. I don't remember the exact date, though she built a reminder into the PIN number she gave my KidSaver account: 1081. It was September 1981. Little Frank was, or was about to be, ten years old. I guess she figured the numbers would make it easier for me to remember my PIN. I did remember it.

'Ten eighty one.' That's what I said as I stepped off the kerb. My lucky number.

There may have been other occasions, but I didn't spot them. I'd lost the habit of looking at things and thinking, What's new? There I was jaywalking at the bad corner of Courtenay Place and Cambridge Terrace and I nearly got bowled by this driving-school car. It was on my beat down to the Chinese Opera. I was thinking ahead. In my mind I was already standing by the red plush drapes looking down at Madame Hee. It was an image I could summon because I went there often. I heard the squeal of brakes and caught a flash of this apparition in the driver's seat. It was a woman in a black cloth tube with an eye-slit. Next to her I could see the instructor's mouth working overtime. The woman was waving her hands around—beautiful, young, rich, slender hands with loose wrists emerging from the dark sleeves. She had gold bangles. I saw her eyes, unnaturally wide in the slit of her headgear. Then the car jerked past me and straightened up. Its dynamo let out an anxious, over-excited whine as it accelerated. I heard myself make a noise just like it. The jostling rickshaws were tooting their squeezy horns, and I made a noise like one of them too.

I guess it was a taste of what it's going to be like to have aged. What got to me was spotting for the first time in years that things had changed around here. That black cloth tube with eye-slits—it nearly killed me. And it brought me back to life. A stutter of images went jerkily across my mind. The place where my mother's neck became her shoulder. A tear rolling out of my Uncle Geek's pee-coloured eye. Video game in the dusty sunlight at the back of Geek's junk shop: a pirate ship like a crimson and gold dragon with rocket launchers and flame throwers. Tusk-grazed shoulder of Halo Jones in a 2000 AD comic. Someone's voice saying, 'Take the low-hanging fruit first.'

I stood there while people enjoyed going for their horns and making various 'you-die-now' hand gestures. I felt the power kick through me again. I turned and walked on into the racket of the street traders in Courtenay Place. I looked at the whole scene as though it was brand new—the crowded, makeshift apparatus of it that every day jostled for advantage, the old shipping containers with generators and fridges, their weathered satellite dishes. If I'd been dreaming, I'd just woken up. If I'd been awake, I was dreaming now. Either way, it was new again. What's that supposed to mean when you're a hundred and twenty years old?

Wet liver lips under a scarlet Guan Gong mask. Amethyst eyes in the mask. The moist siss of a voice: 'But ah—the future!' Dull aluminium sheen of tepid seawater with floating plastic junk. Amber eyes of junk-shop teddy bears. Crimson dragon wrapper of Double Happy firecrackers.

Then the mental stutter stopped. I was holding on to the edge of a stall.

This kid was looking at me. He'd have been in his twenties and he had the unhealthy, dry complexion of someone who spent a lot of time on the street. He had a breathing mask folded back under his chin, the elastic band under his long, dirty hair at the back. He was wearing a sleeveless tee-shirt that had 'Just Hack It' screenprinted on the front. I read the shirt. My eyes followed the text and I think my mouth shaped the words. In the past I wouldn't even have noticed it. The kid's upper arms were skinny and almost unmuscled, like tubes. One of them had a snake tattoo around it. The snake was green and red and it looked limp, like the arm it was coiled around.

The kid's flip-open portmanteau probably had wrist-watches or phones in it, and he'd have been flogging them for a commission. He represented the bottom of the Place's commercial pyramid. Some traders were down there because they couldn't be anywhere else. Others were there because they preferred it. The kid was one of the last sort. He had a swagger not a cringe in his manner. He smiled at me—not the way he would have if he'd wanted me to buy whatever was inside his vinyl folder, but as if he knew me. He had a stainless-steel tooth in the top of his mouth at the front. It was incised with a cross. It was like being come on to by a junkie evangelist.

'What?' I wanted to know. I was embarrassed at getting caught reading his shirt.

'You okay, Pops?'

Some of the other stall-minders and peddlers down that end of the Place were also looking at me. It was as though they and the peddler with the tooth recognised me. I discovered that I knew why but had stopped thinking about it.

The kid flipped his mask up over his mouth and nose, and shrugged. The gesture wasn't unfriendly or indifferent but almost respectful. I had to ask myself why that should be so. Again, I knew.

11

'What?' I asked, spreading my arms at the watching crowd.

Some of them smiled and waved. Others turned back to their business. Yet this wasn't a place where an old bugger like me got noticed. It was going flat out and no one had time to take their eyes off the transaction at hand. The kid with the mask was leaning against a booth a little way off, watching. He made a gesture like a salute, touching his forehead with two fingers. It was between respectful and amused. I lifted my hand to him, feeling I should acknowledge his concern. He immediately turned away and faded into the crowd the way you can if you spend a lot of time down there.

The way he did it was like another little shock—familiar, as though I'd always known it, but also new, as though it'd been years since I'd seen anyone turn sideways like that and fold themselves back into the mob. First, the face becoming a profile, then the profile slicing itself an exit into the mass of masked faces. I hesitated there, feeling the hard air scrape its way into my chest, hearing the cranky whumping of the generators and the sound of voices all pitched to cut through the racket. I wanted to follow the kid with the watches or whatever they were, to ask him why he cared. At the same time I felt my schedule to get to the Opera tugging me that way. I could sense that people nearby were watching me without making their attention obvious. They weren't interfering. That seemed to be about respect as well. I knew why again, but had stopped expecting it. I'd stopped noticing that respect was still paid me.

I was standing there with my arms spread, repeating a silent, 'What?' No one wanted to answer my question. They were looking the other way. I didn't even bother fighting my usual way through the crowd to the Chinese Opera down there at the Oaks. Instead I took a turn south into the Barbary Coast and went to visit Mack.

I like Mack because she's made a virtue out of blurring the distinction between what's original and what isn't. That's been my niche in the universe. I feel at home with Mack. I also like Mack's galah, Boy. Boy chews away on his black tongue and then he says, 'Graaw, bitch!'—a perfect transvestite shriek, followed by a funny little click in his throat like a mike being switched off.

Boy was working his way across the roof of his cage. When he saw me come in he went, 'Bitch, click,' and watched me upside down with his tongue poking out. Mack looked pretty similar, hair all stuck up in a crest, tongue out a bit, peering at me half cockeyed over the back of the sofa.

'Well, Frank,' she croaked. 'And what's the meaning of this? Got our schedules crossed with Fast Pizza?'

At that moment Mack's security bell went again. It played a sonorous ecclesiastical Byzantine hymn with vibrating Russian voices. She pranced across to admit a pizza-delivery man. He was wearing a pointy hat shaped like a black olive, and epaulettes made to resemble melted mozzarella cheese. I'd seen the outfit hundreds of times, but now I had to stare. Everything had a new look and sound—even Mack.

'What's the matter with your friend?' grizzled the man to Mack as he slid the pizza into Boy's cage. I got the impression it'd been a while since he'd wondered how he looked. 'Doesn't he know any other parrots?' he asked, giving me the evil glare and adjusting his pointy black olive hat.

I just had to go back from there a few steps. Nothing had been this vivid for years. I was staring at Boy as he tore the topping off his pizza. The man with mozzarella epaulettes was staring at me. Mack was staring at the ceiling and rolling her inflamed eyeballs.

I pictured myself on the other side of Mack's door, on the landing by the dusty plastic avocado plant in a pot. Mack had a card pinned there with some gnomes on it and an inscription that read, 'Heigh ho heigh ho it's off to work we go.' The gnomes were marching in single file, each of them reaching around to hold the outsize dick of the gnome in front. There were bulgy toadstools shaped like body parts on the card as well, and a leering sun grabbing the pointy end of a sickle moon. I'd always understood Mack's key professional theme was pirates, but since I'd hardly noticed the gnomes for a while this anomaly hadn't occurred to me. There was a video surveillance camera in a bracket above Mack's door. It was so obviously fake that no one had bothered to tuck the wires back into it when they'd come loose years ago. This, too, I noticed afresh. The doormat outside Mack's place read, 'Home is where the tart is.'

No particular reason why I should have remembered this tacky stuff. But even it was vivid to me as I took my refreshed awareness back through the morning. I pictured myself on the fringe of the Barbary Coast, by the Chinese Opera there at the Oaks. I'd gone down that way without entering the Opera. I'd jumped my schedule and I had to remember why. Expectationers didn't switch—didn't switch and didn't know they didn't. But I had and I did.

Boy was holding a black olive in one foot and scissoring the flesh off it with his curved beak. 'Graaw bitch, click.'

The pizza guy was leaving. 'Better keep an eye on this bozo, Mack,' he said bitterly from the door.

'Oh, Frank's a friend,' said Mack from the sofa. 'He's been around. He knows the score.'

The man said something like, 'Single digits,' as he walked out, but I wasn't paying attention to his bad manners. He plucked the shiny seat of his pants out of his arse-crack as he went. I didn't take the opportunity to tell him he lacked grace in general, and in respect of his manners in particular. I was mentally backtracking through the crowds up Courtenay Place. They were all there, all the regulars, defending their patches. I saw that I didn't even stop—Little Frank didn't, not once. I wouldn't have noticed when someone called my name. 'Hey, Frank . . . ! Effendi!' It would've been Gabber. He'd have had a cup of coffee ready for me, and an argument all set to go based on some media misinformation or other. I'd probably walked past him. What had happened with the purdah woman with lovely wrists and astonished eyes and with the young guy with a Christian false tooth—this had been pushing me forward, away from my beat.

14

Expectationers didn't 'walk past' the regular stops on their tracks and didn't know they didn't. But I had and I did. This wasn't like Little Frank, oh no. In all the long years I'd operated out of Courtenay Place, in all the years I'd been the boss of the Place, I don't think I'd once walked past Gabber, or anyone else. Such behaviour wasn't in Little Frank's character. I can say this, because some things you do and don't know that you do them. You pick your nose on the bus. You mutter your little mantra: 'Ten eighty one.' Some other things you do out of mindless habit. But some things, even those that are most like old habits, you do knowing that you do them. Courtesy that declares itself to be specific. Anger that is specific and directed. You do these things deliberately. You watch yourself do them and you make yourself do them. They are parts of the character you build for yourself. They are parts of that character's discipline, its power, its leadership and authority.

In Courtenay Place I knew, and it would have been said, Little Frank never walked past an associate, or anyone, except the lowest deadshits. And he didn't class them as deadshits because they lived on the street in reduced circumstances. He did so because they'd clearly demonstrated that they were deadshits. In any case, many of them lived above the street and weren't encountered down there. If Little Frank walked past anyone, you could bet your life it was a certified deadshit. I had an eye for the real thing, as for the fake. I was quality control. I could tell the difference. Everyone said so.

What that grubby young trader's two-finger salute told me was that this ability, my character, was remembered down in the Place. It was me who'd forgotten. I didn't know I'd stayed in character all those years. I'd been acting myself. Then I woke up.

Back at Mack's place that momentous day, a thought began to nag at me. It had to do with Madame Hee at the Chinese Opera. What was the difference between those elaborate, masked characters and the Madame Hee inside them who I felt reaching out urgently to my trader's appraisal? What was I missing? Why did she compel me? Looking at Mack's ruined make-up made me realise how little Mack hid. Why, despite my skills, couldn't I crack Madame Hee's codes? Why did the need to do so obsess me? Why was my Expectationer's life of thoughtless habit centred on this painted singer at the Chinese Opera? Why was Little Frank even bothering with these thoughts?

That day I nearly got bowled off my track down to the Opera and woke up to my surroundings was also the day I lost my habitual grip on the character I'd made for myself. A gap opened up. It wasn't just the kid with the cross-engraved silver tooth who saw me. I saw myself. And Mack saw something different too. She was giving me a fishy look.

Boy was swiping gluey cheese off his beak against the bars of his cage and Mack was staring at me over the back of the sofa. The place smelled professionally sordid—of other people's cigarettes, alcohol, melon- or peach-scented lubricants, the operating-theatre acridness of specialist pharmacology, the clean smell of very bad habits.

'You all right, Frank? Shall I turn the radio on? You want to listen to the shopping report?'

'I'm sorry, Mack,' I said, ignoring her sarcasm. 'I nearly got skittled earlier by a Moslem. A learner driver. It's made me think.' I replayed the moment when the black cloth tube with the eye-slit had stopped, flung forward over the steering wheel of the car, the instructor's mouth going crazy, those beautiful hands waving, thin gold bands flashing against the loose sleeves. Then, the shriek of the accelerating dynamo. My own demeaning shriek.

'Well, what have *they* got on you?'

'Who, who got on me?'

'The Moslems.' Mack sized me up. 'But I'd have to ask, which Moslems, Frank?'

'Just this Moslem woman in a learner-driver car. We're not talking fatwa, Mack, for Christ's sake.'

Mack was staring at me with a pissed-off look. 'This may mean something to you, Frank, but you've got me beat. Have you lost some time, Frank?'

'No, Mack,' I said. 'It's just like I told you. This woman in a burqua nearly bowled me in an Apple School car down by Courtenay Place there.'

'"You can make a fresh start with your final breath," Bertold Brecht,' quoted Mack, lowering her puffy mascara'd eyelids at me. She was full of surprises like that.

'No, Mack,' I said again, crankily. I wasn't sounding like myself. I felt like the pizza guy, aware of my own absurdity. I felt like I was picking my crack, undignified. 'It wasn't the narrow-squeak aspect. It was seeing this woman in one of those black cloth tubes with an eye-slit.'

'Christ, Frank,' said Mack in her rusty voice. She sat up straight. She was in her old peignoir with the coiling dragons on it. She had a heavy stubble with talc trapped in it. Her siliconed bottom lip was looking petulant, and her hair was like the galah Boy's crest in a high wind. She went into full Mack performance mode. 'There's Red Indian war bonnets down there, Frank,' she yodelled. 'People with bones through their noses. On Saturdays you can see those Hassidim in fur hats. Sundays all the Chinese are going in there for yum char. There's Fijian taukei warriors down there've revived ritual cannibalism, Frank, while they study engineering, Frank. What's so special about some straight little sheikette— they're everywhere, man.' Mack struck a pose, her body a stout question mark.

'Settle down, Mack,' I said. 'I know. But I'd stopped noticing them. I was just walking through it. I was going down to the Opera every other day. Just doing the numbers, Mack, just routine.'

But this is exactly what Expectationers do and don't know they do. I saw this thought in Mack's bloodshot eyes. 'Well, Frank,' she said after a pause, during which we listened to Boy stropping his beak on the cage and tearing up the pizza dough. 'Seems a bit late for you to be having one of these crises. Hardly "mid-life", Frank. What are you now, slipped a digit?'

'Well and truly,' I said. 'One hundred and twenty.'

'Well, there you go,' croaked Mack, slumping back on her sofa. She was thinking this through. 'You'll pull out of it. You've got the experience. You've got the years.' She was trying to seem bored now.

And that was about it for Mack, that day. We sat around for a bit while she told rough-trade stories and complained. But she kept looking at me hard when she thought I wasn't watching. I kept catching her at it. We kept giving each other these little 'Why-are-you-looking-at-me-like-that?' signals. She was on full alert and she didn't want me to spot it. I told myself it was nice to know she cared. But it was creepy as well, because I don't think I'd had any notion of people being aware of me for donkey's years. Now I was seeing myself as a kind of fixture. Set your watch by Little Frank. Figure out the points of the compass by his position along his track. Know the seasons by his coat, his haircut, his summer Panama or winter fedora hat. His cosy Pashmina muffler or loose Venetian silk scarf. His light summer cane with the greenstone knob or the wet autumn one with the rubber foot. Is he wearing dark glasses? Is the sunshine bright? Know when to wake and when to sleep—or perhaps not.

The sheikette's gold-bangled wrists, windsurfers flying up into the blue at the Raglan bar, Chou clown mask on the face of the goon before my shotgun blast made his head fly off like a swarm of red bees—and Madame Hee, Madame Hee. The flicker of images was hard work in my mind astonished by wakefulness. I had to hold my thoughts down. The effort made my face ache. 'Ten eighty one. Ten eighty one.' Trying not to say this aloud.

Then Mack had to get shaved and brighten herself up, so I left. Boy watched me with his head on one side, but he didn't say anything. From the landing, by the picture of the gnomes, I could hear Mack at her big mirror shrieking her catch-cry: 'Demolition *derby*, baby!'

Once, years ago, when Mack was still young and before his nip and tuck, he used to hustle around the grubbier joints up what passed for the Barbary Coast. Then it was an amateurish zone where squads of politely pissed Korean and Taiwanese squidders would get a bit rowdy sometimes. Mostly it was where sad middle-class sacks would converge after big football games to watch exotic dancers fire hardboiled eggs along the bar. Mack was a big kid, he had shoulders on him like a lock forward, hands like legs of hogget dangling off forearms that looked short because they were so thick. But he was a girl. He said he'd always been a girl and that he'd watched his body turn into the dark, hairy hunk it was with grief at first, but next with an attitude you didn't want to encounter on a bad day.

On such a day, Mack was sitting having a cold beer at the bar of one of the Coast's daytime sports joints. It usually filled up with blokes who preferred to yell at the ref in a pub. Mack was wearing his red dress; he'd kicked his high heels off and was resting his big brown bare feet on the rail below the bar. A beefy guy with a sculpted moustache had got brave on vodka shots with beer chasers. He made the mistake of giving the huge kid in the red dress some cheek. The way I heard it when they brought Mack over to my place, the guy ended up head-down in the Cuba Street fountain. The spear tackle that Mack administered broke his neck. That seemed like a good time to turn Mack into herself.

'Here's what I owe you, Frank,' Mack had said more than once. 'Myself. As long as myself is alive and kicking, Frank, Mack owes you.' This had been a source of comfort to me. It was comfort based on a gift of life I understood better than the comfort I had from the children I'd fathered, love them as I had done.

Outside, late-morning sun shone down through dust between the buildings, golden light. In such light even the crumbling buildings could look grand. I suddenly felt good, leaving Mack's place. Little Frank was back in business. I didn't know what the business was, but I was looking forward to it. It had been a while since I'd 'looked forward' to anything other than my Expectations. Them, and Madame Hee down at the Chinese Opera.

One day not long after this I came out into my own neighbourhood and it was full of Greeks. They were driving past in large cars. Mothers were holding their kids up. The kids, in frilly bonnets, wobbled their spoiled faces against the windows. Their fathers, grandfathers, older brothers or uncles rested their owner's elbows on the driver's window ledge. Gold chains glinted against their hairy chests.

Noticing the Greeks wasn't another major episode. I just hadn't registered them. Now I began to see overweight Greek fathers puffing across the hilly streets of my neighbourhood, shepherding their sons and daughters with soccer balls or beach towels. While their kids biked on expensive new toys, they'd be strolling along the big reinforced sea wall above Evans Bay, sometimes with their womenfolk, sometimes in loud-mouthed manly groups.

In the delicatessen at the top of the hill, by the big old run-down Gateways apartment block, responses to the Greek presence caught my eye. The olives, feta cheese, pickled vine leaves, filo pastry and gooey cakes had been there for decades. For generations, youths with the mousey beginnings of moustaches had been blowing their cigarette smoke into the gusty wind that whipped paper napkins away from the little tables on the footpath. They'd looked lasciviously at their prospective brides and the mothers of their future children when they got off the bus there. I'd watched them become the portly fathers who would later shepherd their plump, peach-faced kids down to the beach. I'd watched their scruffy moustache fluff turn into jowly stubble. I'd watched the fat jowly guys glare at the over-sexed youths who were hoping the wind would lift the skirts of girls descending from the bus—the girls who would one day be their daughters, whom they'd protect from the lewd attentions of the kids smoking on the footpath outside the deli.

But I hadn't noticed. Like the nose on your face, you take what's in front of you for granted. And then, one day, you feel the air going in and out of it. Your own breathing feels like an amazing accomplishment.

The Greeks weren't even noteworthy. Nor was their food. It was just there where it was needed. And above it were these lines of ordinary Asian washing hanging off the rusting balconies of the old Gateways apartments with pigeon coops for edible birds on the roof and a wet market with live chickens, big plastic trays of bony herring and half a dozen food stalls under open corrugated-iron sheds where the school used to be down on the promontory.

My kids went to school there. Where the Asian wet market is.

For days I walked around feeling like a tourist in my own city—gaping at the obvious. I didn't visit anyone for a while. I didn't even go down to the Opera. I just went around looking. It was fascinating to me that people were doing shopping in places like the Gateways wet market. I watched with amazement as they pinched the breasts of trussed, dopey chickens. The place where a skinny Chinese guy in outsize shorts rattled sacks of shellfish into wide plastic bins filled me with nostalgia for memories I didn't know I'd had. It wasn't that I'd forgotten the night my daughter, taking part in the school's Christmas production on the site of the rattling shellfish, had executed a too-enthusiastic ballet leap across the stage and disappeared with a crash into the spare chairs in the wings. I hadn't forgotten how the audience had gasped first with shock and then immediately begun both to laugh and to repress its laughter—the choking and snorting of polite restraint. I hadn't forgotten, either, the appalled, dead silence that fell when Little Frank stood up from the front row to go and see how Bella was. It was as though these memories, the nap and substance of my reality, which I'd been accustomed to rub and heft with the knowing touch of a trader, had gone vague. The memories had faded into an unremarkable effect like daylight. Who notices daylight? You'll answer: the person who's lived in a dark cellar and forgotten what daylight looks like. But that wasn't me. I woke up to—I re-entered—something I'd been in all along. It was as though I'd spent my life in daylight only to realise, one day, that it was bright. I didn't so much get memories back as remember that these vague effects *were* memories. I stood in the wet market, an old man crying at the vividness of little Bella's crash landing offstage, while the Chinese bloke ignored me. I was also hooting into my handkerchief because I hadn't felt emotion like this for years. Hadn't felt anything and didn't know I hadn't.

What I realised, in the days after the sheikette near-miss, was that there was a trade-off for using Expectations. I'd known there would be side-effects and that they differed from person to person. But once I was inside the side-effects I stopped being conscious of them. Now I realised that my uptake had thinned out across the extra time. My feelings and perceptions were thin. It must've been something like that for most of us. Can I bring myself to say it? 'Us Expectationers'.

In my own neighbourhood it was rich Greeks in the substantial hillside houses and not-so-well-off Asians in the Gateways building that had filled up the spaces hollowed out by memories I'd forgotten I had, or had forgotten were memories. But elsewhere other populations had flooded whole city precincts, just as the sea had in reclamations when things hotted up. And I saw that everyone now took these population floods for granted. As they did the invading water. My astonishment belonged to a former time. When I'd been walking around in my Expectationer's fog, I'd resembled everyone else. Now my tears on the ghostly site of the school hall in the middle of the busy wet market alarmed the shellfish guy. My unnerving vigil where the randy Greek kids ogled each other's sisters made them glare, shuffle and light cigarettes. Where Little Frank had gone reliably

22

unnoticed for years, he now had visibility again. But not the visibility of his days as the Sheikh of Courtenay Place, the guy who'd remember your favours or slights. Now I saw how Frank was the funny old bozo who did laughing, crying and staring. Now I thought that people pointed me out not in order to say, Don't mess around with *him*, but to wonder, What's come over that Expectationer who lives by himself in the big house? The one who used to run the whole show, that they call Little Frank? To be honest, I didn't know what they thought. But I saw myself and I saw them seeing me too.

Lots of these populations I was noticing were people with historical refugee status. Now they all seemed at home. It was me who found my home strange. A lot of them had overflowed from one filled-up place to another—from Hong Kong, Singapore, Bangladesh, Somalia, the Pacific Islands. They'd just moved along. Some of them were running those floating restaurants in Oriental Bay. I could remember the fuss that was made about the first one. Now rafts of them were pontooned together, three and four storeys high. Families and dinner parties got taken out there in Mogadishu fizzboats flying restaurant flags. There were neons with flashing pictures of food, and signs saying 'Rojak Tow Kua Pow Cuttlefish,' 'Ice Chee Kong' and 'Ling Chee'.

The other night, on one of my gawping tours, I stood there among the food carts and the sidewalk falafel stands, the parallel import and facsimile peddlers and taxi-touts along the giant sea wall of Oriental Bay. I looked out at the glowing restaurant island like a stack of rice steamers. It seemed to be steaming up into the sky. I could hear its distant hum and clatter and its music above the racket of the beachfront. Its jumble of flashing and scrolling neons blurred into a writhing mass like the giant dragons that performed at Chinese New Year, before the Festival of Hungry Ghosts. Further out by Matiu Island the floating casino whirled its laser-lights. They looked like the fireworks of Hungry Ghosts. The taxi-copters that rattled back and forth from the casino in the city night sky made a racket like firecrackers when they battered the air close to the tower blocks.

I never did sleep much, and being an Expectationer hadn't changed that. But these days I was sleeping even less. My mind was ratcheting away—running images and trying to stop them. One night about three in the morning I was sitting on a bench at the quieter end of the Oriental Bay esplanade. I was looking at all these rowdy pyrotechnics going on in my head and out there on the Bay. Getting my fresh take on the scene, trying to remember, when two things happened simultaneously—a now thing and a memory thing.

I saw the glow of a cigarette by the stinky garbage bins of a small seafood joint a little way off. I paid no particular attention to it. The crowds had thinned out along where I was. I looked over at the smoker in the shadow by the service entry of the restaurant, and parked a mental note that someone was there. Probably a kitchen hand having a quiet cigarette before going back in for the final hour of the night. I was looking over at the floating restaurant-dragon in the Bay and at the lasers out by the casino when I saw the spurt of flame from a cigarette lighter in the garbage-bin shadows and registered that the kitchen hand had lit another smoke.

So it was with an edge of watchful unease that I remembered how, when I was a kid, the Bay had only a freshwater fountain in it that they used to turn on for half-full buses of bored Japanese tourists. Back then you used to be able to look across the Bay at the hills on the far side. Below the dark night shapes of the hills, the city had never added up to much. Though when I was really small its lights had seemed wonderful from the lookout on Mount Victoria. Now those lights went to the skyline; the sky was too lit up or smogged for you to see stars; and the foreshore on that side of the Bay was jammed with the neons, holograms and lasers of Chinese and Japanese merchant banks and insurance companies. Their advertising screens filled the sides of the buildings. Outfits like FLOW were there too, but the place got called Toyota City just the same—the name went back a long time.

At the same time as keeping tabs on the smoker in the shadows, my mind was struggling to reel in a memory. The people who lived in the apartments zotted into floors of the insurance company and merchant towerblocks didn't drive domestic *Toyotas*. You couldn't see through the windows of the vehicles they were conveyed in. You never saw babies held up or proud hairy elbows hanging out. Cyber-joint engineering, infra-red-by-wire—those vehicles never seemed to stay in the traffic flow for long.

Little Frank rode in them more than once in the course of his business, and often enough that business was with the Binh Xuyen—the Pirates. But what I was hunting for now, with one eye on the smoker and against the backdrop of the garish Bay and the lit-up towers beyond, was the aching memory of one Binh Xuyen car ride in particular.

This one hadn't just faded back like the rest of my pre-sheikette Expectationer's memories. It seemed, rather, to be somewhat hidden—present but inaccessible. I wanted to remember when my life became the way it was. There had to be a moment when it began to be that way. There had to be a reason. I must've made a decision. When, what, why? The smoker by the fish joint lit another—the previous butt scattered sparks on the pavement where he flicked it. Gawping and out of date, my memory of my life as an Expectationer went back to one ride. I had to remember the ride. Everything since began there, in that luxurious vehicle. I had to get back in that car.

If I'd lived across the Bay, I might have woken up one day to the fact that all the neon was in Chinese or Korean. In Russian Cyrillic, for that matter. I might nearly have been skittled by one of those Mandarin ghost machines. That might have been what woke old Frank up again, instead of a rich Moslem girl with lovely wrists learning to drive up Wakefield Street.

Watched by the smoker, I was remembering how, when

the Pirate's car door opened, air that was cool and slightly minty came out. It was as though the space inside the vehicle extended into a fresh landscape with mountain pines and a crisply edged lake. This was in spite of the fact that Tamar was smoking one of his thin, dark cheroots in there. I saw the glow of its tip, and a little cloud of aromatic smoke followed the refreshing waft of air out across the footpath where my way had been politely barred by a young woman holding a hospitality flag in one hand and what looked like a cell phone in the other. Tamar's waft of smoke passed my nostrils like a low-key, tasteful brand announcement. Then the minty mountain air came back. It was invitingly fresh and cool. So was the young woman's smile. She gestured respectfully with her hospitality flag at the car's open door. I knew who was in there and I knew I had no choice but to accept his invitation to take a ride in his vehicle.

Little Frank was sixty years old then. Ten eighty one was how I measured time. Fifty years since I got my own PIN. Thirty years since the start of the Terror. Something like twenty years as the boss of the Place. I wasn't accustomed to being told what to do.

Ducking my head and smiling at the young woman as I entered the car's roomy interior, I had the sensation of going into space that was extended and secret, like the geographical dimensions of its fresh air. It was like going somewhere bigger than the cramped, hectic world outside the car's tinted windows. It was a relief. That sensation increased when the door shut. The atmosphere was dim and spacious. I heard the small sound of the cheroot being stubbed out and an ashtray closed. I looked across at the facing seat and saw that Tamar, as usual, was wearing a red mask based on the Beijing Opera's Guan Gong war god. His amethyst eyes were recessed within the shiny lacquer. The mask's black beard sat below his mouth, and he spoke formally as was no doubt appropriate for such a high-ranking Lao Sheng.

'We can put the past behind us,' he said. His lips were the colour of freshly sliced liver.

26

As soon as I remembered this during my late-night vigil down on the promenade of Oriental Bay, I felt a rush of urgency about visiting the Chinese Opera. This was something I hadn't done for days. And at that moment I stood up suddenly from my bench and may even have made a sound of some sort, a grunt or bark of surprise and recognition. I remembered getting into Tamar's car, his mask, the fresh luxury of the interior, his unhurried voice offering to put the past behind us. And that was when I saw the smoker in the shadows by the fish restaurant's garbage-disposal unit step forward. It was a man by bulk and dress, but more than that I couldn't see. He dropped his cigarette but didn't tread it out. He seemed to be on alert.

At the same moment I shocked myself by putting together my meeting with Tamar in his red Guan Gong mask and my habit of visits to the Chinese Opera, the smoker in the shadows revealed himself as my watcher. He was clearly there for me. Whether he was there to look after me or to watch me didn't matter. Even if he was someone that Mack had put on the job, which I doubted, what I knew at that moment was that I still mattered enough to be watched. Mattered enough to someone.

The little narrative that dropped into place in my head as I stood trembling and looking at the dragon of the Bay, and remembering Tamar's car, went like this. The Pirates' trademark, and especially Tamar's, was the Chinese Opera masks. He was wearing one the day we made our peace in his car. After making the truce and starting my long life as an Expectationer, I got fascinated by the masked performances at the Opera. When I 'woke up', I was being watched.

I was Little Frank. I had to remember this too. I was nobody's fool. It was hard to keep this narrative simple. It had to be as simple as ten eighty one. I needed to keep its three components intact: Tamar, Chinese Opera, surveillance. It was tempting to rush out in all directions. But this simple shape was the key to understanding what had happened. I needed to push my memory back into the conversation in Tamar's car.

I walked off along the Oriental Bay promenade and noticed that my watcher was following without making much effort to be discreet. It was as though if I'd been watched before now he hadn't expected me to notice, or as though it didn't matter. In the light of the Parade I could see that he was a big black guy with a tight furze of whiskers on his face. I saw him make a phone call using a lapel mike. He saw me looking at him and simply paused, his face expressionless, his gaze mostly somewhere else, on the crowd, the traffic, the night sky.

There was a dumb, shameful logic in my little narrative's connection between Tamar in his high-ranking Lao Sheng mask and my subsequent Expectationer's habit of frequenting the Chinese Opera. I passed over the complication of Madame Hee. My sense that something was going on down there would have to wait. I wanted to stick to my three simple components: Tamar, Opera, surveillance. What I needed to sort out in order to get back to the moment when Tamar and I had made our truce was whether this big calm black guy was watching me on behalf of the Pirates. Because if he was, then their interest—Tamar's interest, if he was still alive—went straight to the terms of the treaty we agreed in the mint-fresh interior of his car.

How did that go? Something like, Settle down, Frank. Stay away. Be peaceful. And we'll see to it that you enjoy a long and comfortable retirement. Was that how it went? I couldn't remember. The world around me was vivid again but this memory shut me out. I needed to get back in there but it was shut. I was awake, now, but this memory was a dream that slipped out of range every time I tried to get it back.

Travelling in the car was like travelling in a pine wood. I remembered that. I remembered that Tamar's smile, where the mask opened below his nose to make room for cheroot-smoking, was calm and friendly. We were alone together in the back of the long vehicle, facing each other. The driver and the young woman were behind me in the front seats, but I knew I couldn't see them if I turned around because they were sealed off behind a glass screen. We drank cool, slightly fizzy mineral water from little bottles that hissed when uncapped. This wasn't recycled or desalinated water. It tasted of piney vistas with lakes. It tasted of nowhere I'd been. Tamar fitted the neck of the bottle between the liver-coloured lips in his red mask, above its black beard. When his smile returned, it had been moistened and his voice, too, was irrigated and effortless. The violet-coloured eyes seemed wetter.

'The present, Frank—what a mess. But, ah—the future!'

The big black guy watched me approach him. He didn't move and didn't change his expression.

'Don't ask, Frank,' he said, before I could speak. 'Because you don't need to.' His voice was a pleasant one, deep and rough with smoking or yelling, maybe both. Maybe he was also a blues singer.

'And why would that be?' I asked him. My head came up to his chest, but I wouldn't crane my neck to look up. He was content to bend politely in order to speak at my level.

He didn't answer my question. 'I seen you looking around,' he said, 'all over.' And then he spoke some words in a language with nice little clicks in it. 'That's Yoruba,' he said. 'What we speak where my folks come from.' He was looking at me without expression but with a certain deference as he bent to be polite and not make me crane my neck. 'You been away a long time, Mr Frank,' he said. And then he added, as if the two statements belonged together, 'We been here a long time too, you know.'

'What say I do ask?' I said. 'What happens then? You going to tell the Pirates?'

He shook his big finger at me. Stood up again, out of the conversation, into the airspace of his own stature. He reached into his bomber-jacket pocket and took out his cigarettes. When he lit one and began to smoke it slowly, looking across the Bay at a hologram of a desert flowering and green below the tower of the water consortium called FLOW, he wasn't so much ignoring me as indicating that I was free, as before, to continue wandering about. Maybe I'd hear some Yoruba spoken next time I mounted an expedition into my home city.

But there it was. Tamar as Guan Gong, the Chinese Opera, the black guy. And the truce and its treaty. Because that was what was hidden in my memory of the car ride. In its pine-fresh space of opportunities and possibilities. I got that much.

'But ah—the future!' The sharp rim of Tamar's teeth, bright and expensive, between those purplish lips.

So Little Frank was worth watching. Even the people in the Place, whose demeanour was between watchful and discreet, had gone on thinking so. Even the kid who'd saluted me on the sheikette morning—who'd been forty years off being born the night I rode with Tamar in his pine-fresh car—had inherited this thought. If there was business to be done, then Little Frank needed to live up to their estimation. He needed to remember his guile.

I went on big reconnaissance sweeps through my home city. I walked around and rode the bus with my little plot in mind. It was my GPS. I had confidence in its three vectors. I was clear about the big fresh interior of the car where I'd reached an agreement with the Pirates. I remembered the water—a kind of taunt. I remembered the red Guan Gong mask worn by Tamar—elite Lao Sheng. These items didn't shift in my vision as they would have if I'd had doubts. I didn't feel that nausea of the fake, the copy, the simulacrum. I had no sense of what Gabber used to call decoy truths. I'd hesitate to use the word truth to describe objects recovered from a sixty-year-old trance of longevity, but I had no doubt that they were certified in their way. I was confident I'd recover the details of this memory. Patience was what I needed—patience and guile.

I went to have lunch with the polite family of Mr Qureshi, my 'domestic security' consultant. I couldn't remember the last time I'd done this.

'Why we don't see you, Mr Frank?' Mr Qureshi wanted to know. I didn't have an answer for him but I knew what it was.

'Busy, na?' said his wife. I nodded—that would have to do. Busy with repetitions that stopped me noticing how the Qureshis spoke in familiar accents but with twists and turns in their sentences that should have reminded me why they were here.

Mr Qureshi fitted his glass of water to the smile beneath his moustache. The water flowing past his teeth told the story of WW—World Water or Water Wars, depending on your position on the issue. The melted Himalayan glaciers, dam-bombing, delta catastrophes and river warfare were why his parents came here. It was the family left behind that twisted their son's speech into politely different shapes. I saw the fresh water in Mr Qureshi's glass rise into his shining, dark eyes. I thought he was about to cry, but he was too polite for that.

I sat in the nice garden at my house on the hill, where the video surveillance didn't trail the cables of fake deterrents. The celebrations and feuds of the Greeks reached me through muffling hedges and windbreaks made of thick brush. I knew the hedge concealed motion detectors and an electrified wire, because it killed cats. The gardener took them away, grinning and stiff. I ate the lunches prepared by my housekeeper, Mrs Flitch, a woman with whom I preferred to have no relationship. Before Mrs Flitch there'd been someone else, and before her another housekeeper whom I'd never paid because that was all taken care of. I'd never had a conversation with any of them. It was the solitude of my house that I liked. The lunches were salads with ingredients I recognised as fresh beyond the capacity of natural environments. The salad greens, tomatoes and bell peppers, the lightly boiled green beans, the raw carrots and heads of broccoli that I dipped in warm olive and anchovy sauce, the organic hardboiled eggs, the small servings of fresh cheese were all brought to me from the privileged zones of water-purified hydroponics or, in the case of the eggs, from 'free-range' environments recreated under climate-controlled conditions. The Mrs Flitches told me this, as though it was part of their job to make me feel lucky.

The lunches, like the aerated mineral water in the back of Tamar's car, tasted of worlds I didn't know and had never visited in person. But the visits I enjoyed through my lunches were enough to convince me that these worlds existed and were real. They came to me courtesy of my retirement plan. They belonged in Tamar's luxuriously moistened promise: 'But ah—the future!'

I'd begun to think of the lunches served by Mrs Flitch as created by the truce and its treaty—the one with the Binh Xuyen Pirates, the one I'd agreed to with Tamar a long time ago, the one I couldn't remember the detail of. I sank my teeth into the yielding cowl of a hardboiled egg. I snapped off a vividly orange bite of carrot. I stuffed a forkful of lettuce sweet with pure irrigation into my mouth. I rubbed creamy curds of cheese against the roof my mouth with my tongue and I asked these things that I'd been taking for granted for all the years of my retirement: What were the terms of the treaty that was providing my lunch? My probably not 'free lunch'? What did Tamar and I agree to? What did I trade for this housekeeper whose only speech to me was about the health of my food, this slice of tomato whose satellite fragment of pungent sweet basil endorsed the authenticity of my survival? What had I traded for this muffling hedge that seemed to be keeping someone's promise of security? That killed innocent cats? That resembled the border beyond which the Bangladeshi family of Mr Qureshi was sealed off at the mercy of World Water? What was the deal? What did I give up? What were they afraid of? And then: Who were they? And: How long since I'd cared about the misfortunes of others?

When Mrs Flitch took my plate and glass away from the table in my garden, I didn't thank her. I never did, but now I didn't because I was still interrogating my meal. I captured a bit of parsley stalk from between my expensive teeth—my lunch had been a piece of lightly seared fresh tuna—and I needed to know from it why the link between Tamar's Guan Gong mask and my habit of watching Madame Hee at the Opera by the Oaks was an impeccable link. I needed to get clear in my mind why my certainty about this impeccable link went so far past my instinct and intuition, which were in themselves considered impeccable—had themselves been considered impeccable when Little Frank's quality-controlling eye had been at work in the tricky transactions of the Place, before this time of peace and tranquillity, this 'future' that had become the endless present, the retirement plan of Little Frank, my trance, my dream, my reward—for what? And most of all I needed to know why the third component of my plot, the polite Yoruba-speaking watcher with the smoker's grain in his thick-furred voice, was keeping an eye on me.

What were they worried about, the Pirates? Had they always watched me? Were the Mrs Flitches watching me? Was my security system designed by Mr Qureshi watching me? Had they all been watching me for fully half of my unnatural life? In my garden, with the lunch plates cleared away, picking thoughts from between my teeth, Little Frank even managed to laugh. Through the french doors I saw Mrs Flitch watching me laughing out there, all by myself, as if someone else, someone invisible, was telling me jokes. Who was it? The bit of parsley stalk was telling me a joke.

Or, I wondered, picking away at my guile, were the Pirates only watching Little Frank now that I'd shown signs of waking up to something? What was I waking up to? Why did it seem that people had gone on respecting me? What didn't I know?

I thought that I might just have been losing it—that the surveillance was benign. I almost found myself saying that to Mrs Flitch one day when, after going out, I'd hopped back inside quickly to see if I could catch her reporting on my movements. 'Do you think I'm losing it, dear Mrs Flitch?' Maybe the part of my brain that lives in the Now is going soft and all I'm going to be left with is memories. But I didn't speak to her.

Mrs Flitch didn't even notice my silly behaviour as I went hopping past her kitchen door, miming fake irritation with my fake forgetfulness of something or other faked, jerking my head to see what she was up to. Or if she did notice me she treated it as normal. She was writing a shopping list in the kitchen. She had a row of household cleaners and bathroom products in bright, almost-empty plastic bottles lined up on the sink bench. I saw her lips shaping their brand-names as she entered them on her list. 'Zephyr', 'Glade', 'Savannah'. And my favourite, 'Hammam': the essence of pamplemousse and cardamom with which I infused my sauna. Then she'd phone the delivery service. I'd seen this a thousand, a million times. I'd seen my Hammam steam-bath essence replaced every month of my life since the pine-fresh treaty with Tamar. If I lined up all the empty Hammam bottles, I'd see, in a kind of brightly coloured sculpture, how far back it was that I'd forgotten what I'd committed myself to, what I'd given up for that fragrant steam.

Outside the electric fence of my present, beyond the cardamom-infused trance of my habits, Global H20 and World Water had once begat Water War. This I remembered because I'd seen a 100PC mercenary thug toss a satchel bomb into the protest mob held back by police barricades outside FLOW. He was thickset with a couldn't-care-less hoodie pulled over his face. He stepped out on to a first-floor restaurant balcony where I was enjoying the spectacle with business colleagues. His underarm chuck of the satchel was calm and practised. So was the movement with which he took out his cell phone and activated the bomb as he stepped back inside. The nails and other rubbish in the bomb sprayed through a group of school kids holding up a long banner with PURE painted on it—People United for Renewable Energy. My own business and that of my lunch colleagues was flourishing off varieties of renewal not accommodated by the PURE slogan. But the amount of blood I saw when the smoke cleared stopped me in my tracks. The kids were lying there mostly torn to bits, some moving a little, and their shredded banner had somehow fallen across many of them. Was that when hard-hearted Little Frank began to long for peace? Was that when I began to be ready to enter the Binh Xuyen limousine where my tranquil future was already drafted?

I moved on. But it wasn't so long after what got called the FLOW Incident that I was handed a chilled bottle that hadn't been filled at a communal tap in Dhaka and heard the moist siss of Tamar's voice say, 'But ah—the future!'

And now, here I was—in it.

But I doubted that I was losing my grip. We're talking about Little Frank. After my near lapse with Mrs Flitch I exercised some discipline. I went out into the city without glancing back, knowing that I'd find what I was looking for. I'd recover the terms of the understanding I'd come to with Tamar, and through him with the Pirates, sixty years ago—sixty years of Hamman-scented steam ago—in the fragrant back-seat alpine forest of his limousine. All it needed was patience, and Little Frank had always had that. I went out there with my little narrative, my GPS strategy. I set off nourished by the wholesome lunches that refused to tell me their secret. I embarked safe in the knowledge that Mrs Flitch saw my behaviour as normal. I went out to see what else had changed that everyone else but me had stopped noticing because it was just how things were, now. I'd heard the little twist of tragedy in Mr and Mrs Qureshi's polite speech. I'd seen my neighbourhood Greeks. I'd stood in the racket of the wet markets under Gateways apartments and watched shoppers pinching live fowl while I blubbered remembering Bella's balletic catastrophe. Now, I went out to hear Yoruba spoken on the streets of my city. It seemed more likely that I'd find what I was looking for in what wasn't familiar than in what was. It seemed likely—and the black watcher on the Parade had almost told me this was so—that I'd find out what I didn't know by listening to a language I didn't understand, rather than by consulting the banal oracle of my daily salad, the salad that knew everything but would only tell me, stupidly, to keep in shape—for what?

There were a whole lot of Armenians, I discovered. They had a coenobite community of recluses living in walled-off buildings attached to an ornate church. Here, they commemorated their exile by the Turks to the deserts of Syria and Mesopotamia. This is what they told me. I drank little cups of gritty coffee in the back of a shop selling carpets, cheap household implements and kitchenware made of plastic or aluminium, and refilled gas canisters like the ones people used to drive generators. The coffee tasted of cardamom and reminded me of my Hammam sauna essence. The Armenians seemed determined not to be rich, though making money was mostly what they talked about. How hard it was, here, at the end of the earth. There were lots of them bottled up on the valley-flats where the entertainment district petered out through Newtown. The men worried that their daughters were going to become prostitutes. It was clear they'd had this worry for generations, with no visible justification that I could see. The women worried that their sons would forget their roots and fail their parents in their old age. Again, this myth seemed to be without foundation, since the families were large and there seemed to be at least three generations of men involved in drinking coffee around the uneconomic shops. None of them seemed to be sure why these worries were traditional, or why they were never rich. But they were all sure about the justification for the coenobites. The coenobites' task was to commemorate an exile to the deserts of Syria and Mesopotamia. No one knew where Syria and Mesopotamia actually were, or if they still existed. They were also unsure about the location of Armenia. They hinted that it had always been somewhere else, anyway—in Turkey, in Russia, in Iran. Now it was also in New Zealand.

There was something very real about these people. A man tried to present me with an ancient gun after I'd sat at the back of his shop for a day, listening to stories and drinking so much of the sauna-scented coffee that my thighs trembled uncontrollably when I stood up to pee. It was a Kalashnikov sub-machine gun made in Russia. Why did he have it? Apparently, the gun had belonged to a family member who'd been involved in 'liberation' in the 1990s. Though not as old as the memory of the Syrian exile commemorated by the coenobites, the details of this 'liberation' seemed, now, to be lost. Perhaps that's why he wanted me to have the gun— to free his family from the responsibility for remembering the reason it mattered. He was formally sad when I politely declined. Hefting the weapon, smelling its ancient metal, reminded me that I didn't like guns. I remembered why. The guy who drove his bull-bars through the doors to my depot had a cheap Chou mask on, and cheap shoes made of car tyres. I never used the shotgun again after that. The sight of his head flying away like a swarm of red bees was a turning point.

With the Armenians I, Little Frank, began to learn that I was not alone in having to deal with difficulties in respect of memory. There was comfort in this. A sense of collective enterprise.

Some of the Armenians still spoke a language other than English, but I don't know what it was. It seemed presumptuous to assume it was 'Armenian'. The gun left a smell of rusty oil on my hands after I'd held it for a while—to show respect and to suggest that I was tempted to take it—and the coffee made my pee smell of cardamom. The man's wife kissed a little crucifix around her neck as part of her goodbye to me when I left.

I caught a cab home. It intrigued me that the Armenians were so real yet seemed unsure about where they'd come from, about why they went on fearing prostitution and ingratitude, about why they remembered an exile in the Syrian desert, about why they kept an old Russian gun.

I asked the cab driver where he came from. 'Lower Hutt,' he said. We left it at that. At home, Mrs Flitch had my supper ready. It was a half bottle of Bordeaux, a skinless breast of organic turkey and some steamed courgettes. I didn't bother to microwave the food but ate it cold, wishing I could have had dinner with the Armenians. I'd heard the sizzle of something tasty and unhealthy in the back of the shop. I felt lonely for the first time in years. I wished I could visit Mr and Mrs Qureshi again, but it was late. I found another half bottle of wine, an Australian merlot. It was labelled 'Tuesday', which was tomorrow. I drank tomorrow's wine and overslept, waking with a thick head and a bladder still bursting with Armenian caffeine. I went out again as soon as possible. I didn't shower or shave, concealing my previous day's aromas of research, frustration and loneliness under squirts of the cologne I found in my bathroom but had no memory of buying or requesting.

It seemed to me, as I looked for other strangers at home in a country where they were free to forget the details of their history, and as I listened out for languages I didn't understand, that these exiles had taken root where their history stopped. Their cases resembled mine. My exile began in the back of a luxurious limousine filled with the future promise of a pine forest. Now, I couldn't remember what I'd agreed to. But here I was.

I kept looking. In one place, on the fresher hills above the jumbled-up Armenian valley-bottom with its bad drainage and stormwater culverts that backed up against tidal bores, were quite a few Tibetan Buddhists. I joked to myself that they must have thought New Zealand was a nice place to bring up kids. My Uncle Geek, who did most of my bringing up, used to say this phrase and show his yellow beaver teeth at the contents of his second-hand junk shop in Kilbirnie. I'd have been taking a television set to bits in the corner or, some years later, furtively sorting out the quality vintage postcards to sell on the side for myself. Geek used to hang out-of-date calendars of lovely New Zealand landscape scenes in his office. When he made his usual joke about this being a nice place to bring up kids, he was likely to be positioned on a line between a glacier lake neither he nor I had visited and me in my corner, perfecting my discrimination between what was new and what wasn't, what was the genuine article and what was a fake, what retained its provenance in one way or another and what had never had a memory in the first place. The Tibetans had a building where they did amplified humming. You'd see their priests wearing headphones down in the shopping area near the Armenians. The guy I spoke to was wearing dark glasses, and he had excellent false teeth. He also had the sweetest breath I've ever encountered in a man. He was carrying a shoulder bag of early summer artichokes, big, purple, spiny ones.

'Love 'em,' he told me. And when I asked him if they preferred food made from yak products, he assumed I was pulling his leg. He laughed and laughed, slapping his orange-robed thigh—that was when I saw his teeth and smelled his breath. It was a stupid question and didn't deserve the compliment of being treated as a joke. I didn't bother asking him where Tibet was. I had the feeling I was best to leave him chuckling about yak products and crediting me with a sense of humour.

I didn't go home for lunch. I jumped schedule, again. I didn't bother looking to see if the black guy or some other minder was hovering about. I didn't care. It was like being on holiday, at once lonely and fascinating. It was the territory of my quest. It was the destination promised by my retirement package. If I kept going, something would happen. Then I'd understand what I'd paid for this, my trade-off, my sixty-year-old memorandum of understanding with the agents in Chinese Opera masks. With Tamar. His slickly smiling mauve lips, the moist siss of his smile. The alpine fragrance of his car.

I kept on prowling. I couldn't stop. Every twenty minutes or so I'd sit down somewhere. There'd be kids in a makeshift playground with old cable drums and a swing made of security fence chain-link. In some places, the sit-down facility was occupied by semi-permanents. Someone's kit would be there, and their dog lying in bliss on the dusty ground. Once, there was a skinny guy who danced, with no shirt on, to some music in his head. He made his dark glasses jump up and down in front of his face by pressing on the bases of their ear-pieces. He had a dog that lay in the dust next to a dish of water and another small plate for donations. The dog's dry, greyish nose was pointed at a handwritten sign that read, 'It's not just the thought that counts—a small gift for life please.' His nostril rims were dark, dilating slightly with the gentle rhythm of his breath. He opened his eyes without moving anything else when I sat down next to him and scratched his head. Every other time I stopped for a rest, I'd buy a glass of water from one of the street vendors. This time, I tipped a glassful into the dog's bowl and dropped my small change in his plate. His owner didn't even notice—his head music was too loud, I guess, or his jumping-up-and-down sunglasses affected his vision.

On-the-street water always tasted to me like the smells in Geek's warehouse—dusty and metallic. I'd been spoiled lately. The early summer sun was lighting up the golden and purplish dust and smog haze above the streets. I could hear a babble of languages I knew nothing about and Pacific Island ones that were familiar though I didn't understand them. They were being spoken in the vicinity of the hospital, near the dry-nosed dog and the dancing man. I guessed it might have been because a lot of Tongans worked at the hospital. My gardener's wife did—in the laundry. He'd told me this, and that he minded the flower beds there, before he discovered that I didn't pay attention to his attempts at conversation. After that, he'd avoided me, walking past the corner of my vision with a stiff electrocuted cat in his hand or re-coiling the hose on its reel after washing dust off the shrubs.

Finally, something did happen. Something my life turned around, like the time I blew the Chou-masked goon's head off, only this time it seemed unsensational at first.

Coming out of the Newtown hospital after an Expectations appointment a couple of days after meeting the dry dog and feeling the hot, coarse hair of his scalp under my fingernails, I found a postcard from Tonga that someone had dropped by the front entrance. It must've been from a patient who'd gone back to the Pacific island Tonga, whatever that was. It wasn't from the Tonga that was near the hospital, the one my gardener and his family lived in. It'd been written from the island Tonga to someone who'd been in the same ward, here. I was taking care coming down the steps at the front of the hospital. I saw my nicely polished shoe about to tread on a picture of palms and blue sea. It was a vivid, miniature window into another world. The existence of this world became plausible when I saw its picture. I picked the card up and saw the caption referencing Tonga. My first thought was that I wished I'd taken the time to talk to the friendly gardener at home.

Then I looked at the stamp—some amazing shell. Who still used stamps? Where were shells like that? I put the card in my pocket. It was like my first piece of forensic evidence. It testified to a world beyond my surveillance. It was as good as the Armenian sub-machine gun, but more portable. The Tibetan's laughter would've been good, if I'd been able to record it. These things were telling me what I'd been missing. Maybe they'd tell me what had set me on my track of unthinking routine, of not talking to my friendly Tongan gardener, not feeling the hot, dry pelt on a dog's head, not smelling my piss infused with something different like cardamom. And not remembering the terms of my treaty with the liver-lipped man in the spacious car when he sold me the future that had become my habit in the present.

The card with its little window opening on to blue sea wasn't in an unknown language like Yoruba, or Tongan for that matter. I read the simple message on it in the peaceful surroundings of my garden. It said:

41

Mrs Crane,
        I hope you still remember
me, I won't forget you lady with your
blue eyes and your kindness to me while
I was in the Hospital. I'm alright only
a few sore on top of my wound but I hope
it will be alright soon. Our temp is
warm and sunshine. I still remember you
with your cold hand and trembling body.
I missed you.
            Best wishes and good
                Luck
                Mrs Malena (Tonga)

I read this and then I turned the postcard over again so the picture was showing. I tried to put Mrs Malena in the little scene with the blue sea. I tried to look through this little window and see her. I tried to imagine her writing the postcard under one of the palm trees. I even tried to imagine her in a fresh hospital smock from the laundry where my gardener's wife worked. I tried to do this and was looking forward to the result.

But I couldn't do it. I could be aware of the instruction I was giving myself to imagine these things, but I couldn't imagine them. 'Think of a woman called Mrs Malena in a hospital smock under a palm tree near the blue sea' didn't turn into an image of her there, any sense of her there. The instruction just fell back, lifeless. The words were dead. I could be amazed by what was newly vivid in my present. I could work out that some of what amazed me now was old hat. I could get some of the way down a memory lane towards the moment when my retirement plan had commenced in the fresh atmosphere of Tamar's limo. Now I sat in my secure garden where I knew every detail of every tomato plant and I felt my blood freeze. Because I couldn't imagine anything that wasn't happening or hadn't happened. The place in my mind for imaginary worlds was gone.

Little Frank began to tremble, looking at Mrs Malena's postcard. I could see that the dancing man with the dusty dog was hearing imaginary music, but I couldn't do that. If I was going to dance, it wouldn't be to music I made up. I remembered how the sweet-breathed Tibetan guy had imagined, momentarily, a Himalayan meadow with yaks in it, where he'd never been and whose possibility was only a joke to him, including what yaks looked like. This imaginary memory made him laugh happily. The Armenians had imagined a Syrian desert, not to mention their daughters prostituting themselves and their sons abandoning their largely imagined histories. But I couldn't do anything like this. I tried to imagine a lunch that Mrs Flitch hadn't prepared, ever, such as a sucking pig on a spit. I couldn't. I could assemble the words but I couldn't make a picture of it, like a postcard. The words I used to call up the picture had no purchase in my mind.

Without difficulty, I remembered the only time I ever held a gun, aside from the ancient Kalashnikov the Armenians tried to give me. The sawn-off shotgun nearly tore my arm off at the elbow when I fired it. I remembered that it did pretty much tear the head off the guy who'd driven the bull-bar car into my depot. I remembered how the frames of his dark glasses lay on the ground almost intact but without lenses afterwards. I remembered what people looked like after they'd trodden on Claymore mines that exploded upwards. The details were very clear, like the tomato plants in my present. But I didn't imagine these things. I remembered thinking they were unnecessary, the bad memories, and wanting them to go away. I remembered wanting to be left in peace to go about my business. I recognised that this was, indeed, now, my peaceful condition. I wasn't imagining the peacefulness of my current condition any more than I was imagining the stiff cats that my Tongan gardener retrieved from my security hedge. There were things I'd chosen not to recall and others I preferred to avert my eyes from. But they were not imaginary.

I tried to imagine the Chinese Opera and Madame Hee in a costume and character I'd never seen. I couldn't do it. This was the most painful of my failures to imagine. Little Frank sat in his garden and was watched discreetly by Mrs Flitch as he wept over the empty place where Madame Hee didn't appear dressed as an airline stewardess, or even in the tee-shirts I remembered my mother wearing, the ones that revealed the bowl between her neck and shoulder. I didn't know I couldn't imagine until I found Mrs Malena's postcard. That was when I discovered that a part of my mind had been removed. It was as if my ability to imagine something had been cauterised. It had been removed as effectively as the feet, genitals and chins of Claymore-mine victims.

I knew I'd been able to do this, once. I vividly remembered Uncle Geek's beaver grin when I'd told him my imaginary version of the holiday we never took by Lake Wanaka. The one when we'd (never) washed a fortune in gold out of river sand and (not) been entertained by two Swedish backpackers. Behind him, the old dog-eared Lakeland promotional calendar was empty of people, especially us, but I'd imagined my uncle tipping bright flakes of gold into a bottle of pure river water where they whirled and glittered in the same golden sunshine that sparkled in the tiny blonde hairs on my imagined Swedish girl's thigh.

'Christ, son,' Geek had remarked, squinting past the golden dust mites hovering in the air of the old warehouse. 'Don't overheat that thing. Your brain, I mean. Only gold you'll ever see's in there, somewhere.'

I remembered this, and it was a very old, callow memory. I remembered imagining. I remembered my sadness for Uncle Geek, the sadness in his hopes for me. I remembered pitching my imaginary holiday at his sadness and I remembered how it had felt when the imaginary holiday only made him sadder. I remembered the dancing dog man's imaginary music, and that was a very new memory. In his case, I didn't remember imagining anything myself, but I remembered recognising the imaginary nature of his music.

Expectationers didn't know their minds had been changed once it had happened. But mine had and I did. There was a fence in there that I hadn't noticed because, like Mr Qureshi's privacy hedges and the barriers at my home, it was just part of the scenery. I'd sat in the garden of my mind and smiled at the well-tended plants, at my pride-and-joy tomatoes. But I saw that there were motion detectors in my mind and an electric wire that killed my prowling thoughts when they went too far. Especially when they tried to put two and two together on the basis of what I knew. When they tried to imagine.

I sat in my garden and made mental lists of what I knew. I knew a lot and I remembered a lot, but every so often I drew a blank. My thoughts began to stall or freeze after the time of the depot shooting, after I blew the Chou-mask guy's head off. Then, there was nothing I could do to sneak around the side of the blank space and time in Tamar's car. The wet-liver sheen of those lips, the taunting siss of that voice, the gloat in his proffer of pure water—these might as well have been etched on the front of my consciousness by a neurosurgeon. 'But ah—the future!': the voice as clear as if alive in the present. As if revived over and over in the present. As if I met it again, over and over, in the present that was the only time I had left. But around it, during it, after it, after that moment in the pine-scented car—nothing. And Madame Hee, immovably factual in the many masks of her make-up, taunting me.

I needed to interrogate my jailer. What did I know about Expectations? It was what the treatments got called if they extended life by acting as cell-replacement agents. They regenerated cells from deep inside the body tissue. The cheap treats were called Creepers, and so were their users. The unsympathetic called these people Creeps. For that matter a lot of Creeps called themselves Creeps. The physical effects of low-end Creeper products were unpredictable. They caused local mutations, isolated growth accelerations and 'epidermal irregularities'. Some Creeps got to be very old, but with extra ears, breasts and enlarged lips. They grew scales and feathers. They had hairless or hairy skin in the wrong places. There were clubs where they hung out—no pun intended. There were radical Creeps who cultivated their freaky bodies. Creep competitions were reported in the media. Some Creeps were the products of laboratory testing that they'd done for money. This I knew to be true because I'd hired them.

The most expensive GTX products were compounds that did more than one thing. They balanced side-effects and controlled cell mutations. You weren't going to look like a snake, a chicken or a veal bratwurst. They were more expensive than Creepers by a factor of millions. This was because GTX varieties were unstable—they continued to evolve. 'Exponential obsolescence' was the official term that explained why the development of these products was good business. Then there was a high-end bracket of hyper-expensive Expectations. You needed power as well as money to keep the beat with the kinds of GTX that would always be scarce. Whole herds of mosaic chimeras and generations of Creeps went into sustaining the global base of this product pyramid. Its pointy end belonged to clients you didn't bump into in the street. Their clubs were the ones that ruled the world.

Those who could afford to combined Expectations with cosmetic surgery and organ transplants. Little Frank had a thorough clean-up at the start. There were cryogenic rest homes where you could take five-year naps. Some Resters didn't wake up. Some Expectationers used blood dialysis. I'd had a few fresh tanks—they perked me up. Of course there was a trade in blood and organs at street level. The rich could afford blood and organ banks if not chimera herds. They didn't need to know why the products were young and fresh. There wasn't much that Little Frank needed to imagine about this world, even if I could have.

There were countless hormone replacement treatments whose job was to supplement life expectancy. Sometimes, their job was to extend sexual life. I had little use for them. The occasions when they might have been useful were too rare to matter.

There were said to be nanotech memory chips that could help old brains. I'd seen no evidence of anything that worked. There were also said to be nanotech body cleaners that did maintenance work on arteries and stomach linings. These were mostly rumours. There was no shortage of prosthetic gear. No one over a hundred needed to be deaf. I myself had an implant the size of a grain of rice. I tuned it with a remote, and had turned it down years ago after hearing a tiny, shrill, high-pressure fart coming out of one of the Mrs Flitches as she swiped her security card to leave the house. I had a good full body set of artificial joints. They didn't come cheap and were one sign of the quality of my retirement package.

Then there were the chimeras that grew spare parts like heart valves and the vital components of GTX cell regrowth. The herds were good business and consequently the focus of competitive commodities speculation. Rumours about cloning and artificial life, not to mention miraculous births and alien inseminations, were rife. They'd been so long before Little Frank started his treatments. They'd continued ever since I'd made a habit of my future. A cloning breakthrough was rumoured monthly at least. Less unreliable was the regular news of ethnic cleansing.

I was feeling sprightly as I climbed on the bus outside the hospital that day I found the card from Mrs Malena. It was only later that I got the shock about losing imagination and sat down to review what I knew. A man in a flat tweed cap got on the bus too. He was dressed in clothes not seen for the best part of a century.

'You drive very well,' he said to the bus driver. 'I'd like to see you in a Porsche 225. You handled the traffic lights beautifully.'

He got off at the end of Oriental Bay and so did I. I caught the Samoan bus driver looking back. I guessed it was at the man in the flat tweed cap. I don't suppose it's often that bus drivers get complimented on their driving technique. Not often they see someone dressed like that, either. Plus-fours with brogues and a shooting stick. And what would he do with an internal-combustion Porsche 225? GTX got some people that way. Their bodies went on but their minds stayed back. They locked into character as the drugs stopped working. Creeps grew scales and extra tits. But declining high-end Expectationers grew hard-wired character.

The Porsche 225 guy reminded me of other stuff. If you stopped taking GTX you 'lost time' at a rate that accelerated in proportion to the time you had in credit. Say I missed a dose and got back on schedule a week later. That week would age me by a factor relative to my extension. Not only could I get a whole lot older quickly but I'd also get a whole lot sillier.

I hadn't given any of it a thought for so many years that all this also surprised me, like the randy Greek kids on the footpath outside the deli and the Asian wet market on the site of Bella's famous school-hall stage crash. And I was hunting for what I knew about imagining. You can only imagine what you haven't experienced. Perhaps, sometimes, imagining is deducing: putting two and two together and getting something logical. But, logical or not, it will still be something you haven't experienced. You have to be able to imagine what you deduce.

This work was giving me a headache. I went inside to get a glass of water from the filter in the kitchen. Mrs Flitch was shaking salad greens in a wire basket over the sink. The spray from her efforts fell on my sleeve as I got my glass of water.

'Sorry, Frank,' she said. 'I didn't notice you there.' I guessed she'd been lost in thought, as we say. Perhaps she'd been imagining. Her face had an unfocused look, as if what made it vivid in the here and now was somewhere else, in another time or place. I took my glass of water back out to the garden. I was trembling again, and spilled some water on the patio table as I put the glass down. What was the point of being angry with Mrs Flitch because she could daydream?

What else did I know? GTX dosages were inexact sciences and kept changing. Too much too often made time thin out. Speeding Expectationers went catatonic. They experienced mental flashes like electrical discharges, together with teeming sensations in the body. They lost control of their speech, and their brains scrambled language and visual perception. They tried to talk pictures. They thought they were seeing what people said. This had all happened to me, but it wasn't imagining. Too little too seldom and Expectationers had time loss slumps when body functions would suddenly cave in, without warning, as if exhausted by the effort of keeping up with the rest of the team. But this wasn't imagining, either. It wasn't even imagining death. I knew because I'd had this experience too. But long ago, before Dr Smiles got my calibration sorted.

I didn't know about withdrawal. I'd never done it. They said it was bad, followed by a period when you recovered brain functions, followed by proportional acceleration towards death.

All this made Expectationers predictable. We seldom strayed from routine. Most of us had automated our schedules, and we had cell phones and pagers to keep us regular. Some of us had smart clothes that imparted knowledge through contact with our epidermal nervous system. See, I read the promotions. But I baulked at the idea of having my underwear tell Little Frank what time it was. I now thought with increasing bitterness that one of the things that made us model citizens was our lack of imagination. I'd never lacked the ability to second-guess what the competition, including the Pirates, was thinking. I used to be able to imagine that. I had that advantage. As sad beaver-teeth Uncle Geek had observed all those dusty years ago in his Kilbirnie junk shop, his nephew's real gold was his mind. The reach, the sunlit glitter, the cunning of that mind. As Gabber always said years later, I could tell the difference.

I hurled the rest of my water over a tomato plant. My petulance only made me angrier. I heard the sounds of Mrs

Flitch preparing to leave, and I longed for the sounds to finish with the security chime of the front door. For once, she didn't come out to say goodbye and tell me my supper was ready. She was fed up with me. The front door chimed then slammed. I got up and threw my chair across the garden. 'But ah—the future!' That liverish smile, those teeth. What kind of promise was that, when it stopped short of meals I could anticipate without knowing? When it baulked at memories that needed the lubrication of fantasy to get them back into the present? Another thing I could tell myself for free: the drugs thinned out your consciousness. You didn't know that you were doing what you were doing. You could go on and on for years and not know what was making you tick other than your schedule.

I didn't know why or how yet, but I'd stepped off that track. I'd gone off to the side of my schedule—to a place I could watch myself from. Even if I couldn't imagine the result, I could begin to put two and two together. First: I knew my life as an Expectationer had begun in the back of Tamar's limousine. Second: I knew I went often to the Chinese Opera. Third: I knew it was Madame Hee who compelled me. Fourth: I knew I was under surveillance and that the Binh Xuyen had something to do with it. Fifth: I knew my mind couldn't imagine. There was no glitter left in that mind. No gold, not even fool's gold. No foolishness. I had no future. All I had was in the present my schedule managed for me, that managed me, that made Little Frank what he'd become.

These were the things I knew. Here's what I didn't know. I didn't know what had happened to my old gift. Had I lost my knack of spotting what was new and what was old? Or what wanted to be new and what couldn't help being old? Or what was out on reissue and what had never been tested? What came from the opportunity shop and what came off the rack? Or what had taken a tuck in history and was now out there on the streets masquerading as an original?

I'd caught Uncle Geek looking at me one day—sadly, but

50

with his buck-toothed yellow grin that made him look even sadder.

'Reckon you'd recognise your mum, if you saw her again?' Geek's expression was cagey. I thought he was probably asking something else.

'How do you mean?' I asked. Some young guys were looking at the guts of old PCs to see if there were functional CPUs in there. I was wondering if they'd see I'd already swapped them. 'Do you mean would I want to?'

'You can please yourself about that, kiddo,' said Geek, sourly—he'd never made a secret of the fact that he thought my mother was a selfish little cow. I could see that the guys ferreting about with the computers lacked the confidence to decide they'd been tampered with. Put this another way: they lacked the imagination to visualise me tampering with the CPUs and them getting duped. They couldn't play. They were no fun. I wanted to move in and push a sale past their lacklustre minds.

'So what, then?' I was only half paying attention to my uncle. I could see him measuring my interest in stalking my dumb marks fucking around down the end of the shop against my interest in his weird question.

'I mean, suppose she'd changed a lot.' Geek's smile stuck right out of his face. It was so inappropriate that I had to deflect my predator's attention on to it. The guys I'd have trapped into a transaction the moment I'd spooked them into not asking me about the traces of solder were slipping away towards the safe territory of second-hand porn magazines. I didn't know why Geek was looking at me like that. His shocking grin was threatening to make the front fall out of his face. Why did he look so sad when he thought my mother was best left out of my life? Why did he bother to ask such a question? He never had before. Every month some money still went into my 1081 account. It always did. Geek never asked for any.

'Why?' I asked his smile, staring straight into it. 'Have you seen her or something?' I suspected that he got money too, which was why he never wanted any from me. But I never asked him about that and he never told me. My own memories weren't bitter. Any sadness I'd felt as a little kid had gone. I remembered my mum's play, her make-ups, our pretends. Our imaginings. These were memories I liked. I guessed I'd probably like her if I ever saw her again.

The guys were showing each other centrefolds and making rooting noises down the far end of the shop. I knew it was only a matter of time before they tore one out of its magazine, trying to do it so quietly they might as well have asked permission. But I couldn't be bothered with them. This was because a tear had run out of one of Geek's nicotine-coloured eyes, something I'd neither seen before nor imagined I ever could.

'Bugger it,' said Geek, closing his face over the beaver teeth. He pretended to have a bit of dust in his eye. Then he tried to finish what he'd started. 'You never know,' said my uncle in his best flattened, uninterested trader's voice, as if someone had brought my mother into the shop for him to appraise. 'You might see her one day. Then it'd be interesting.'

'She might see me first,' I said, playing along. I remembered imagining a non-specific sort of woman stopping and staring at me, or whipping her head around to look at me after I'd gone past her. I'd imagined my mother's almost childish face on a middle-aged body. It didn't work for me then, and I couldn't do it now.

'I wouldn't count on it,' said Geek, and that was that. He meant, Don't count on her recognising you first. The hurt of that remark made me cheat the first idiot to come into the shop. I needed everyone else to be more stupid than Little Frank—than the kid who was fast becoming Little Frank, I should say. I remembered, now, how Geek had turned away, back into his character, back into the hard man. But I also remembered his look of sadness. I guessed it was because he'd seen that my talent for spotting the real thing might one day recognise the mother who'd walked out on me. The mother who'd be in a different-looking body and another life from the one I'd known as a little kid. But maybe there was another reason.

'I wouldn't count on it.'

Sitting in my carefully tended garden on the chair I'd retrieved from the bush I'd chucked it into, wiping and then closing the little folding knife with which I liked to slice my peach or melon, smelling the pleasant aroma of leaves and soil wet from a hose-down, feeling my rage subside, all I could think about was the single tear that had crept out of my uncle's amber eye, his eye that resembled the pee-coloured glass eyes of the scruffy teddy bears in the toy section of his shop, so many years ago that the memory was like a postcard whose utter factuality made my heart squeeze painfully around a grief I couldn't understand but wanted to grasp, somehow.

'I wouldn't count on it.'

Hunting in my memory of the Kilbirnie junk emporium I found the teddy bears with the eyes of their proprietor, my seldom-teary uncle. I found the garish old video games, especially the dragon pirate ship one with rockets and flame throwers. I found the scent of my mother's neck as she bent to prise me away from the console and the screen with the boat like a dragon with a great ballooning sail on its back. I found the 2000AD comics and my first love, the intergalactic skinhead punk diva Halo Jones whose long neck was not my mother's—my mother had gone by then—whose neck arched away from the approaches of General Cannibal but whose smooth shoulder was grazed by his tusk.

'I was General Cannibal,' I said to my memory of the acned, motherless little wanker with a perpetually aching cock like a divining rod dipping and nodding above the piles of crap in the back of the shop, the pee-eyed bears, the crimson and gold dragon boat, the bounty-hunting punk girl. 'My intergalactic cabin cruiser had free lunch drive.' I was a hundred and twenty years old and talking to myself. I was Little Frank, the vizier of Courtenay Place, and I was weeping all by myself in my garden made secure by Mr

53

Qureshi's cat-killing wires. 'My tusk bit Halo's shoulder. I was going to reduce a planet to rubble. Ten eighty one.'

I went inside. It was a hot night and the haze had a metallic stink. In my bathroom were some new products, or rather some replenished but familiar items. There was a fresh tube of toothpaste, a newly unwrapped cake of olive oil-based soap that didn't irritate the skin, a mouthwash flavoured with 'real lime', the pamplemousse- and cardamom-scented Hammam infuser. The cologne I doubted I'd ever chosen. It must've been the beginning of the month. That was usually when the products were changed, whether they were completely used up or not. I think Mrs Flitch took the unfinished ones back to her place as a perk. It had been a whole month since I'd seen Mrs Flitch mouthing their brand names as she checked off her inventory. I had no sense that so much time had passed. At the same time I felt as though a greater workload of time had passed than ever before—ever before, that is, dated from the moment when the promise of a future had locked me in this world of regulated nows. The now of my lunch, the now of new products, the now of memories like factual entries in a catalogue.

'I wouldn't count on it.'

In the mirror I saw a little elderly man whose right hand had reached across to clutch at his heart, as though he was making a public oath or salute of some kind. His face was not properly shaved, and white stubble glittered across cheeks that had a nourished look—except for the dark bags under his eyes. The eyes, too, looked nourished and tended, and I knew they could see clearly because I was looking out of them at myself. I saw the tears coming out of my eyes at the same time as I appraised the squalid state of my haircut and the fact that my shirt was unbuttoned to a careless scatter of little dark melon pips in my sparse white chest hair.

I watched myself mouth the words, 'I wouldn't count on it.'

I'd been living in no time at all and now there was

54

unbearably too much of it. I needed philosophy. It was time to visit Gabber down there at his stall in Courtenay Place.

I had my barber visit me before I went back into the world in which I was expected to set standards. In which I expected myself, Little Frank, to set standards. He did my hair and removed the long, tusky bristles that grew vigorously in my nostrils and ears. He didn't comment on the state of my haircut, but he did allow himself a gentle, 'I should think so,' when—a small luxury—I asked him to shave me as well. I lay back under the luxurious covering of warm, cologne-scented towels and let myself enjoy these simple pleasures. He did my fingernails, and he also clipped my toenails, not counting the big toes whose hard, ingrowing monsters had been surgically removed many years ago.

'Anyone I should know?' he quipped.

His name was Honour ('Don't ask!') and to me he was a parody of the gentleman flirt, the gossip, attentive and trivial. He wasn't the first to have his card in the professional services folder by the hall telephone of my house, but I couldn't remember his predecessors any more than I could the previous Mrs Flitches. He'd been nattering on about the headlines. The Sino–Russian conflict had removed another instant city from the natural-gas belt up along the uncertain Arctic borderlands. A popular American film star had been caught with what looked like a small harem of under-age Tutsi, but they were probably a living organ or chimera bank. The local conflict over water rights had flared up again, and there was another tribal insurrection on the Wanganui River against WW's subsidiary FLOW. And had I read about the suicidal *omertà* involving Stemmies?

I told Honour, from beneath my muffling towels, that I didn't read the papers and that he probably knew that, so why was he bothering to ask? I felt his huff of irritation on the back of my hand, where he bent over a cuticle.

'You expect me to believe that?' he complained. 'A man of

your stature?' He gave my hand a little smack.

These fragments of soft news, these gossipy, probably inaccurate hints at factuality in the wider world, hit my awakened consciousness like small meteors. They, too, were shocking in a post-sheikette way, though not news. I knew that the Chinese had been throwing up vast instant cities across the Siberian gas-lands. That the Russians had been violently removing them was of interest to me. These had been territories from which the Pirates, who were indifferent to nationalities and borders, had drawn down resources, including black-market nuclear junk, much of it bought with dirty gas money. The item about the chimera-organ stable made the heart I'd clenched the day before hurt again. I gritted my teeth under the towels, because this had been a place of danger for Little Frank. I vividly saw most of the Chou-mask guy's head fly off when I shot him in my depot. Such sharp recall was unwelcome—it was another kind of memory I wanted. The tribal water insurrection on the Wanganui pierced me because that's where Hokkaido lived now. I hadn't thought about her for years, or didn't think I had. This was a hurt I'd begun to return to in my catalogue of what I knew. The last *omertà* pact of silence I remembered had wiped out my best friends a long time ago. I owed my life to them, even the life I was now living as a prisoner of my retirement plan. That memory was painful because I'd shelved it. I didn't know for sure what Stemmies were, and I was too proud to ask Honour. I knew what they sounded like. I thought Gabber would help me with that one, too.

I gave Honour a decent tip and threw in the bathroom cologne which I'd decided I didn't like because I couldn't remember preferring it. He gave himself a squirt with it as he went out the front door into the thick, smoggy sunlight. He'd told me to 'lighten up', but I let him away with that. Then I caught a bus down to the Bay and made my way along the busy promenade towards Courtenay Place. I felt fresh yet bruised. I was apprehensive about seeing Gabber—I hadn't done so for weeks and may even have walked past him. But I had my collection of clues in a satchel. I was looking forward to hearing what he'd have to say about them. Little Frank approached the Place with freshly shaved cheeks and a light amber-topped cane from Genoa whose provenance owed something to the *omertà* that Honour had reminded me of. I had the word 'Stemmies' tapping at the soundproofed window of my consciousness.

I saw my black Yoruba-speaking watcher down where the old yacht marina had been. I didn't acknowledge his presence and he didn't signal his own to me. He pretty much blended in there with the Mogadishu water-taxi operators, though he wasn't skinny like Somalis. I saw the black guy hang his big head down over his flickering cigarette-lighter in the gusty wind off the Bay. I vividly saw the yacht marina as it had been when it still had room for such leisure craft tucked up under the armpit of the city. That was before the polders and their dykes, and before the museum got washed out. My watcher seemed to be standing guard over my memory of cruising into that neat marina past the breakwater below the museum with Hokkaido on our little *Cao Cao San*. He was watching over my memory of Hokkaido's denim shorts up by the jib halyard where she lifted the mooring aboard with a gaff and dropped its weedy orange loop over a crucifix on the *Cao Cao San*'s bow.

Following my amber-topped cane along the teeming walkway, I remembered how the Courtenay Place neighbourhood had been back when Hokkaido and I used to walk through it, getting our land-legs back. We'd looked for a cold beer at a table on the footpath outside a bar, eaten sushi, gone back to the little rocking cabin with its permanent salty smell and the sound of the dinghy tapping at the hull next to our bunk when the wind shifted. It had been tacky and innocent, then, the Place, with too many young drunks and music that was always louder than it needed to be. It was where Little Frank had started up. It was where Hokkaido had stopped being next to him at the sushi bar. Now, the Place stretched from the floating restaurants of

Oriental Bay and the big retaining dykes, up the apartment and nightclub slopes of Mount Victoria, and back up to boho Newtown where the Armenians held the low ground and the Tibetans had the slopes. Above the crowded streets rose the entertainment towers and media complexes of the big networks: Globeaid, Time-Life, Spacelink, Transworld Corp. The water companies like FLOW and the banks and venture-capital outfits made one perimeter of the Place, over beyond the Barbary Coast and along the western flanks of the hills. Saline groundwater had risen into the roots of these buildings. We'd been used to the buried thump of the pumps for so long we'd have been surprised when one of the towers fell on us—even though the pumps were telling us it was time they did.

I wouldn't have been seeing any of this if I hadn't woken up and needed to get back the terms of my MOU with Tamar. I wouldn't have been noticing my watcher, either, with his cigarette dangling at the corner of his mouth as he slouched with loose, ambling strides at four o'clock to my midday. He was just behind my lateral field of vision, just far enough back for him to see me having to turn my head to notice him, just close enough for me to see that he didn't much care if I was watching him watch me. Watcher was at home in the Place the way it had become. Little Frank was wondering how many people remembered that these noisy, filthy streets had once been contained within the peaceful confines of some bus shelters and a wide two-sided boulevard. And a couple of little trees doing okay, for that matter, and some City Council beds of flowers!

Sitting in my garden made secure by Mr Qureshi's surveillance and security plan, in my mind made secure by the terms of a contract I couldn't remember or imagine, assembling catalogues of what I knew, I'd realised that the phrase 'at the back of my mind' had no meaning any more. There was no back. If anything was there, it was in the front. It was vivid in the way high-resolution digital images were vivid on the expensive data wall of my house. What I knew or remembered could be viewed only on the flat surface of my mind. I could view these images or action sequences by calling them up. How things looked when I was a kid, how Hokkaido's beer glass left a wet ring on the table in Courtenay Place when she lifted it to her lips, Geek's orange-coloured beaver grin, the raw-liver shine of Tamar's lips under the red mask. Other images and action sequences arrived whether I wanted them or not, and this was happening more often. The frying sound of the burning deadshit after he got torched near my outfit at the back of Barbary. The shredded PURE banner over those twitching kids. The Chou-mask guy's head flying off like a swarm of red bees, his sunglasses frames without eyes. The sound of Tamar's hissy voice: 'But ah—the future!'—that too, of course, whether I wanted it or not. But it was all on the surface. There was no back. There was no imagination.

Little Frank walked steadily through his former caliphate. I saw that people moved aside from my Genoan cane. From time to time I lifted its amber top in a salute to someone I no longer knew and perhaps never had but whose obeisance I recognised as proper. I was the ghost of myself as well as my own impersonator. No one who saluted me could see that I was walking through a phantom territory that had ceased to exist before they were born.

Courtenay Place! It was like saying 'flat tweed cap', or 'Tonga', or 'yak'! Now, in the noisy bit of city that still had its name, all that was left of the original shape was the wider defile that ran from the flasher Mount Vic clubs through the centre of the gaming belt and the old markets with their rusting shipping containers, thudding generators and jerry-built stalls to the perimeter of Cuba. To the north were the stinking swamps and clogged culverts above the harbour dykes, and the floating shantytown of boat people. South was the Barbary Coast, where sailors could still get flogged if they wanted to be sailors and if they fancied being flogged. Where, behind the fake surveillance deterrent and the single file of penis-grasping gnomes, Mack catered for a different kind of pirate from the ones with a capital P that I needed to relocate in my memory. My memory that had no 'back', that was all vivid present.

And one memory in particular, the man with lips whose slimy sheen was like freshly cut healthy liver, whose promise—'But ah—the future!'—had begun to fill me with rage. Whose red mask of a Guan Gong war god I wanted to rip from the sharp smile that had bitten off my imagination, that had consigned me to a drudging role whose contract terms those smiling teeth had also chewed from my mind. Or worse, the teeth that had smilingly duped Little Frank—who'd never been duped—into a retirement plan whose secret code had locked him into his slavish schedule, his beat down to the Opera, the bungy that snapped him back there to his position by the plush red drapes. The compulsion that was making Little Frank feel sick with need again as he strolled down to Gabber's after not showing his face in the Place for long enough to be noticed again when he did. Or for the people who noticed him to be saying, Frank's back. He's over whatever made him stand bawling in the middle of the Gateways wet market, thank god.

'Frank—good to see you. Looking great.'

They saw the casual blessing of my cane. They noticed the fingers I raised to my hat's brim. They appreciated the inclination of Little Frank's groomed head. I saw how deferential they were. They didn't see how my guts were being hauled forward like ropes towards the winch of the Chinese Opera. Towards the vivid Madame Hee: the place where her neck and shoulder formed a cup that filled with my longing. Where her voice like a jade dagger stabbed into memories of video games, books and comics in dusty sunlight at the back of Uncle Geek's junk shop—a red dragon coiled over the prow of the pirate dhow, golden towers in the distance beyond a thorn-fenced garden where a princess slept entranced, tusk-grazed shoulder of Halo Jones surveying the wasted planet.

It was at the end of this defile, where the touts began to hustle their marks from the entranceways of the specialist clubs, that the Chinese Opera stood. Big names came across from the Mainland and got accommodated in luxury above ground by the tower blocks of the Chinese banks. Around the time of the Festival of Hungry Ghosts, little folksy companies showed up and played the Opera as well as doing late-night makeshift off the backs of carts in the surrounding streets and around Oriental Bay. But the Oaks Opera had its core company. Its female star was Madame Hee.

I'd got into the habit of going down there to matinees not less than twice a week. There was something about Madame Hee. I didn't know what it was. I stood down the back where I could get a better view, by the red plush drapes at the dragon-coiled entranceway. I stood there and looked down the sloping interior at the artificial world of the Opera. Perhaps Madame Hee reached past the front of my mind into the places I'd lost. But before I woke up I didn't know she could do this. And now that I was awake I couldn't go into those places anyway.

I devoted time to the Opera in the privacy of my home. At 2 a.m. I sat by myself in front of my screen wall in the early performance night of high-quality 10 p.m. Shanghai or Beijing, or in the frantic, pixilated folksiness of Sheng-cam back-street Singapore or Shenzhen. Outside, the late-night sirens began to go off as things hotted up over on Oriental Bay.

The guy whose head I blew away at my depot had been wearing an el-cheapo opera mask, as well as the dark glasses whose frames miraculously survived the blast. It was a Chou clown mask, and that seemed appropriate, though I wouldn't have known what it was at the time, since it pre-dated my hobby. The other thing I remembered about the clown was his shoes. They were crappy recycled car-tyre sandals. At the time, I thought my real foe, which the contract goon's mask identified as Binh Xuyen, wasn't showing me the respect of committing decent talent to harassing Little Frank. Later, it occurred to me that the goon may have been trying to pass for Binh Xuyen. Either way, it marked a moment at which

61

Little Frank began to measure the strategic limits of such bloody conflict. Despite the clown's shitty footwear and disrespectful Chou mask, his sponsors may have been capable of drawing down reserves secured by Siberian or Arctic oil and nuclear-waste residuals. That made it a matter of time before the Pirates sent round a chauffeured *sheng* wearing buffed Florsheims.

Mrs Flitch called my interest in Chinese Opera my 'hobby' and I noticed, now, that she'd been sorting my printouts into a tray.

When did I first go in there to the Chinese Opera at the Oaks? Why? I couldn't remember. There was a link to Tamar's Guan Gong red face, but the jade drill of sound that Madame Hee drove into my unimaginative Expectationer's mind was in a class of its own. Her voice had been trained away from any human sound. It pierced my armour of habit and became my habit. It drilled straight through to my old instinct for appraising difference. Madame Hee was usually dressed in costumes whose ancient origins were at home under modern stage-lights, lasers and 3D VR props. Her face was masked by thick make-up. Sometimes this represented a natural face, though very white with pink around the eyes. Less often it was something elaborate, accompanied by complicated vocals. I could pick her out even when she was playing those artificial roles.

Madame Hee's squealing voice, her white face and endlessly repeated gestures focused my life, my schedule. She was my destination. Walk through Courtenay Place, have a coffee with Gabber, then stand at the back of the Opera by the dragons, with one hand wrapped up in the red plush drape. What was under that mask? How old or new was the Opera? How new was Madame Hee?

I was looking at something I couldn't imagine. And my desire to do so covered my body with craving gooseflesh like antennae. My desire to know her made me sweat and stiffen my sinews with the effort of paying attention. When the performance was over I'd be exhausted. There was a roar in my ears and a frightening headache of pressure in my skull. Before entering the Opera I'd have turned my hearing aid up, and when I came out I'd have to turn it down because the street's noise was too real.

Though not awake to it, was I already bored by the future that went on packing itself so predictably into my present, day after day? Like the household products Mrs Flitch replenished monthly? From my first visit to the Opera when Madame Hee had plunged her jade dagger into my heart, something had begun. Something had begun to wake up after an unimaginative present that had lasted close to sixty years.

I needed to get back to that initial seduction at the Opera. Why did I go there in the first place? I needed to get back past that moment to the red Guan Gong mask in the back of the limousine full of fresh air. That siss of promise: 'But ah—the future!' I needed to know why they were connected. I needed to know the terms of the contract that connected them. I needed to know why I couldn't imagine what those terms might be. I needed to know why the Binh Xuyen, the Pirates, thought it was necessary for me not to know these things. I needed to know why I'd agreed to be ignorant. No—I needed to know if I'd agreed. Why I began to go to the Chinese Opera. Why I was being watched while I asked these questions.

The citizens of the Place were stepping respectfully aside from Little Frank as he made his way to Gabber's. I tried to look dignified and serene but my guts were knotted. It was an effort to stop myself moving my lips around the questions I was asking.

I needed to know how Madame Hee had primed me, Little Frank, for the moment when the rich sheikette with the beautiful wrists of gold bangles would wake me up. When I'd cough out the thing that had put my imagination to sleep.

'I wouldn't count on it.'

I was being shadowed carelessly by my Yoruba-speaking watcher. Maybe he wouldn't have paused to light another lackadaisical cigarette if he'd been able to see how I was beginning to sweat at the thought of Madame Hee's icy voice slicing into my guts where my old dynamos of consciousness had begun to spin again. The watcher was coughing like a phlegmatic elephant in the awning shade of a smoky grilled-chicken joint at about four o'clock to my noon. All he could see was Little Frank dressed to the nines, papery cheeks rosy after a fresh hot-towel shave, summer Panama tipped a little over his dark glasses, pale lightweight suit a bit loose at the shoulders, a sprig of pale Clementine mandarin blossom in his buttonhole and an expression of impassive courtesy on his face. Little Frank strolling through the scorching, foggy light, the racket and mayhem of the Place, as if it was an elegant boulevard somewhere in his senile mind.

The lanes of rickshaws, handcarts and assorted other traffic that came down the Cambridge Terrace throughway to Wakefield Street and the sea walls often backed up across the end of Courtenay Place. If the wind was blowing along that way you'd see a pall of purple gritty smoke fanning across the vehicles from the stalls that were jammed in there.

It had once been my habitat. I'd been the vizier of the Place. I'd looked up at the heli-cabs delivering execs to the rooftops of the media towers there, and thought how class was now organised according to those who never set foot on the ground and those who never got off it.

But down there in the Place I'd ruled consistently. When I gave it away even my enemies seemed to have nothing to gain from harming me. The media was full of stories about the grisly fates of those whose off-the-ground existences were as carefully guarded as the blood banks and chimera harems they bought shares in. I'd never had any more protection than was prudent. Yet here I was entering a new youth of consciousness, with a personal bodyguard courtesy of friends I didn't know and didn't know I had. Or of enemies I thought I knew, whose desire to protect me was one of the unanswered questions I struggled to stop myself muttering in public.

Gabber came to the Place courtesy of the Egyptian secret police, of whose torture Gabber said, 'You forget the milk that you have been fed from the breast of your mother.' But that was long ago. 'When evening comes . . . How long ago were we here?'—he liked to quote an old guy called Naguib Mahfouz.

Gabber did everything from high-level meteorological scans and UV profiles, through news, Futures forecasts, the big water and hydrogen markets, inside stock-market data, political muck, classified industrial stuff, IP research files, the lot. He was as at home in the city's computer databases and wireless frequencies as Mack was in dry-dock sailors' fantasies of rum, sodomy and the lash. He planted viral sleuths. He joked that he 'put two and two together, not one and zero'. He boasted that he built huge from tiny, like an archaeologist. He discovered pyramids in a scatter of masonry chips. He saw stocks going down in sheets of flame. He predicted new IP rendering whole corporations out of date. 'You and me, Frank,' he used to say. 'The A Team.' In digital entrails he divined pandemic transgenic outbreaks that would decimate whole nations and make the market share of certain pharmaceutical R&D corporations and PCR clone libraries explode exponentially following trends of global paranoia. 'You and me, my little sheikh. On shari' bayn al-sarayat.' And he'd pour me a little cup of his coffee.

I was coming to Gabber with a question I'd never needed to ask before now. Where did Gabber stop and his machines begin? How did Gabber's imagining work?

A little girl just able to walk and run, her hair in a couple of dark twisted-together ponytails, and wearing little blue cotton shorts and pink plastic sandals half the size of my newly manicured hands, ran experimentally down an uncrowded stretch of road next to me. Its hazards were flooded pot-holes and slicks of old cooking oil, the edges of the food stalls and generator housings. Her hands and arms flapped beside her as she worked to keep her balance. She was shouting something in a high, laughing voice—in a language I couldn't understand. I feared for her safety. Then I saw the big black arms of my watcher reach in and pick the child up. He hastened in to the one o'clock zone to my noon, well up on his surveillance quadrant of three or four on the dial. I heard him say laughing words to the child while he kissed her, in the same sounds as the words she'd been babbling when she'd run close to the edges of the hot oil vats and improvised power cables of the booths. I heard that the child and my watcher both spoke Yoruba.

The black guy looked over at me. His face was expressionless. He'd managed to keep a cigarette in the corner of his big, loose-lipped mouth. He was speaking Yoruba around it to the tiny girl who'd just learned to run in her pink sandals and blue shorts. I might have been part of his workday world but I wasn't part of the one that had the kid in it. No one chose to share his domestic moment with him. They weren't going to pick up his child. We walked on together, Little Frank, the watcher and the little girl in pink sandals, as if screened off from the crowds. I'd thought it was respect that put the screen there. Now I had to wonder if it was something else, like fear.

The people who controlled the information that Gabber interfered with all had Gabbers on their payroll. But Gabber's digital entrail-reading services were at the disposal of the Place. He preferred to keep his head down. And our association wasn't without profit.

'They're all palace eunuchs,' he used to say of the corporate spooks, wrinkling the thin, stretched skin at the edges of his mouth. 'Small-time plotters. Gossips. Good lieutenants.' He made perfunctory throat-slitting gestures.

Gabber had a framed, glossy colour photograph of a tomato in pride of place on the wall of his lab. The tomato was the legendary Flavr Savr of early GM food experiments, a kind of ancient matriarch, the product of genetic union between a tomato and a deepsea bottom-dwelling flatfish.

'Flavrsavr,' Gabber would mutter, 'Flavrsavr. Flavrsavr.' It was his mantra. 'Don't talk to me about "natural",' he'd snap. It had never occurred to me that we might share the same kind of unnatural consciousness. Some music was always playing, ancient Oum Kalthoum epics with orchestras of clattering coathangers and maudlin zithers, or Mozart, or his favourite, Puccini. He ran around his consoles like a dervish DJ. 'Flavrsavrflavrsavr . . .' He'd pause and sway his tiny torso and skinny neck to the music. And then he'd be yapping away through skin so tight the unnaturally perfect teeth in it were always grinning. Keeping a big marsupial eye on the street to see who was passing.

When Gabber spotted me in the doorway of his lab that day, I saw him looking out at me with eyes as big and wet as a night possum's. Then the grin reappeared, like something luminous on a screen. Gabber was already talking even as I stepped in out of the smoggy scorch of the glare.

'Salaam aleikum, Allàhu akbar, my little sheikh, what's this I hear?' Gabber wanted to know. 'They're saying if Frank's got friends they wouldn't know it because he's forgotten them. Who's wearing the fine clothes you have on, Frank? Anyone your brother Gabber knows?' He came forward to embrace me.

I didn't answer him. I sat down before he could kiss my cheeks, and opened my satchel of clues. I wanted to see how he thought, more than what he thought. I wanted him to read my portents.

Gabber clicked his tongue peevishly at my bad manners.

First, I showed him Mrs Malena's postcard and a clipping out of the morning paper. The clipping was a blurry photograph of an overweight boy about eight years old. He was wearing a miniature military uniform with braids looped across the chest. The kid had a weaner's mouth. His pouty bottom lip was hanging off his teeth and his eyes were very dark. Though I didn't like supposing that eyes could have expressions, his seemed sad and scared. The message with this snapshot, which I'd clipped from the personal notices section of classified ads, read, 'Happy Birthday Jason You Rule in Samoa—from Dad'.

I thought Gabber might wonder what Jason You Rule in Samoa's picture meant. The kid was trying to get a message through, but I couldn't hear it. I wondered if Gabber had any ideas. But I kept my trap shut. I waited for him to finish looking at my items. I had more in my satchel. I saw the warped reflection of my Yoruba watcher slouch across one of Gabber's screens that faced out into the Place. He had the little girl on his shoulders and her pink sandals were hanging down against his wide chest. The kicking sandals had pushed his bomber jacket open, and that's when I caught a reflected glimpse of his gun. But I didn't bother turning around to see where he'd stationed himself. I was watching Gabber.

He pushed my items around in front of him for a bit. He was sitting on a swivel chair next to the screen where Watcher had been reflected. There was a talking head on the screen, a newscaster, but no sound. The only sound was the music—Mozart, with a flute. The atmosphere between us was tense. When Gabber looked up at me again, his smile had stretched itself into a thin downturned hoop.

'Turn that thing up, will you?' snapped Gabber, pointing at his ear. His meaning was clear. I adjusted my hearing aid while he glared at me. 'What do you take me for, Frank, a fucking oracle? Who's Mrs Malena? Who's Samoan Jason?' His voice was tinny and loud. Then the Gabber smile switched on again, no more real than his teeth. 'This isn't like you, my brother, a man who used to know who his friends were in this world. Take my advice, go and get your cup read.' He made a formal gesture of turning aside to spit.

I'd never seen Gabber angry before. I didn't know what to do. There was a silence during which the various screens and things in Gabber's place began to blather away because he'd turned their sound back on. The Mozart was the Concerto for flute and orchestra No. 1 in G Major—some things lasted even if patience and friendship didn't.

When Gabber still didn't say anything, but just glared at me with that fixed, angry grin on his face, I put my clues back in the satchel with the others and stood up. Terrible loneliness and disappointment had gripped my heart, the same organ that had felt other spasms of grief or anger over the past weeks. But before I got to the door, Gabber grabbed me by the back of my suit jacket. He did it violently, so that his bony fingers dug into my shoulder blades.

'Not one word, Frank?'

It was true. I hadn't said a thing. I sat down again in the spare chair—the one I'd sat in hundreds of times for coffee and a yarn. I'd seen that Gabber had no magic. But I'd forgotten that he was also my friend. I heard again the angry door slam of Mrs Flitch leaving that morning. I replayed my hairdresser Honour's flounce of irritation. I saw myself walking into my old mate Gabber's place for the first time in weeks, not saying a word, and then leaving. I'd done something similar at Mack's the other week.

'Sorry, Gabber,' I said. 'I just needed to have a bit of a yarn.'

'Does the camel forget how to fart?'

This was an old joke between us. I couldn't speak past the lump in my throat.

Gabber tried again. 'So what did you think this was? A Tarot booth? Show me your palm, effendi.' But his anger had gone.

I just went right into it. 'You can't imagine stuff either, can you, Gabber?'

Usually his eyes blinked all the time, but now they were staring. His false smile quivered, as if waiting for time to move again.

'I used to be able to think ahead, Gabber.'

'Yes, you did, effendi.' The Adam's apple went up and down in his neck like an elevator on the façade of one of the venture capital houses he pried into.

'No one ever fooled me. They gave up trying.'

'You were the best, my brother.'

'*Were*, Gabber?'

'Sure,' he whispered. 'You were.' He reached out and lifted my hand from the top of the cane. 'Didn't you retire?' asked Gabber. Then I saw a movement like a speeding tsunami passing just under the plastic-tight skin of his face, fast, as though his brain had shivered. 'Don't you notice? No one's sure, Frank. What you can do. They're all still scared.' Now he was blinking flat out. 'They've been scared of you for years, Frank.' Gabber paused. 'Your abilities,' he said delicately. I could see the pressure of the next thing he wanted to say pushing his smile back into a snarl of fear, like a Rhesus monkey's. 'People think you might've hooked up with them,' he whispered, as if sharing a secret. 'With your old enemies. With the Binh Xuyen, Frank. The Lao Sheng.' He grimaced, as if uttering blasphemy. 'With the Pirates.' It was inconceivable that Gabber could be afraid of me. 'But you and me, effendi. We know what you can still do.' Gabber rubbed his forefinger and thumb together.

'I reckon I just stopped paying attention, Gabber. I stopped knowing anything. I was just passing through, Gabber, those days I used to come and see you, doing business.' His shoulders lifted in a shrug. 'Just doing business, Gabber.' I felt an unfamiliar pain—a sadness unlike the emotion I'd felt remembering Bella's ballet leap offstage at Roseneath primary school where the Asian wet market now plied its trade.

'Retirement blues, Frank? You ever thought of a hobby?' That was another Gabber joke.

'I've been going along to the Opera a fair bit,' I said. 'The Chinese Opera.' I knew my lips were trembling and that he could see this.

'My god, Frank, all that yowling?' Gabber had a malicious look on his face now. 'Besides,' he said, but then he didn't go on with it.

'I think it's got something to do with the lead singer,' I said. 'Madame Hee.' I wanted him to finish the 'Besides . . .' he'd started. I pressed the top of my cane to my trembling lips.

70

'Prayer is better than sleep. The sleeper admits impure thoughts, brother.' Gabber was grinning like a jackal. 'Remember Puccini's *Turandot*? The "Chinese Opera"? Where all the princes get their heads whacked off because they can't answer the riddles? That what you had in mind, Frank?'

'I damn near did get my head whacked off the other day. It woke me up. I wanted to talk to you about it.'

Gabber waved his remote at the consoles and the screens went silent.

'There's no one else I can talk to about it, Gabber. That I know of.'

A strange, almost wrong little flute arpeggio flitted out of the Mozart, followed by some mockingly correct orchestral chords. Then the music, too, finished. The hubbub of the Place came in, but we sat there as though in silence. My hearing aid was sifting out tiny metallic rubbing sounds, like insect wings.

It seemed a long time ago that right-wing thugs like the 100PC would come through the Place and beat the shit out of new coloured immigrants. Who'd bother now? Tolerance didn't come into it. With the possible exception of the upriver insurrection against FLOW and World Water, the only conflict now would be about survival. The racket out there in the Place was all about survival. In a way it was soothing. As the boss of the Place I'd found ways of dealing with elements like 100PC, and I couldn't rule out the possibility that one of them later turned up dressed as Binh Xuyen in a shitty Chou mask. If so, it might have been because I'd had his mates rounded up after a rampage through the Place. On my orders they were detained under the path of a rockslide at Owhiro Bay. There were legitimate reasons for people to be afraid of Little Frank, with or without the Pirates.

'*Besides* what, Gabber?' I asked him. Enough beating about the bush.

When Gabber pursed his lips, his chin almost entered his mouth. 'Tell me about this junk you've brought me,' he

71

said, 'these *riddles*, and I'll swap you for the "Besides".' He wrapped the word 'riddles' in contempt.

I fished my items out again. Mrs Malena's postcard to her friend with the 'cold hand and trembling body' came first. I stared into its tiny bright window with the view of blue sea and coconut palms, and Mrs Malena wasn't there. 'Where's Tonga, Gabber?'

Gabber held the card at arm's length in the thick light that shafted through the door of his place. 'Oh, Mrs Ma-lena?' he called. He shook his head and put the card down. 'Nobody home,' he said.

'But Gabber,' I said. 'I can't picture her.'

'Too bad,' said Gabber. 'You can only forget things that existed. Think of it as a positive.'

I was fishing in the satchel for my next item. 'What about Jason of Samoa?' I passed Gabber the clipping from the personal notices section of classified ads. Gabber looked at the poor little fellow with the weaner's mouth and the ridiculous military uniform. He was shaking his head. 'Fair's fair,' I persisted, poking at his emaciated chest with the top of my cane.

Gabber was looking at the cane. It was meant to remind me about the price paid by those whose *omertà* on my behalf had cost them their lives. He pushed the cane aside respectfully. 'This guy's Samoa isn't where he'll go to die peacefully. It's wherever he'll eventually tell his own sons to kill people. His punches sound like him kicking another kid's football over the fence. He's already a psychopath. He's going to hurt a lot of people.' I let most of this pass. Gabber was playing tric-trac with his own memories. He looked exhausted. 'Hayya' ala falàh, my friend, tell me what you really want?'

The light was fading outside. I wondered if Watcher had gone off his shift and taken the little girl in pink plastic sandals home. I pictured the sandals hanging down either side of his gun. I could see that Gabber hadn't imagined anything. But I still needed him to look at my three-part riddle. Tamar's Guan Gong mask, my attraction to Madame Hee, Watcher with the little gun strapped up next to his big breast. Or, put another way: my contract with the Binh Xuyen, my habit with the Chinese Opera, the surveillance. Or: 'But ah—the future!', Madame Hee's mask that I couldn't see through, the way no one shared Watcher's family moment back there in the Place. I needed my old Egyptian sphinx to look at this riddle in its various forms. He had to run it through the mind he'd constructed, his vault of unimaginative hieroglyphs and fragments. A tiny tremor had begun to agitate Gabber's chin. I was running out of time with him.

'One more riddle, Gabber. Then you have to tell me what you were going to, a few moves back. Your "Besides".'

Gabber's face was straining to be calm. '*Besides*, effendi, don't pretend you don't know that the Chinese Opera you bless with your eminence is where your old mates unveil their new product?' I must've looked blank. 'The Binh Xuyen, Frank. It's their shop window.' The tremor was advancing into his limbs. 'Sorry, Frank, have to call it a day.' He stood up. He looked tiny when he didn't have his full energy. 'People see you going in there, my brother. Like it was your storefront, too.' His voice was fading. 'A'ùdhu billàhi minash shaitàn ar-rajeem. Your history's not unstained, Frank,' he finished, sipping the stale, ionised air of his den.

I felt a chill of understanding and wanted to push his 'Besides' further. But I hurried on. The attention in his big night eyes seemed to be fading. 'Run this through your system, Gabber,' I pleaded.

He was edging towards the back of his place. Silent screens flickered in the dim room. His teeth were showing. He was approaching the fridge at the back of his workspace. It was impolite of me to stay.

'It's Madame Hee,' I said, hurrying. 'At the Chinese Opera. It's like I want to get inside her, Gabber.'

Gabber tittered in the shadows but I didn't know if I really had his attention any more.

'There's something I have to find out. I started going down there all the time. I couldn't stay away from the place.

Just looking at that Madame Hee, Gabber. Wanting to find something. Wanting to get into her.'

Gabber was waving his remote. His screens went dead. The place was nearly dark.

'What's happening to me, Gabber?' I picked up my satchel but left the postcard and the clipping behind. I thought they might remind him. 'Run it through,' I pleaded. 'Find out what I'm doing.'

I stood across the threshold of the doorway to Gabber's place. It was too warm on the inside from the equipment and the lack of ventilation, and there was an old smell of backed-up stormwater, salty and bacterial, on the outside. Inside, in the deep gloom, Gabber's face was briefly pallid and visible in the bluish light from his fridge. Then both he and the fridge door sighed, and I was standing half in darkness and half in the thick, murky glow of early evening in the Place. The dull remnant of daylight was soaking back into the tawdry low-wattage flickers of the stalls. I could hear Gabber's rustling movements with one hyper-tuned ear and the transitional sounds of the Place with the other, as the traders shifted gear for the night's activities.

Gabber let out a big sigh from the back of the shop. It was bigger than his tiny shrunken lungs. It seemed to go on much longer than he'd have had air for. I thought he said a word that sounded like 'Bellerophon', but it was so much a part of his sigh that I couldn't tell if it was a word.

'Maternal surrogates.' My hearing aid picked up the insect-wing whisper of his breath. 'You're looking for your mother, Frank,' said his small, evaporating voice. He had a morsel of humour left. 'At the age of one hundred and twenty. In a Chinese Opera singer.' Gabber's expiring laugh was a succession of little glottal clicks, like an old machine ratcheting to a standstill. 'It's called imprinting . . .' The old Egyptian's voice faded out. I heard 'Bellerophon' again.

'Gabber,' I said reproachfully, spreading my arms to show him my age. But he'd gone. I knew he'd find my clues in the morning and be unable to resist them. I closed his door behind me. The security system announced it was active by playing the opening bars of Eric Satie's first *Gymnopedie*—a few sad wee notes on a piano.

But its tearful simplicity didn't deter me. I felt both hot and cold. The hot part of me knew that although Gabber was older than me, he couldn't imagine anything either. All he knew was based on the entrails he looked at and what his machines told him. The hot part also knew, now, that I'd been right to put the liver-lipped man in the red Guan Gong mask and the Chinese Opera together in my riddle.

The cold part of me was dealing with what Gabber had said about people being afraid. I remembered the young guy with the cross incised in his metal tooth, his salute that had been both respectful and ambiguous. A feeling of shame chilled me as I pictured myself strolling through the Place like a benign capo. It chilled me to think that whatever I'd been doing mattered enough for the Pirates to put Watcher on me. He'd been on the job long enough for it to have become his domestic routine, with room for the little girl in pink sandals—long enough for his presence in the Place to have lodged inside the perimeter of fear that sauntered through there with Little Frank, the Place's erstwhile protector. And that it must have been the Pirates' interests, not my safety, that kept the kid in pink sandals' dutiful parent employed. That he might have been protecting me from the people I'd thought were my friends, not the ones I'd always known were my rivals and even my enemies—the ones Little Frank had made his truce with. The wisecrack about my mother I left in the margins of my thought, though its hurtfulness took me by surprise.

I headed off toward the Opera. I was burning and shivering. I avoided eye contact with the friendly, respectful people who saluted me.

There must've been a bad convection, because the smog was sitting right down on the rooftops. It was going to take a real Cook Strait blow to shift that and bring back the blue.

All the evening snacks braziers were smoking away, the generators were grunting out fumes and quite a few people had masks on. I'd never used one myself. I might always have been skinny, but I had a set of lungs on me like a racehorse and I could afford to get them serviced. But that night I felt the bad atmosphere burning my throat. I went flat-tack down to the Chinese Opera where the air conditioning was pretty good.

Right away I got the first test of my new consciousness reconditioned courtesy of Gabber. I paid my money to Half Ton Jack who runs the ticket window of the Opera, and he caught me looking at him. In the past I'd just been going in like an automaton, not looking at anything other than Madame Hee as an acrobatic horsewoman or woman warrior, or as a quing yi or dao ma dan, an aristocratic lady in extraordinary costumes who did things with her sleeves and hands that made me grip the curtain at the back of the theatre.

'Yes?' said Half Ton, pushing his big face up to the window. It was hardly a polite enquiry. That wasn't why Half Ton got employed at the Opera. A lot of punters came in there thinking the place had to be a front for something else. Half Ton could cope with optimists. It was said he killed by sitting on his victims. This rumour was a powerful pacifier when Half Ton was around. I was grinning at Half Ton there in his little den with its floor covered in sandwich wrappings. The cold part of me was thinking about all the people who had bits and pieces in them from cytogenetic vaults and various organs from stem banks and chimera herds. I thought about the abducted kids from the plague lands who got implanted with mosaic cells and harvested to keep someone else's brain from packing in. I thought again about the ambiguous salute and the cross-incised smile of the skinny guy with the snake tattoo around his flabby bicep. I saw people stepping aside from Little Frank as he passed through the Place on his way down to the Opera. Now, with a frozen grin on my face, I was confronting the monster in the ticket booth. I felt the heat of his watchful patience.

'Sorry,' I said to him. 'No offence. You just reminded me of something, that's all.'

He pushed his face right up to the window and the little talking-port there. 'Just tell me it's the last arse you kissed,' he said in his rich-gravy voice, 'that I remind you of, Junior, and I'll find you in the dark.'

I could see why his services were valued by the management of the Opera. 'No offence,' I said, 'have a nice evening.'

Half Ton was sitting back unwrapping another sandwich and he didn't look at me. I went on inside through the dragon's-mouth entranceway. The place was half full, the lights were dim and I could smell it straight away, the ancient and new mystery of the Chinese Opera.

Tonight's show was one of the Maoist social realist rehashes they sometimes dug out of the repertoire. Even without knowing it you could guess that the story was about a wicked landlord who got his arse kicked by the Collective—ironic when you consider what the Chinese did to their economy, not to mention the world's, not much later. Time does strange things to value, because without any comment the company could haul out some feudal character, some landlord warlord baron type, or his woman counterpart, one of the dao ma dan that Madame Hee was great at, and she'd be the hero of some outrageous costume drama in which the peasants were just the people who did the lights and the special effects.

I sat there while synchronised dancing with banners went on, and while the orchestra worked its way through what Gabber would have had down as the Puccini sample module in a midi. I felt cheated. Sometimes Madame Hee wouldn't have a part in the productions and I guessed that the mid-twentieth century wasn't her natural speciality.

But then she did appear, with rosy apple cheeks painted on to that white mask, and with her hair in two braids under a blue fatigue cap. She executed some wonderful dance manoeuvres, which were new to me. She pivoted on the ball of one foot and her other leg came up so high behind her as she leaned her torso down that I thought she would surely fall over.

But no, at that moment her voice—which I thought could cut through lies, difference, value and time like the Matiu Island casino's laser through the night-sky smog—pierced the interior of the Opera.

As Madame Hee thrust her flag-bearing arm forward and lifted her chin up, a cup of space appeared between her neck and shoulder. It was back-lit by the heavenly blue of the stage flat. Then she brought her flag arm back across her chest with martial precision, and the cup between her neck and shoulder filled with emptiness. I wanted to be sipping that emptiness until it filled me up. Until I contained it. Until Little Frank was complete. Until I filled that blue space.

I immediately got up from my seat down the back and stood with one hand wrapped in the heavy red drapes by the door. My heart was thundering away as the spotlight tracked Madame Hee past a giant holograph of a mountain. My heroine was in some leadership role, because she was leading the cadre towards an ominous build-up of forces stage left.

'Ten eighty one. Ten eighty one.' My calming mantra.

There was something about seeing her in a role emphasising her youthfulness that made her seem more artificial than usual. I found this almost too exciting to handle. And just then I felt this gust of zoo air on the back of my head, breath like you might expect from something big and stir-crazy.

'I already spoke to you, Junior,' said Half Ton Jack right by my ear. 'How come you can't sit down like any normal citizen and enjoy the show?'

'Hey,' I said. 'I like the view from here. I'm a regular.'

'Let me tell you about "regular",' said Half Ton. I could feel his body heat wrapping itself around me in the cool, air-conditioned interior of the Opera. 'Today's show is called *Taking Tiger Mountain by Strategy.* It's a revolutionary classic. Now if you don't like it the *regular* thing to do is to forget you've ever heard of refunds. The regular thing is not—' and a big digestive sigh came right down over my head—'to do strange things with the drapes back here, Junior.'

That really pissed me off. Here was Little Frank, with my reputation in the neighbourhood, and this talking hamburger was treating me like some juvenile nuisance.

'Whoa, now hold it,' I began.

'Oh dear,' said that amazing voice that seemed to be speaking through a mouthful of half-chewed lunch. And then these enormous arms wrapped themselves around me from behind, I was hoisted up on to the hard sofa of that great belly, and Half Ton Jack walked me out into the foyer. 'I been watching you,' he said. 'Who are you? I should know you, right?'

'Why?' I said. 'Why should you know me? What can I give you? You've got a good job, plenty to eat, a nice cage.'

He let that pass. 'I see people looking at you,' he said. 'They know you. They know who you are. You're *somebody*.'

Half Ton made my amber-topped cane seem absurd, and I resented that. I wanted very much to be back inside with *Taking Tiger Mountain by Strategy* and Madame Hee. I wanted it so much I felt sick. And I could still feel my heart going crazy.

I said, gasping, 'Somebody, hey? Well, these days that's not so hard. I hear they can even clone something human off a steamed pork bun.'

Then it went black. I didn't feel any pain at all.

When I woke up, though, the pain was in my chest and up through my left foot and arm and into my head. Half Ton Jack had me on the floor of some room. I saw his big, joined-together fists coming down at me again, and then they stopped just above me. Next thing he'd got this mask over my face. It was oxygen and the pain slowly subsided.

What was poor Little Frank to do, awake after sixty years of habit to a world in which I couldn't tell friends from toadies? Where I feared I might have fallen under the spell of a Chinese Opera singer because I'd made a pact with my enemies and because my mother had left me where I would grow wise too young among the disposable commodities of other people's lives?

Either I was Timing Out or this was the real world. The first scenario made sense, but I was going with the real world. Because when the blue comes back, my God. Allàhu akbar, as Gabber would say. Especially when it's a good bright southerly blow that does it. Then you see the cloud cover rolling back like a big grey drape off the sky. The heat and the smog rise up out of the streets. You can breathe. The city looks beautiful around the harbour. The water has that glitter, like crumpled aluminium. As I remember, that's how it was most of the time when I was a kid horsing about on the beach there at Lyall Bay or on the swings by the surf club when I lived with my Uncle Geek.

After Half Ton had brought me round the time I keeled over in the foyer of the Chinese Opera, it was that blue coming back I thought of first. Because the pain going away was like the smog blowing clear. I lay there remembering old Uncle Geek. Half Ton was good. I had to give it to him, in his capacity as front-of-house. He had the equipment there. I didn't have to explain to him that heart-stops like I'd just had weren't uncommon. Sometimes you'd see an older Expectationer drop. The organ just couldn't hack the continuous maintenance. Then you had to get a new one or a new bit, or you'd die.

He'd given me a massive ding on the chest. That's what the pain was mostly about, but he'd done it right. What impressed me more was that he'd wanted to. My impression was that he'd cheerfully have tossed this overdressed corpse into the street and thrown its silly ornamental cane after it. I didn't think it was his sweet nature that made him save my life. He went on acting surly, and even though he brought me a drink of water without my asking for it he managed to give the impression he hoped I'd choke on it.

Meanwhile, there I sat getting my breath back and remembering when I was a kid living with Uncle Geek. If we could organise the way the brain worked we'd be less than human. Little Frank was thinking this too as I sipped my water and felt the breath going in and out of my nose and lungs. My nose whose cartilage wasn't mine until it became part of me, and my lungs that had both been grown in a patient resigned body somewhere I didn't want to think about just then. There was no way any parahuman was going to come up with 'riddles', as Gabber jeeringly called them, that would join up Madame Hee's inhuman voice, a temporary death, the blue coming back, my childhood with Geek in Lyall Bay and the day my mother left me. My ten-eighty-one day.

But I just went with it. What I remembered best about that ten-eighty-one day was the way Uncle Geek dealt with it when he came back from one of his mysterious expeditions and I was still there. My mother usually picked me up from the warehouse section of Geek's second-hand joint when she finished work.

'Aren't you home yet—where is the bitch?' said Geek. It was just his manner. He always behaved as though time was running out. Never time to cook—we ate takeout food. He only ever caught the second half of soccer games I played in. Used to drop me off at school an hour before everyone else so he could 'get cracking'. I was a public swimming pool and national museum orphan during the school holidays. That's how he was.

The day he came back and found me still rattling happily around in the junk shop after his minder had shut up and gone home, he had this kind of 'I told you so' look on his face. If he was sorry for me he didn't show it. He just stood there rubbing his bald spot with one hand and pulling his moustache with the other, showing those big yellow teeth that always made me think of pictures I'd seen of beavers.

'Where is the bitch?'

And a fair bit later, when I was properly settled in with him and I asked him where my father was, he said he didn't know but he guessed it was a long way from my mother. And that wherever she was it would be a long way from me.

He used to call the money that went into my 1081 KidSaver my 'share'. Only later did I guess this meant he got a share too. Only much later did I wonder how it could've come from my little mother. By then I didn't care one way or the other.

All summer we used to play down at the beach, us kids. It was blue right out to the horizon, sky and sea. There'd be surfers speeding along these breakers that went on unfolding right across the bay. You'd see the big jets wobbling down out of the sky all shimmery with heat. Now the airport's been shifted because of sea levels. The Kilbirnie flatlands have mostly gone too.

What I knew had gone. But it amazed me how much I remembered again with each of these shocks to my system— the beautiful-wristed Muslim, the Greeks, Watcher, Gabber, my heart-stop. Each one brought the blue back. Brought more blue back. I remembered the piddly smell by the wall of the surf club. To my shame, I remembered the smothered breathing of our adolescent wanking competitions next to the women's changing sheds. I remembered the sulphur stink of the fireworks we bought from old Mr Chan and then tossed over the fence into the yard behind his greengrocer shop where his ancient, bent-double mother would be stacking crates. I remembered her spine-chilling curses. I remembered the fabulous glitter of the dusty air in Geek's warehouse. I remembered the video games there.

What I couldn't remember was whether I'd missed my mother. I guessed I had. You'd expect me to have cried myself to sleep in the porch-room Geek had cleared of overflow junk for me. But I couldn't remember. When she went, my feelings about her seemed to go as well. And I soon refilled the porch with other junk.

She was between sixteen and seventeen when she had me. One day my father departed on a Railways bus. I remembered his narrow leg and his boot with a wonderful silver buckle that I'd loved and desired on the step of the bus. My mother used to play this game with me. 'I'll be the mother,' she'd say. 'You be the kid, now act like one.' So I used to run around the flat, banging doors and acting a tantrum, and she used to do this exaggerated mother routine: 'Don't you *dare* bang doors like that when your poor father's tired after work!' We'd fall about laughing. Then we'd pretend to cook proper tea and we'd pretend to have good manners when we ate it. We had competitions to see who could make their pinky finger stick out furthest from their cup. My mother was really young and maybe that was why she invented the game of being real.

Geek knew something that he never told me. He made no attempt to find her. But then he didn't try to find me either, when I ran away a few years later. He probably knew what I was up to and kept an eye on me from a distance. He poked around in most parts of the city and he'd have heard something. He'd have heard from the cops a couple of times, too, during that period in my life.

'When the blue comes back,' I was saying aloud when Half Ton Jack came back into the Opera office.

'You're alive,' he said, making it sound like a disaster. 'I checked you out,' he added. He had a whole bunch of clips and rings in one ear, and I was fascinated by the way the flesh had pouted around them. You don't usually think of ears as being fat, but even Half Ton's eyes were. They bulged out of his face. And where a twisted queue of hair came out the back of his skull there were folds of flesh in the shaved parts of his head.

'Okay,' he said. 'Tell me. You think I'm ugly. You'd rather still be dead than share the planet with something like this.' He had my hat, suit coat and my fancy cane. He put them down carefully on a chair.

I can appreciate a joke, but Half Ton wasn't laughing enough for me to get smart with him again. Besides, I wanted to know what checking me out amounted to. 'I don't think you're ugly,' I said. 'Not to mention you saved my life. Around here they call me Little Frank. Ask anybody, they'll tell you. If there's something you need. I'd like to pay you back.'

'*Little Frank*,' mused Half Ton in that wonderful voice. 'You're the dealer. I thought you were a big shot.' He had a way of turning compliments into turds. But I'd begun to get the idea that the real Half Ton Jack deep inside that enormous body was a decent human being. I'd just have to get used to his style. 'For a start,' he said, doing his I'll-find-you-in-the-dark routine and shoving his face up close, 'you can tell me, now that the show's over, what you were doing at it. You've been here regular.'

'I had something more concrete in mind,' I said. 'Something you might want.'

'Hey,' breathed Half Ton. He made the word sound as long as a sentence. 'What I want is, I want to know what's your interest here. What you're doing standing up the back all the time?'

'You been watching me?' I kept the irritation out of Little Frank's voice.

'Say I began to notice you, Junior. That's my job. What're you looking for? You waiting for someone? Using this place for some Little Frank monkey business? Because don't.'

'I'm retired,' I said. 'This is my retirement hobby.' But I wasn't going to escape Half Ton's patience. The question would be back and I wasn't ready to go anywhere just yet. 'What're you looking for?' It was my question, too.

The big face just stayed there, waiting. The breath went in and out of it very calmly, very slowly, with a kind of sieving sound deep inside the grave, stoic flesh of his trunk under the tank-top dark with sweat and streaked with the day's mayonnaise.

I thought, What the hell. 'Okay,' I said. 'You win. My interest is Madame Hee.' I made Little Frank's voice easy and noncommittal. 'Sensational.'

Something very fast moved in Half Ton Jack then. Suddenly the huge face was several feet away, and if it had seemed inscrutable before now it was the Great Wall of China itself.

I guess Half Ton's original nickname would have been spelled Won Ton. Won Ton Jack. That might not occur to you if all you ever saw was the big man in the cashier's window, one ear full of clips, pigtail sticking out of his shaved head. Then again it might. But say something wrong, like it seemed I just did, and you'd find yourself looking at a one-man Mongolian horde. Half Ton's reaction to the name Hee was so obvious and at the same time so hidden that my first disgraceful thought was, Maybe he's her pimp.

'Now talk to me about "interest",' whispered Half Ton. The sieving sound of his breath hadn't sped up but it seemed to have increased in volume, as though he'd opened the mighty valves in his chest and was methodically flooding himself with oxygen.

'I already answered your question,' I said, politely but firmly. 'Sorry, I'd like to stay and talk, but I have to get this sick puppy to the doctor.' I clasped my hands over my whimpering little heart, combining the gesture with a salute of some kind to the big man who was steadily emptying the room of breathable air. I thought Half Ton should make the next move if there was going to be one.

But he just nodded his head very slowly. 'Yes, you can go now, Junior,' he sighed. 'You take it easy. See a doctor. Look after yourself. Tomorrow we're doing *The Romance of the Three Kingdoms* with that Cao Cao creep. It's a classic.'

'Tomorrow I'll have to go up to the hospital again,' I said. 'Thanks all the same.' I resisted the urge to say to him, 'Talk to me about Cao Cao.' I badly needed to get out of the trajectory of these memories.

'Yes, yes,' said Half Ton in a voice that poured smoothly out of him like warm caramel sauce. He might have been trying to put a fractious child to sleep or hypnotise a psychopath into confession. 'Yes . . . the Hospital. Junior.' And then, to my amazement, he seemed to smile. 'I go there, too,' he said, as if that made us complicit in something. The mass of his cheeks dimpled and his eyes disappeared completely. 'Junior,' he said, his chuckle slopping about somewhere deep in the echo-chambers of his chest. 'Little Frank, Junior Frank. Tell you what, Junior Frank, maybe one day you *can* help me.' His face was expressionless again and he was looking at me very hard. 'Yes, I think so,' he rumbled.

Maybe it was Half Ton's idea of a joke, or maybe he was being friendly, but those eyes bulging through their slits of fat were paying very close attention to me. He helped me into my coat while I disguised the shallowness of my breathing and tried not to inhale the composting aromas of his own. He passed Little Frank his cane without a trace of mockery. Still, he was appraising me.

He left me at the lobby without saying goodbye. Preparations were under way for a late-night show at the Opera. Little Frank walked out into the crazed jostle of the Barbary Coast perimeter. The night people were taking over. No one knew me now. These were not my hours. I walked with care, pushing Half Ton's breath out of my lungs, drawing in the acrid nourishment of the Place. There was no sign of Watcher. Either he'd taken the little running child home or I couldn't see him in the crowd.

The speed of Half Ton's reaction to my confession about Madame Hee—I added that to my list of riddles. It answered one and made another. There was something special about Madame Hee, that was certain. But I didn't know why it mattered to the enormous freak whose job was to make people very afraid before they paid to watch Madame Hee putting on the act of being different from herself.

When I got home there was an email from Mrs Flitch explaining that she'd resigned because I 'frightened' her. Her replacement would introduce herself to me in the morning. She pointed out that the replacement's name wouldn't be Mrs Flitch either. She reminded me that I had a hospital appointment in the morning. Of course my supper was ready. It was a tabbouleh salad with falafel. I began to eat it but then threw it in the waste. I fell asleep without getting out of my underwear.

I'd have been going up to the hospital anyway, next day. It was my regular appointment. But that heart-stop at the Opera made the trip urgent. The thing with Expectations, the body *thinks* it's young but the concentration span of its workers like the heart isn't great. There's only so much the drugs can do by themselves. Nor is failure confined to the underprivileged. I once saw a big-shot biosecurity suit continue her under-rotor helicopter crouch all the way to the tarmac, where everything failed at once. The contents of her body left it any way they could. I was incentivised at the time and remained diligent subsequently.

It seemed obvious that Half Ton Jack was someone you could trust. This was a hunch I had yet to test, but Little Frank's antennae were all saying so. No way they'd ever have said that about Doctor Smiles.

I'd known Smiles for years. She'd come with my package. She was part of my management team. As well as managing my health, she looked after the demand side of the 'retirement business' Little Frank kept ticking over as much out of habit as for the cash flow that groomed my legitimate appearance. Smiles was part of my habit. She'd done a good job. And since she'd been part of my habit, I'd paid her only as much attention as was necessary to notice that she had a brilliant bedside manner and could be delegated to match an inventory with a balance sheet. But many a less pampered patient must have experienced a moment of blind panic at the thought, Is this smile on the doctor's face to do with sympathy or a love of slicing? What's at play here, the Hippocratic Oath or the desire to trial a new product?

The name Smiles wasn't a nickname, though it was so apt most people took it that way. There was something seamless and matching about every aspect of Smiles, including her smile. She was like a scar that had closed smoothly over some perverse experiment. This was probably a clinically truthful description. I wouldn't have trusted Smiles to cut up the cat's meat for me, were it not for the fact that habit and my package had locked us into a safety zone. But now I was on alert again and remembering her bedside manner's queasy proximity to our mutual commercial interest.

The doctor was giving me the once-over. Usually, she'd

have taken care of my Expectations, held my hand briefly between her own warm, dry, violet-scented talons, showed me her deft, moist smile and her uncrinkling eyes of cool amethyst whose colour seemed to match her perfume, and left it at that. I'd have walked out feeling refreshed but followed by that old-fashioned perfume and the clinging trace of her violet scrutiny. I attributed her appraisal to her investment in me as a showcase of her skills. Not to mention our mutual business interest.

Today, though, I'd been through a scanner and was now lying on a gurney with alcohol-damp swabs that attached sensors to parts of my body that no one but Smiles and I ever saw. Her watchfulness had moved in close to the old dope who'd been parading around the place for sixty years dressed up as himself.

'Goodness me,' said Dr Smiles in her slightly mannish voice. I wondered if she saw the gooseflesh rise on the exposed parts of her specimen's body.

Earlier that morning it had been clear the replacement Mrs Flitch already knew what I had for breakfast—she'd read the manual. I caught my usual bus up to the hospital. I recognised the Samoan driver. It was the same guy who'd looked back at the fellow with the flat tweed cap and the shooting stick—the one who'd suggested the Samoan could handle a Porsche 225.

I noticed several things. I noticed the driver, for a start. How many times had I made this trip? How many times had this same man driven the bus? How many times had I caught the same bus at the same time and the same one home again? How often had I noticed this? Never—until now.

Next, I noticed something else obvious. I was wearing a different lightweight suit from the one that had ended up on the floor of the Chinese Opera foyer the night before. The replacement Mrs Flitch was, without comment, sending that one to the dry cleaners. The one I was wearing to see Dr Smiles was a dove-grey silk and wool mix with a nice airy, pleated drape to the front of the trousers. I realised as I put my foot up on the bottom step of the bus that I never wore it without a creamy Dutch white linen shirt whose brand was replaced as regularly as the toilet cleaner in my lavatory, though not as frequently. The shoe I saw on the bottom plate of the bus steps was a comfortable Italian one with a basket-weave top on the instep that let air through to the cotton socks within. I'd worn the same kind of socks my entire unwaking life. I saw that I had a sprig of budding musk rose in my buttonhole, and I knew, with a sick, sinking heart, that this was what I always wore with this suit and this shirt when this rose was in bud at this time of year. I was wearing an alternative summer hat, but that was only because the other one had been scuffed at the Opera.

The Samoan bus driver was looking patiently at me as I hesitated with one foot in his bus. I was paralysed by the obviousness of the realisation that, the other day, the driver might as well have been looking back at me as at the fellow in the flat tweed cap. The day I'd noticed Tweed Cap's comment about the Porsche 225 but not the weirdness of my own dress-up as Little Frank.

The bus driver raised his eyebrows at me in a friendly way. I climbed up and put my ID card through the scanner. I was noticing the third obvious aspect of my morning as I found an empty seat and looked at the tiny image of Little Frank on my card, this dapper little stranger with the neatly trimmed white moustache and the expression of placid indifference on his face. I was noticing how dumb habit was until you got dislodged from it. Until something gave you a kick up the arse. Until a woman with gold bangles gave you a fright. A watcher made you watch yourself. Someone who had no reason to saved your life. And then how shameful it felt to have been the prisoner of behaviour everyone could see but you.

I put the ID card with its picture of the smug little man I didn't want to know any longer back in my wallet. The wallet was a nice one, made of thin, pliant leather with a slot for my phone—the phone that called me and told me to do the same thing I always did at a certain time, on a certain day, at a certain season. I recognised the wallet as the one belonging to the dapper man on the ID card, the man called Little Frank, whose face peeped out from the wallet's card-holder window between the soft folds of handstitched yellowish pigskin.

I tried not to glance back as I got off the bus by the hospital in case I saw the driver looking at me the way he had at Tweed Cap. I wondered what kinds of weird conversation the dapper little dandy in the dove-grey suit might have forgotten he'd attempted to have with the Samoan bus driver over the months or even years he'd been driving the hospital bus. Had these politely ignored attempts at chitchat been up there with the Porsche 225? And I found myself wondering about Jason You Rule in Samoa. Maybe if you were Jason's dad and you saw smug old crooks like the little guy with musk rose buds in his buttonhole, or another one who still lived in the world of the Porsche 225, you could be forgiven for wanting your son to live in a world where the power relations were different. Where being a bully might earn him the right to wear a uniform of his own choosing. Perhaps you'd be forgiven for instructing your son in the correct machete arc for taking the old fuck's head off his shoulders.

Smiles watched the dials on her machines for a bit. Then, with a radiant grin, she said, 'Little Frank, I think I'd recommend that you act your age. Your alpha waves look like a cheap perm and your poor old ticker's rigid with stress.' Smiles's voice had a tendency to accentuate the sibilants, and when she spoke the word 'stress' it had a menacing effect. She made as if to hold my hand, but she must have seen my expression and changed her mind. She folded her hands in her trim lap and went on: 'Now what reason could there be for that, at your age?'

'I had a bit of a near-miss,' I said. 'It gave me a jolt. I've been on edge for a few days.'

'Well, Frank,' she smiled. 'I'd suggest you put your feet up and stop running around. There's nothing wrong with exercise, but at your age, really!'

'What are you suggesting, Smiles?' I knew what she was suggesting. It was an old routine I now recognised as habitual. I took refuge behind the anonymity of habit.

'Now don't be coy with me, Frank, you're all agitated. Even modern science knows there's nothing like romance to raise the pulse rate. Especially since yours hasn't altered in decades, Frank. Not even when the Pirates were firebombing your concessions all those years ago? Remember? Never even took your hands out of your pockets.'

This last bit was a departure from routine. Also, she'd reminded me of an old trademark that had lain buried all the years I'd been coming to see her: Little Frank's legendary cool, the hands in his pockets. Smiles was pushing the envelope of habit. The Binh Xuyen weren't normally part of our rote flirtation. I preferred not to remember them, but what Dr Smiles was saying was true.

'You're right, of course, Smiles,' I said, just to shut her up.

'Really, Frank?' The doctor's thrilled smile was as radiant as sunlight on a shark-infested lagoon.

'Too right,' I said, irritated now, grasping the first out-of-Little-Frank-character crudity that came into my head. 'One of yours, actually, Doctor. A factory job.' *Why not?* I thought. 'And she can sing,' I said. 'She's an opera singer.'

Smiles's face froze on a grin that wasn't going to change until she forced it to. Her reaction surprised me. But she made a good recovery and smiled at me as though I was her favourite comedian.

'Well, Frank,' she purred, 'whatever it is you're up to, my advice is return to Go. Getting another heart into you would be very exclusive indeed. We'd really have to go shopping, darling. The body's very good, Little Frank, but it expects a lot by now.'

This sounded like a threat to me. 'I know,' I said. 'I'll try and be grown up about it.'

If she heard this as another joke she gave no sign. I slipped back into character. It began to feel more and more like the best protection I had.

There was the business with my arrival at Smiles's clinic to think about in that regard. I'd only taken half a dozen steps from the bus, but I must've been giving off an air of uncertainty. Not the usual Little Frank don't-fuck-with-me routine. My hands-in-pockets chill. I was dealing with the polite Samoan bus driver's gaze of amiable hatred on the back of my neck. I'd tucked the arrogant old bastard he wanted to hack to bits with a machete in the card window of a pigskin wallet. I was dangling the wallet from my hand. This was an unwise gesture when coupled with my air of eccentric bewilderment.

The Creeper who was attracted by these signs of weakness rapidly appeared at my shoulder. She had a bottom lip so enlarged it hung down to expose her lower teeth. It was the opposite of a grin and the opposite of what I would see when I got past the door of Smiles's cool violet-scented consulting chamber. I came to my senses when the poor thing grabbed me by the arm. She made a noise like 'Uzhuzh.' She was trying to stop me putting the wallet in my jacket pocket. The word her dragged-down lip had changed was probably 'Jesus', or it might have been 'Please'. There were scrofulous growths around the glands in her neck and throat which also impeded her speech. The hand she kept on my arm was rough and purple with impending scales. I lifted the wallet with Little Frank gazing serenely from his card window out of her reach. Normally such freaks wouldn't have approached Little Frank. Normally he'd have given a couple of them something to help them along. But this morning the signals had been reversed. The poor thing was trying to pull the wallet down where it couldn't go into my pocket. The old bloke who'd abjured his philanthropic self was trying not to give her anything.

Then her hand abruptly let me go. I saw that she was looking past me. The expression on her face couldn't change but her body language did. Her hands dropped to her sides and she stood there, compliant and watchful, a rope of spit running unchecked from the great ladle of her lip. When I looked back to see what had stunned her into this posture of defiant fatalism, I saw an Asian woman, who could have been Cambodian by the pragmatic flatness of her features, standing smoking a cigar a short distance away. She had reflecting sunglasses on, and she was wearing a nondescript tracksuit and a peaked cap with a sun-visor brim. She'd have melded without trace into any crowd on the streets of the city. But she was looking expressionlessly at the Creeper with the ladle lip. The reflecting sunglasses were as carefully focused as infra-red video surveillance. As I watched, she slowly took her hand out of the pocket of her tracksuit jacket. The reflecting glasses seemed to recalibrate fractionally and focus on me. Then the Cambodian cigar-smoker stepped back into the crowd and disappeared. The Creeper was gone too when I made the effort to get up the steps of the hospital. Gone quickly. And then I knew that my gravel-voiced watcher with the pink-sandalled child wasn't the only one with instructions to keep an eye on Little Frank.

'Feel like a little chat, Frank?' was Smiles's normal invitation after we'd done the medical part of our business. Today when I let her take my arm as we walked along towards the solarium I detected tension in the way she held my elbow against her breast. I strolled like the boulevardier Little Frank in my basket-topped loafers along the antiseptic corridors of the hospital's specialist wing. But I'd consigned that serene fraud to his own compact pigskin wallet where it lay against the heart Smiles had just checked. This was my reminder that since I was being watched I'd better watch myself.

There were two simple questions I thought Dr Smiles might be able to answer. I figured that if I could get even imperfect answers I could ask Gabber to check them out. I wanted to ask the questions so much I had to make an effort to keep my courtly boulevardier's arm relaxed. I made sure my feet pointed out at the stroller's angle. I resisted the urge to hurry Smiles past the fake, shiny aspidistras in their fake soil. I didn't cut her short when she stopped to greet members of her staff. They treated her condescensions with respect.

This was probably because she was holding the arm of an old dandy whose business involved the raw materials of her specialisation.

Our 'little chats' were mostly supply-side demand-side tallies and reports. Since the operational details of Little Frank's business were in the hands of managers like Smiles, the chats were usually mundane. But this one soon strayed. I was trying to insert my questions into our banter. Smiles was smuggling her curiosity about what Little Frank was scheming in there as well.

I wanted to know from the doctor who'd managed my entire life as an Expectationer if GTX could selectively edit memories and destroy the ability to imaginatively reconstruct them. I wanted to know if this action could be reversed. And how.

What did I think Smiles wanted to know? I saw that she was trying to measure not just what I could remember, now, but how I felt about it. I saw that she was another of my watchers.

We strolled along while this unacknowledged electrical charge shot back and forth between us. Between the unyielding silicone bag of her breast and the efficient titanium joint of my elbow. On the way, I bantered a couple of things to see her reaction. I told the smiling doctor that on the bus I'd misread Sheetmetal Worker as Sentimental Worker in the employment pages. Smiles wanted to know what I was doing checking out the employment pages. She wasn't interested in the little neural slip over a word, its challenge to her diagnostic alertness. Frank was taking some kind of interest in the world? Why was this?

'Don't tell me you're looking for a little retirement job as well, Frank?' Smiles enquired with a trill.

I heard the 'as well'.

'As well as what, Doctor?' I asked.

'As well,' cooed the doctor, hugging my arm to her upholstered breast, 'as your romantic interest, Frank.'

'Oh, that,' I said. 'No fear. Not on your life. Ever since

94

I was a kid, Smiles, I've looked through the employment pages, just to check on all the jobs I'm never going to touch. It makes me feel good about my situation.' I thought I'd lay it on a bit. 'As you do, Smiles.'

She gave my silk- and wool-clad forearm a coquettish squeeze. I saw the unblinking amethyst moment of her scrutiny. We walked on like a couple of well-preserved sweethearts and entered the solarium through a sighing door that retained the room's warm begonia-scented air. This was another Smiles touch.

Smiles was humming a tune and looking with satisfaction at the hanging pots of real plants and flowers in the solarium. There were a couple of poleaxed patients sitting on some wicker furniture over by the big outside windows, as well as a balloon-head basketcase with flippers. They were all three swaying very slightly, as though to some sound-track the rest of us couldn't hear. The basketcase was crooning and its volume went up when Smiles entered. It was a good place for confidential chats, Smiles had once been fond of repeating, because no one there could remember anything. This joke had lost its buoyancy. There was a glass-domed ceiling and a soothing little fountain. Through the windows, which had been treated with an ultra-violet screen, you could see the other buildings of the hospital. There was a smokestack that had something to do with waste disposal, and quite a lot of sky, blue again today, or blued by the film on the window.

'But tell me,' continued Smiles. 'Since when have you reminisced, sweetheart? This isn't the Little Frank who defends himself against those awful Pirates without taking his hands out of his pockets?'

She was going around me again. We settled into our comfortable wicker chairs. Smiles lifted the lid of her notebook and brought its screen to bluish life. I crossed one leg over the other and watched her with the phony smile of an absentee company director. I took her nostalgia lead and went with it. I told her how, that morning as I'd come around Oriental Bay in the bus, I'd seen a windsurfer slicing through a cloud of seagulls feeding and diving in a shoal of sprats between the sea wall and the floating restaurants. The windsurfer went right through the middle of them. They flew up in a big cloud. Then they got back to the business of feeding out there on the bright water with the backdrop of floating restaurants and Toyota City. It was one of those rare blue days, I told Smiles with a tremor of old-fart emotion in my voice, all too rare now, what with the atmosphere the way it was, with big clouds towing across and purple shadows racing over the harbour. I watched the doctor's diagnosing face. She watched mine quivering a little with emotion that wasn't entirely manufactured.

'I find myself thinking about my childhood a lot,' I said, hamming a beseeching expression, though what I was saying was also true. Smiles was looking at me tenderly—and waiting. 'Life is so full of surprises,' I said. I dabbed my eyes with the hanky from my jacket pocket. Smiles passed me a box of aloe vera-infused tissues and I blew my central casting nose into one.

The doctor closed the glowing lid of her computer gently, as if pressing down the eyelids of a recently deceased.

'Lucky old you,' she breathed. I reckoned I heard real sadness in her voice. 'What say, Frank, we just park the boring old business for today and have a candid chat about your—' she waited until she had my eye contact above the fragrant tissue with which I was disguising my partial deceit—'about your condition.' A sound like venomous steam hissed out of the word 'condition'.

'What condition are we talking about, Smiles?' I asked, all innocence. 'I thought we'd got that sussed. Is there something you're not telling me?'

'Come off it, Frank,' she snapped, letting the bedside manner slip. She hitched her chair close to mine in the humid sunlight of the solarium. 'You know damn well I've told you everything I know. Now it's your turn.'

'I don't know what you're talking about,' I said, feigning alarm.

'You've got sirens going off all over you,' hissed the doctor. Her smile had turned into the patient grimace of a hire nurse looking at another steaming bedpan. 'I saw it, the machines saw it and you saw it, Frank.'

'You already told me that, Smiles,' I protested. 'You told me to take it easy. Act my age.'

Smiles was trying not to be provoked. 'What's more, Frank,' she went on, ignoring the rhetorical bedpan between us, 'you're taking an interest in aspects of your life that have filled you with indifference for sixty years. I should know, Frank.'

'Because you've been listening to me talk drivel for all of them.' I finished the doctor's sentence for her. 'What's so wrong with that?' I protested indignantly, prodding her knee with a bony finger. 'What's so strange about remembering stuff?' *Come on*, I was urging her. *Get pissed off. Tell me.*

There was a tiny rim of delicate china white around Smiles's sculpted nostrils. Her enhanced bosom was heaving a little. I held her hard, crystalline, amethyst gaze with my own look of self-righteous reproach. She was measuring my intention. She was taking cover. She wasn't going to continue with this. Her face began to recompose itself into the mask of relentless caring I knew so well. My bottom lip began to tremble—because I was making it, but also because I was desperate for her to cross her break point and tell me what I had to know.

'Because you *can't*, Little Frank,' said Smiles as if uttering stones.

I could see that the effort it cost her had made a collar of perspiration encircle her purplish mouth on top of the light, peachy face powder there. She was on the wrong side of her scepticism now. I had to give her something or she would self-correct right out of the room.

I assembled a look of horror. 'What do you mean, *can't*!' squeaked Little Frank. 'Haven't we trusted each other all these years? Have we ever cheated?' I gave it a beat. 'Haven't you,' said Little Frank maliciously, 'benefited substantially?'

I waved melodramatically at the well-appointed solarium—the real, perfumed plants, the benign glow of sunlight filtering in through the glass dome, the tinkling fountain, the dispensing cabinet for refreshing natural beverages. I allowed my indignation to rest, unflinchingly, on Smiles's own superb facsimile of herself. She couldn't have missed Frank's outraged evaluation of the sparkling brooch with which her crisp shirt-waister was fastened over her expensive chest. I glared at the placating hand she placed on my knee.

'Now, now, Frank,' soothed the doctor, alarmed.

'Don't patronise me,' yelped Little Frank, trying to withdraw his hand.

The basketcase on the far side of the room began to moan with anxiety. The sighing door exhaled as the other poleaxed solarium regulars took their shambling leave.

Smiles pressed the hand she held between her own against my knee. The knee began to agitate—I was doing well. Then she let go and sat back. I waited for her to expose my play-acting for what it was. Instead she repeated, 'Because you can't,' in a voice that seemed, for the second time that day, to be tinged with real sadness. 'You just can't, Frank. It's not that I won't let you. The treatment won't, Frank. Every time you top up, darling, you take in blockers. We've been over this.'

No we hadn't. 'What do you mean, blockers?' I began, very gently, to reel her in.

My compliance over the past sixty years horrified me. I had to believe the drugs were why I hadn't asked these questions before. The basketcase was nodding and rocking, and I knew how it felt. But Smiles's tone was now different from the threatening one with which she'd advised me to return to Go, back in the consulting chambers. Now, she sounded tired. She sounded like someone who was sick of her job. I didn't doubt she'd get over it. I pressed on while her self-pitying mood held her on my side of the play.

'Who's blocking me?' I asked rashly, and saw at once that I'd lost the initiative. Smiles went back into character so fast her brief excursion out of it into my faux sentimentality might as well not have happened. She was back across her bullshit-detector divide and she was staying there. But her reaction had told me what I needed to know. The 'blockers' might be drugs, but their effects belonged to someone.

'I never said anyone was blocking you.' The doctor's tone had defaulted to soothing professional. 'I said the blockers in Expectations were. Without them your synapses would melt all over your brain, Frank. Too much information, as we used to say. Besides.' Smiles paused. This was the second 'Besides' in as many days.

'Besides what?' I asked, feeling like a cracked record.

'Besides,' said Smiles with a hint of professional woe, 'it's better if you don't. Not only would you start putting all sorts of things together that shouldn't be, but you'd get sad.'

'*Sad*, Smiles?' I managed to sound amazed. 'Why should I feel sad? Look at me. In the pink, not a care in the world.'

'Bollocks,' said Smiles.

I waited.

'You're heading for a Deadline, Frank. Like I told you. This memory stuff—it's leaking through. Dribs and drabs. You won't get much but, trust me, it will make you sad. It will make you sad because you won't be able to make sense of it. You won't have the imagination to put it together. It will put itself together in ways that will make you sad.' The word 'sad' was striking me as unclinical and evasive. I wasn't enjoying the hiss Smiles injected into it. 'We have to manage the next bit. Can't have you Timing Out,' she concluded. She patted the moisture from around her mouth with one of the aloe vera-infused tissues. 'It gets so humid in here,' she said with an almost audible gear-shift in her manner.

'But what if I want the memories? What if I want to be sad? Why can't I?' I waited a moment. 'Why can't I Time Out if I want to, for that matter?'

There were two answers to that question. One, I knew now, was that someone didn't want me to remember something. Smiles might as well have handed me that answer on a piece of paper with a date stamp and the signature of a Justice of the Peace. The evidence so far said that the people who didn't want me to get complete recall were connected with the Chinese Opera. The Chinese Opera was connected with the slimy-lipped man called Tamar in the back of a vehicle. The vehicle was the property of the Pirates, the Lao Sheng, the Binh Xuyen, whatever they got called.

The other answer had to do with what action to take.

'You'd have to Deadline, Frank,' said Smiles matter-of-factly. 'You'd have to Time Out.' Her tongue flicked over her shiny lips, wetting them. 'If you wanted to get it all back.'

'You mean die?' asked Little Frank with an expression of confusion.

Smiles didn't believe me. 'Did I say "die", Frank?'

I persisted with my stupidity. If I was stupid enough I might provoke the doctor into saying what I'd already begun to know. 'How can I remember anything if I'm dead?'

Dr Smiles glared with her amethyst diagnostic tools at the thin ground-cover of my stupidity. I had the feeling I'd answered as many of her questions as she had of mine. 'I don't know, Frank, sweetheart,' she said in a conversation's-over, crisp tone of voice. 'I've never died. Can't tell you that.'

And then, at the very last minute, proving that even the most polished self-awareness can have a character flaw, I heard Smiles say something she shouldn't have. She said it because she wanted to. No, she *had to*. She had to have her triumph. Because having told me that it was Expectations that withheld memory and blocked imagination, and that the way to get them back was to stop taking the stuff and, sooner or later, unless I got started again in time, die—having told me this, she found the information banal. A huge weight of habit was banked up behind it. I saw that she needed to finesse the sadness of her endless task of keeping the lid on Little Frank. Of preserving whatever it was that made me worth keeping alive. She just had to cap this dowdy moment with something glittering.

'Anyway,' confided Dr Smiles, leaning her shiny lips closer, as though she intended to kiss her proudest professional achievement with whom she was bored and whose success had enslaved her. 'Anyway, Frank, there's something new out there, something exciting. A "new thing".' She put the phrase in thrilling quotation marks for me, as though I was a child. 'Isn't that worth living for?'

The muggy, over-perfumed atmosphere of the solarium chilled suddenly. The hairs on Little Frank's neck and forearms stood up. But I wasn't going to ask Smiles what this 'new thing' that was more exciting than me was, knowing that she'd already transgressed the fail-safe of her discretion. But she warned me off anyway.

'Don't ask,' hissed Dr Smiles with a twinkle.

'Thanks, Doctor,' I said, being unspecific and retreating behind my predictable behaviour.

Then I thought I heard her say, 'Patients.' She'd crossed the room with calm strides and was soothing the moaning basketcase by the big window. The balloon-head flapped its fins at her and made adoring sounds. For a moment it occurred to Little Frank that the doctor was being unprejudiced in the care of her patients. No favouritism around here, except perhaps for the 'new thing'. But in a frantic corner of my brain, bewildered by fragments of memory, by riddles, by my efforts to keep it simple, the word 'patients' wanted to be 'patience'.

I thought I'd give it one last shot. '*Patience*, Smiles?' I enquired in a perplexed tone, emphasising the hiss at the end. 'What exactly am I waiting for, Doctor?'

Dr Smiles whipped around and gave me a last brilliant smile. Once again, her reaction put ink to the paper I'd handed her. 'Not me, Frank,' she said sweetly, while fending off the balloon-head's flippers. 'Bye bye. À bientôt.'

Patience, patience. It was a word the doctor used often in our little chats. Along with the memory jokes. I wondered if she'd been playing a game with me. The word nibbled at my thoughts like a mouse. Like the mice whose foetal brains Smiles injected with human stem cells. On our occasional tours of inspection, our cosy wanders around the scientific playgrounds of Little Frank's 'raw material' supply, I'd watched the mice trying to figure out what they were—what they'd become—in the antiseptic paradise where Smiles's demands and my supplies met in states of innocence.

The solarium seemed to sigh with relief as I left through its self-sealing door. Maybe the 'new thing' mattered, maybe not. I left that issue along with Smiles's flawed need to have the last word. I had enough on my mind.

But a question nibbled at the edge of my thoughts as I walked back along the corridor. Before coming in to see Smiles I'd prepared as usual. But there was an anomaly on my screens of market analysis as I followed my organic orange juice with my two permitted cups of coffee and my nice fibrous bread roll. I sluiced whole grains from the roof of my mouth with the stringent coffee and watched the colour-highlighted anomaly of market heat, a little hectic rash that poured down the screen as the figures scrolled through. There was a minor glut of Harvest. The oversupply was pushing margins down. This was a big part of Little Frank's business, and I wondered why the manufacturers were unloading. Where was the redundancy threat to these excellent, reliable, even classic products? Why had they begun to behave anachronistically? Whose interests were being served by the information leak that had trickled this effect into the market?

Smiles's phrase 'new thing' hooked itself into this thought like a tick. But as I walked along towards what I wanted to do down by the hospital entrance I didn't let the thought with its little attachment get in the way. I parked it with the list of things I had to check with Gabber.

Patience, patience, patience.

A running red stripe on the floor, as well as the ordinary green and white décor, told me I was tracking towards the hospital entrance and also that I'd now left the privileged zone of the clinic Smiles ruled with terror and devotion. I felt as though I was backtracking to my future. I was walking backwards with my gaze on the scattered, unpatterned information fragments of my past. I was heading for a future that seemed to depend on something I'd already done.

This future also depended on my decision about limiting my place in it. Despite Dr Smiles's coyness, there was a moment when Timing Out became dying. There was going to be a decision along that continuum somewhere. I was working the nature of this decision around in my mind. I was twisting it around with the phrases, 'There's a time and place for everything', with 'All in good time', with 'In the nick of time'. *Patience, patience, patience.* This was fun. I felt like someone who'd just had a fresh blood tank through them. Not many of the people I passed as I skipped along the corridor's red stripe looked as merry as Little Frank.

What's the difference between Timing Out and dying? As Gabber enjoyed pointing out, this had to do with a stretch between contingent and necessary. When you died, you stopped. Game over. Nothing to do with time. Timing Out, you began to accelerate through time in inverse proportion to the amount you'd saved. I thought of the time credits beginning to screech out of a kind of vent in my life, like gas from a punctured tank. This was an image Gabber had gifted me by turning his mouth into a little whistling aperture. Like the lispy hiss in Smiles's voice. Sooner or later the credit would be gone. I'd have had a finite amount of time in which to Time Out. There was a necessary end to it and to its contingency. When it ended, I'd die. It would be necessary for me to die.

Patience.

Here's what Smiles didn't tell me: the point along that stretch when contingent tipped into necessary. When it would be too late to change my mind.

I had to Time Out in order to remember what I'd done in the past. There was something back there that I had to remember so as to find out what to do in the future. To stop my future dumping itself into my present like a dull shopping list of products. My pamplemousse and cardamom Hammam infuser, my toilet cleaner, my Dutch white shirts, my unwanted cologne. Once I'd found out what to do in the future, I'd be on a tight schedule. A tight schedule getting tighter.

The thought of a tough schedule fired me up. I didn't like my present any more. The process that transformed contingent time into necessary time excited me. The thought of the ultimate risky decision somewhere along that track made me break out in a gambler's sweat. I wanted a deadline. After the deadline, everything that had happened to me in my life wouldn't have happened any more. It would have gone when I did. But everything I'd made happen during my life would go on happening. My consequences.

I was thinking, *About time*. That was something Hokkaido said a lot, back when I used to be late meeting her. First, she'd said it almost gaily, because she was glad to see me. Later, she'd said it in different tones of voice. And there they were again, the surfers and the wave-jumping windsurfers like the ones who'd been slipping back into my thoughts all week. They were slapping across the wet surface of my thoughts and across the sunlit water out at the Raglan Heads. They were going past the *Cao Cao San* as we dropped sail and cautiously approached the Raglan Bar. Hokkaido was waving at them. One of the wave-jumpers waved back. Why was I remembering his wetsuited arm lifting off the boom of the windsurfer, the flash of sunlight in the board's tail of sea spray as he flicked it across and over the crest of the wave that was lifting the *Cao Cao San*'s prow?

My business at the hospital entrance was going to be twofold. I wanted to trade my GTX home dose for street information, and I wanted to go to the public lavatory there. These things were related. My Expectations treatment with Smiles came in two parts. She administered an intravenous through the little sticky trapdoor in my forearm. Its flap of thin skin, which Smiles lifted with delicate forceps, closed again afterwards like a semicircle of Scotch tape. She sluiced it with a little antiseptic rinse. I felt a slight tingle. The rest I did in the privacy of my home. Wearing surgical gloves, I opened the sealed foil lid of a neat cartridge containing GTX. I inserted a small, thoughtfully streamlined, lubricated bullet in my arse. There it began slowly to enter my bloodstream which, the way Smiles told it, had been prepped by the shot through the trapdoor. 'Clandestinely', as Smiles liked to say with a titter, the arse-bullet began to insinuate to the stuff already in my system that Little Frank was going to die. This whispering had to happen gradually and preferably while I was asleep. Not in public. When I woke up in the morning after a refreshing, sedative-assisted slumber, the components of the treatment would have reached an agreement. Frank's cells would've begun to dispel the death-threat through managed growth.

Smiles's fastidious account of the process was odour free and short on detail, but my bedroom would be filled with a strange, acrid smell. There was a home science product that Mrs Flitch replaced monthly called Glade. I'd open the double-glazed windows and pump the place full of Glade's equally repulsive stink of chemical wallflowers, lilacs, roses or something called Wildflower, depending on the month and the manufacturer's whim. Twice a month, the smell of the struggle of life and death and the stink of defeated nature. Twice a month only, the hundred-and-twenty-year-old man flinging open his bedroom windows at six in the morning would also fling his diaper into the incinerator down in the garden and torch it with the help of a cupful of volatile spirits called Lucifer. My breath would be sweet again and lightly scented with another product, Airwaves, by the time Mrs Flitch arrived at eight. The organic juice, coffee and fibrous roll that went into my digestive system at half-past eight would be received with enthusiasm by a metabolism whose prospects had never looked better.

Patience.

If I missed a couple of weeks I'd age by some mathematical factor I couldn't remember and didn't want to calculate. It wouldn't kill me. I didn't care. I'd be a diaper in credit. The bullet looked like the hashish I used to trade when I was just a kid, bringing the prow of the *Little Frank* and later the *Cao Cao San* around into the deeper estuary channels of the Raglan Harbour across the main channel from the town. The magic but not silver bullet that Smiles prescribed was going to be worth more than an extension of my dreary, *patient* routine. What was I waiting for? I couldn't know unless I found out.

I knew what my smile could do. Uncle Geek used to call it Whitey. He said it would either get me into trouble or out of it—baring his own orange-coloured beaver snaggle that would never do either for him. The first time he caught me making some substantial personal adjustments to his inventory, he just stood there looking at Whitey with his own useless Orange hanging out of his face. He didn't say anything then, and I didn't stop smiling. Maybe I despised him for being unable to confront Whitey. Maybe I just thought he was being soft on me because I was, virtually, an orphan. Either way, I felt the power. I used to feel it when the kids I was gypping at the back of Geek's place smiled back at Whitey. They were still buying shit they didn't want.

Hokkaido saw the smile when she opened the front door under the shady old veranda of Dr Jack's house on the scrubby hill above Raglan. I never found out if Jack was his first or his last name. It was what he was called around the town and the little pockets of habitation up the estuaries. Late-summer cicadas were making the whole baking atmosphere of the mid morning vibrate. The heat waves coming off the asphalt driveway were like graphics of a cicada's raucous music. At first I thought I was looking at a pint-sized boy, because the kid in running shorts, sneakers, a blue tee-shirt and a softball cap opened the front door while looking back down the dim corridor towards someone or something I couldn't see inside.

'Hi,' I said, getting the Whitey smile ready anyway—you never knew. 'Can you help me?'

Then the kid turned around and looked at me. We weren't all that different in size. Little Frank had never seen this tiny, beautiful girl before, but she'd seen smiles like mine a thousand times. The heat and the cicadas made me dizzy. I was soaking wet and sweating from my walk up the hill from the jetty. My silence after my first words must have seemed, at first, like the speechlessness of dryness and exhaustion. But I could feel my smile shutting down. I was poleaxed by the scepticism of this little beauty who'd stepped out on to the veranda in front of me. She made me take a surrendering step backwards. If I'd had a hat, I'd have been wringing it humbly in my clumsy peasant's hands.

'I doubt it,' she said in slightly accented English. This broke another of Little Frank's rules: have the first smart word as well as the last one. She didn't bother to ask what kind of help I needed.

Then Dr Jack appeared from the dark hallway of the old villa. He was a third again the size of the little Japanese woman, but she didn't defer to him either. He was wearing nothing but a pair of baggy khaki shorts that could have fitted Hokkaido and me both, a leg each. He was the colour of strong tea, with a shaggy head of yellow-white hair hauled together in a ponytail that hung down his back. He was built like a brick shit-house, with a few baggy bits around the arse and tits the way old fellows go, but solid overall, with hands like shovels. Though he was huge and strong, he didn't look well. I got a shock when he shook hands with me, which he did without saying anything. His handshake was shocking not because my little hand disappeared inside his, but because his palm was so soft. You'd have expected someone that big and strong to have tough hands, but his were doctor's hands. The nails were short and clean, and the warm, dry palms felt as though they'd been dusted with talcum powder. He looked at Little Frank over the little woman's head with an expression that was just short of visibly angry. And then he stepped back and began to laugh. It was a sound halfway between a truck-engine trying to turn over and a big animal roaring.

'Well, my my,' he said. 'Look at you two.' He was laughing but he wasn't smiling, and I had a feeling he wasn't joking either. It was as if he'd already seen that Hokkaido and I were made for each other. He'd seen that no good would come of it and had moved beyond hostility to a position of reasonable anger. His voice was fantastic: it seemed to come out of the front of his whole body. He was laughing at the pint-size of us, but not so I'd take offence. He was laughing at his own bigness as well. What was also noticeable was that at eleven in the morning he was pretty drunk.

I guessed he'd have been about seventy. Maybe he did his own garden with protective gloves on and his shirt off. The garden was big—a lawn with shade trees, and cabbage trees spaced out along a curving asphalt driveway to an old house on a hill above Raglan Harbour. Further up the ridge was a small complex of white-painted weatherboard buildings with institutional-looking windows and concrete steps painted red. Some elderly people were sitting on park benches under the shade trees up there. The doctor's house had a river-boulder balustrade in front of a big porch where a whole lot of boxes were stacked up. There were larks twitting in the hot, blue sky. A big mean-looking tabby cat was sitting on his spread-out arse on the stone balustrade, glaring at me.

'I want to talk to you,' was all the doctor said then.

'So I heard,' was all I said back. I'd turned Whitey off. It wasn't going to get me out of trouble here, and if it wasn't turned on it couldn't get me into trouble either. I kept my eyes on the doctor's huge sweating mahogany back and the ponytail of yellowed white hair that hung down it as we went along the dim kauri hallway. The house had a smell of old beeswax and cigars. The doctor was trailing his own smell of whisky. The house was a museum of smells.

But what I was clinging to with all the tiny devices of my nose and throat was the sharp smell of limes that had come off the Japanese woman's short hair as I went past her. It was the smell of her hair sticking out from the cap, not the smell of something she'd put on it or washed it with. That tangy smell of something rooted in her skin caught in the back of Little Frank's throat like a million tiny hooks and it never really let me go, not even when I thought I'd forgotten her. Close to a century later, it cut through the antiseptic smells of Dr Smiles's hospital at the moment my life foreswore habit and contemplated death.

It was the smell of life itself, and I sought it like a running mongrel dog with his nose skimming the unfenced wasteland of deadshit, corrugated-iron bach-land suburbia. Not long after my satisfactory business talk with Dr Jack, I ran the lime smell down again. The tiny woman, whose hair had smelled fresher than the salty wind from Antarctica that had first sent Little Frank's *Little Frank* bucking randily towards the sleepy, dope-addled Hicksville where he would meet her, was heaving the boxes from Dr Jack's veranda off the back of a pickup and on to the weedy concrete forecourt of a crumbling, sun-scabbed, two-storey pile down by the motor camp. There was a new, crisply lettered sign outside that read: 'Rooms'. I recognised the laconic style.

I loved the tiny cabin in *Little Frank* where Little Frank barely had to stoop. I loved the smell of the fresh tide when it came slapping along the side of the boat. I loved not having to listen to anything but the gulls and the rare distant bleating of rogue sheep that had run away into the bush. I loved not having to listen to prison inmates, their farts, their wanking and sad boasts, or to any other human sharing my space of habitation. But the next words that came yapping out of my mouth couldn't have cared less.

'Hello, again,' I yelped. 'I just got here, you know anywhere to stay?'

'I rent rooms,' said the little tiny woman in that completely flat voice. 'What do you do?'

I was a bull-artist at that age. I hadn't yet learned that lying was a waste of time: the truth may not have mattered so much as the way you presented it, but it still had to be the truth. But even then I wasn't dishonest. There were those who'd have disputed this with tears in their eyes and sworn affidavits sticking out of their pockets. Nothing I could have done about that. It was just one of the pitfalls of my work.

With Hokkaido, though, faced with those flat, black eyes that didn't blink and that voice sharp with disbelief, I found my natural honesty unable to present the truth in a favourable light.

I dropped my bag of groceries on the footpath. 'I'm just out of prison.'

'What for?'

'Receiving.' I thought I'd better expand on the technical term in case the woman who was drilling her eyes into me didn't know what I was talking about, so I added, 'Stolen goods.'

Her ghost of a grin acknowledged my courtesy. 'Did you know they were?'

'Did I know they were what?'

Hokkaido paused just for a moment. I could feel her making a very quick decision. One honest answer followed by a dumb attempt to stall and I was already losing.

'Okay, okay,' I said. 'Of course I knew. What business is it of yours, anyway?'

'What business is it of *mine*?' She was standing next to the 'Rooms' sign.

'Yeah.' I was losing fast. Inside me a little voice was saying, Don't be a fucking turkey, Frank, learn this lesson while it's still being spelled out for you. It sounded a bit like poor old Geek when he'd visited me in remand. 'Never mind,' I said, being careful not to smile.

'Listen—what's your name?'

'Frank.' I caught myself just in time. I nearly said 'Little Frank' with a big-note emphasis on the capital L—my Witako Prison name: *Little*. To those black eyes of Hokkaido's it would have been about as successful as saying, 'Big Frank, you must have heard of him.'

'Listen, Frank, I don't let rooms to deadshits or crims. Are you a deadshit or a crim?'

I was very impressed. 'I'd love a room,' I said, skipping one whole stage in the dialogue. 'It would be nice to stay on terra firma for a bit.'

At this moment, Hokkaido's expressionless face cracked open and I heard her famous laugh for the first time: 'Kkkkk.' Aside from endless-summer dole surfers and the occasional Canadian vegetarian on a bicycle tour, the only people likely to rent a room with Hokkaido were going to be deadshits or crims.

'You'd better not fuck me around,' she said.

'I won't,' I said. I meant it sincerely. But I did. On my thirtieth birthday. On 11 September 2001. At least, the way she told it I fucked her around, and I would never say that Hokkaido lied, any more than Little Frank did.

Several mornings a week, Little Frank adjusted the magnifying mirror in his bathroom, swinging it towards himself on its cleverly articulated arm. With unshaking fingers I used my special little clipping scissors to trim my nifty white moustache. The upper rim of the Whitey smile was still there, neatly bordered by its hedge of trim bristles. The lips were still pliant, and their raised, fleshy rims, though slightly marked with wrinkles, were still roguish on demand. Dr Smiles had more than once reached across and tapped these lips with a long, glossy-nailed finger. 'Put it away, Frank,' she'd say.

Now, as I approached the hospital entrance and began to look around for my mark, I felt uncertain about what kind of smile to wear. I was out of practice with street signals. As before, it was probably my uncertainty that brought to my side the man who wanted to know what I had. In the mélée around the front of the hospital, transactions went on in broad daylight. This was not Little Frank's kind of place, but what choice did I have? I had to find out if what I was sticking up my arse twice a month was what the man in the street would envy me the supply of. Who else but a stranger could I trust with my ignorance? I wanted to trade a sample of the privilege I enjoyed for the expert opinion of someone without privilege. I'd trusted Dr Smiles for too long. I needed a second opinion. It had to be someone who didn't know me. Who wasn't afraid of me. The guy looked okay. He wasn't a Creeper and he was clean.

I guessed his origins had been Scandinavian, a long time ago. He had that kind of old blond tan, and a stubble of whitening blond hair on his head and cheeks. He was in reasonable shape. His affectation of a pale tropical trader's suit was modest compared to some of the Deadliner outfits you saw.

I was about to tell him that I didn't want money—what I wanted was to trade his quality-control opinion for my dose of GTX—when, across the crowd that filled the hospital's forecourt and spilled over the pavement and street, I saw the Cambodian woman again. She wasn't smoking a cigar this time but she was still watching me. She put her reflecting dark glasses on when she saw me, and just stood there, waiting.

'Give it a few minutes and then find me just inside,' I said to the pale-suited Swede without looking at him. I covered my mouth with my hand while talking. I suspected the Cambodian woman's reflecting glasses of being fancier than they appeared. 'Don't look as though you're listening to me,' I added, 'and don't look across the crowd out here, either.' I felt like a ham actor.

'Why not here?' he complained. He complied with my instructions at least up to the point of pretending not to talk to me.

'Do you want this shit or not?' I said, and walked back inside, miming an old geezer who'd decided he needed a piss, now, before risking the bus.

To myself, I sounded like the little fresh-out-of-the-can dealer I'd been back when the smell of limes had risen through the follicles of Hokkaido's hair and snagged my whole being. 'Do you want this shit or not?' I heard myself saying this a thousand times back then. It was absurd that the century that had passed since phrases like this were my stock repertoire had shrunk to a wait of mere minutes in the hospital's public convenience foyer.

Back on the fateful morning of my first meeting with Dr Jack, he'd tolerated me in his house because he had a use for me. I saw what it was before he told me. He wanted a bad person as a third party between himself and someone else. He wanted to protect himself and the other party. Just in case.

'You want me to do your dirty work, don't you?' I'd said as soon as we got into the big, dim dining room of the house above Raglan Harbour. This time, I wanted to get the smart word in first and give myself a chance of having the last one.

Dr Jack turned around. His big chest was working a bit harder than I'd noticed at first. He didn't look good. 'I don't know if you're a bad person, son,' he said. 'Probably not.' He watched my pride take a hit from the casual 'son' he'd used to talk down to me. He was making me shorter and younger than I felt. Then he made it worse. 'Would you like a glass of grapefruit juice?' I wondered if he was going to offer me a straw. He poured two peanut butter glasses of juice from a jug covered with a beaded doily. He didn't add a shot of scotch to mine. He looked at me while taking a slow sip of his whiskied fresh juice with lips that were trembling slightly. I could see that we were going to remain standing in the room with its old oval table and gauzy curtains shutting out the glare. I may have got the first smart word in but I couldn't think of anything to follow it up with. I stood there waiting while the doctor did the same. He wasn't waiting for me, that was clear, but for his own careful thoughts and his observation of me to come to the point of speech.

'Not a lot of people are bad,' said the big old man as though finding the shortest, simplest way to say something that could otherwise take a long time. 'I'm not a bad man but some people think I am. You're not a bad boy but you're probably trouble. So I hear.' He put his glass down softly on the table. All his gestures, including the slow pad of his walk, seemed designed to be gentle. It was as though he didn't want to jar himself, just as he didn't want to bash the world. I was intending to get stuck into the 'So I hear' bit, but he talked deliberately and methodically across my opening mouth. 'I hear this from my patients who grow marijuana in the bush around here,' said the doctor. He anticipated my vengeful thoughts. 'The only reason they tell me this,' he said, as though willing me to stand still, take a drink, relax, 'is because I've asked them what's happened to my supply. They tell me . . .' He didn't finish his sentence. He didn't need to. He drained his glass of whisky juice and put his big mitt out, palm forward, as though stopping traffic. 'Before you say anything, son, let me tell you how you can help. I'm not threatening you. Besides, if I dobbed you in you'd only add to my troubles, not to mention my conscience.'

Dr Jack ran a hospice. People came to his quiet, sunny hilltop to die. He administered marijuana for humane purposes and was closer than he'd ever been to prosecution. He didn't want to buy from the locals anyway, because that placed both them and him at risk. He'd considered buying the dope back from me, which would have distanced him from his sources. In my line of work, this was known as a left-hand thread. He was prepared to do a left-hand thread in the short term. But what he really wanted was to get away from the local supply altogether.

He also rescued kids like Hokkaido who'd come into the country in the snares of prostitution and passport slavery. This I found out later.

Yes, I could help him. I could left-hand thread his supply right out of the country if need be. He made me feel worthy— redeemed from the language of 'Do you want this shit or not?'—but he didn't make me feel welcome.

It was later, too, that I found out he did euthanasia. He tolerated me in his life because I was useful to these larger needs. He tolerated me in Hokkaido's because that was up to her.

Here at Dr Smiles's hospital my smile and I were familiar regulars. I'd be tolerated for a while. But I didn't want a sign that I was up to something to get back to Smiles, the second doctor in my life. When the nineteenth-century-trader Swede came in I let him see me, and then turned and hurried towards the men's lavatories. I affected a slightly distraught air—as though my indecision was about banal, old-man worries such as piss now catch the bus later or catch the bus now and hang on.

The place was busy under the inattentive gaze of a janitor behind a glass window. He handed out toilet paper on demand and emerged when he thought something fishy was going on. Little Frank stood at a urinal and pretended to pee.

'I don't do that!' hissed the Swede, taking the next unit.

'Nor do I,' I said. Then I pretended to recognise him. 'Olaf!' I exclaimed heartily, clapping him on the shoulder with my free hand. He'd feel the foil packet with its capsule in my palm. 'What are you doing here?'

'Taking a piss,' said the Swede, with admirable humour. He clasped my hand with his free one, and the packet passed between us.

'You must give me a call soon,' I said, heading for the basins. I dried my hands and fished out a business card. The Swede was looking at me with a 'That's it?' expression. The janitor was watching us both as though he wished we'd stop pretending and get it over with. 'There's something I'd like to discuss with you, Olaf,' said Little Frank, unfurling his best smile. It was every bit as clear as the Swede's mute enquiry, and I saw him get it. 'I'd value your opinion.' Little Frank paused, holding the smile. 'I'd find your opinion extremely, but extremely, valuable,' I said, and pushed the door open.

Scratched hastily on the cowl of the hot-air hand drier had been a short verse of Deadliner wit. It read:

My love it is a flower
that mostly blooms in spring
but twice a week my GTX
I stick it up my ring

Without intending to, I'd killed two birds with one stone. I'd wanted to find an on-street tester for my Smiles-supplied Expectations. Also, I'd wanted to sight vernacular evidence that the privilege I enjoyed within the soothing environment of Smiles's exclusive clinic and laboratory was not a hundred miles away from what went down at the ends of corridors painted in practical, wipeable green and white. With the red stripe for those whose navigation equipment was on low beam. Who confided their thoughts to the wearily overpainted walls of the toilets. I'd read them before but never with any intention of taking meaning from them. I'd never seen a code to decipher. But then, would I have considered decoding the view every afternoon I'd sat on a bench at the end of Point Jerningham, after lunch, and seen a vista that changed only because the weather did?

'Twice a *week*.' Mine was twice a month and it was also called GTX. Whatever Gabber did was daily. My ignorance astonished me.

'Ten eighty one.'

I walked down the front steps of the hospital with an air of annoyance—as though the piss had cost me my bus. I didn't see the Cambodian but that didn't mean she wasn't there. I didn't see the black watcher and I hoped he didn't let the pink-sandal girl come down here. I didn't look around to see if Olaf had followed me out. I decided to visit Mack. I believed the Swede would call me. I hadn't taken a risk for sixty years. And I was flagging Mrs Flitch's healthy lunch. I'd hardly missed one of those for sixty years either.

Before Hokkaido came on board and renamed the yacht *Cao Cao San* after the Three Kingdoms warlord and poet, it used to be called the *Little Frank*. Before that it was called *Why Not?* I got it while I was still with Geek and before I did my time in Witako. Geek's and my relationship had settled. He let me do what I wanted, and never had a word to say about the money I made off the back of his business any more than he did about the remittance that still went into my 1081. He taught me to drive so I could help with collections and deliveries. But I mostly drove my own ute around and left him to haul more loads of stained inner-sprung mattresses into the warehouse. Little Frank, who was about to earn his business name 'up country', was already getting above that stuff. The sad maps of uncertain continents and lopsided faces contained in the mattress stains depressed me. So did the small change that rattled sporadically in and out of the till. Geek found another minder for the shop-front, a fat girl who was doing midwifery at night school. But her boyfriend got himself into a jealous fantasy about me so she left. Geek didn't bother with anyone else after that. If neither of us was available to mind the till, he'd just shut up shop. He didn't seem too concerned about his cash flow. A lot of his stuff was going out to new immigrants in the suburbs and coming back again the worse for wear. This was depressing to Little Frank as well. Just like school had been.

But the boats around the harbour didn't depress me. Not even the fact that I didn't own one. They made me happy and they gave me something to aim for. The *Why Not?* was in a cradle up on the hard over at the Evans Bay marina near Kilbirnie, walking distance from Geek's establishment. I used to go over there to the yacht club on good weekends and bum crew chances during the regatta season. One day I saw the guy who'd been down there every evening all summer, toiling away at this big, beamy cruising hull. But now he was sitting on a crate with a bottle of wine in his hand. I had a hunch. It came from his shoulders and the way his feet in old paint-splattered sneakers were turned outwards. It came from the fact that he was drinking alone, which no one did, down there. It came from the cigarette that hung out of his fingers as if he couldn't be bothered with it. It also came from the fact that he'd done nothing about the hull all evening. The electric sander wasn't out, he wasn't caulking, there was no paint, nothing.

'Want a hand?' I asked, smiling at him. I was eighteen. I had a ute that I'd swapped for a filing cabinet of liquidation office gear Geek hadn't bothered to check. I had fifty thousand dollars in 1081. I didn't pay rent. I sold lids of dope to high-school kids who walked back and forth twenty times in front of the ute when I parked at the surfer end of Lyall Bay and sat in it, until I tooted the horn at them and made them jump out of their skins.

The *Why Not?* was mine. The *Why Not?* had to be mine. I would make the *Why Not?* mine and sail away from the pissy watery blood maps of Africa on the immigrant mattresses.

The guy's hair was black, curly and hadn't been washed since yesterday's session. I was looking down at it. It was dull with old paint dust. He took another swig of red wine and another haul on his smoke. He didn't look up.

The boat was mine.

'Want a hand?' I asked again.

The guy looked at me, letting smoke out of his nostrils with weary absence of effort. I wasn't big but I had Whitey.

'Want a boat?' he replied. His wife had left him. He'd got the sack. I hated the taste of the red wine but I swapped my ute for the boat hull, and we agreed I'd bring five thousand dollars in cash to cover the sails and rigging. He threw the second empty wine bottle into the bushes along the retaining wall. The boat was the only thing he loved, next to his wife.

'You can't,' he said when I told him I was going to rename the boat *Little Frank*. 'You're not allowed.' But I just did change the name, anyway, anticipating by a couple of months my own upcountry rebranding as 'Little'. Maybe it was a sign. Hokkaido changed the boat's name as well, after she left the rooming house full of inevitable crims and deadshits and came on board with me. I'd told her she wasn't allowed, too. Dr Jack didn't tell her she wasn't allowed to leave the backpackers he'd set her up in, and he didn't forbid her to hook up with Little Frank, but he told her he thought she was making a big mistake.

You could hear the breath collapsing through the doctor's huge, rickety lungs, and the way his big old bare feet plodded softly down on the wooden floor of the beeswaxy villa made you feel tired too. But Hokkaido walked away when Little Frank asked her to. I felt smug that day, getting offshore from the wrecker's coast with Hokkaido tucked into the cockpit like a little tern pointing into the wind. But in my heart I'd known this wasn't something I'd made happen. It was one of the things that was happening to me. The little woman with the secretions of citron in the follicles of her hair was doing this to me. Little Frank was one of her consequences, like the renaming of the yacht.

We were still lying around on the double futon we'd squeezed into the cabin of *Little Frank*, Hokkaido and me, ten o'clock in the morning. After a spell in the jug, it was things like this you valued. Hokkaido was lying on her front. Her little smooth body had a big sash of sunlight across it from shoulder to hip. She was turned around with her head at the sunshine end of the bed, sipping tea. I was propped up at the other end, looking along Hokkaido at the open hatch where the sunshine was coming in. It was fierce out there—not hot so much as so bright you'd have got a headache if you went out without a hat. Hokkaido always wore this softball cap and a pair of shorts and running shoes, and she looked like there wasn't a milligram of wasted weight or effort in anything she did. Even the best part of a hundred years later I now remembered this morning—not just because I was crazy about Hokkaido but because my satisfaction was nearly perfect. We were little and we fitted each other. We ate the same little amounts. We drank the same little amounts. I had a lot of appraising talent but I'd made mistakes. Hokkaido didn't make mistakes, ever. We were going to be invincible.

One day she decided for herself that she was making a mistake staying with me, but not at first and not then. What I became was one of the consequences of that decision, too. I remembered that dark moment and I remembered the earlier one, the sunlit one, that early summer morning of my life with Hokkaido which I thought was perfect and deserved to go on for ever because perfection did.

'*Cao Cao San*,' she said, sipping her tea. 'Why can't you change a boat's name?'

I wanted to put my hand on her smooth calf, to show her I wasn't arguing. 'No,' I said. 'You just can't.'

But she could and she did. We didn't argue, either.

Normally, I'd have had the whole afternoon to kill before my early night in diapers. Normally I'd have gone home and taken it easy in my neighbourhood. With the rich Greeks. I'd have had something to eat and drink, but not much, just in case. I'd have taken a walk along the dyke by the sea. I'd have looked blankly at the evidence of weather in the view from Point Jerningham. I'd have sat in my garden if it was fine, or I might have spent an hour with my business affairs. A quiet evening with 'my hobby'. Probably not a final stroll down to the Bay after dark, nor a drink looking at the floating restaurants or the casino. Then, up she goes. Nice and smooth. Next thing: Glade, Lucifer, Airwaves.

Instead here I was breathing the thick air of the Place just as the afternoon traders were getting cracking. There were already a few punters crowding in. The shawarma grills, kebab stands, woks and seafood concessions were going flat out. I didn't much like to eat there myself, given the good care that was taken of me by the Mrs Flitches, though there were concessionaires who'd treat Little Frank's occasional appetite with respect.

'No, no!' They waved my money away.

Lots of people were walking about with food on a stick, in a bun or a pita bread, or in a bag—walking, eating, and looking at what the markets had turned up. I was keen to get to Mack's before her commercial hours. But the portability of the food caught my eye. I was standing there like the tourist I'd become, gawping at people walking around eating.

I saw this skinny Somali woman with a kid in a trundler. She was gnawing away at a chicken leg. The kid had a sausage-on-a-stick that was dripping red sauce down his shirt. She was rummaging through a pile of cheap kids' clothes while holding the piece of chicken in her mouth. Her kid had a propeller-on-a-stick in his other hand. He didn't have much control over the dripping sausage. And as I watched this pair, both dressed in brightly coloured clothes with white sneakers on the ends of their very dark legs, a mangy-looking black and white mutt with sores around its nose walked up and gently took the sausage thing out of the kid's hand. The dog swallowed it in one gulp and stood there chewing on the stick for a bit, a patient expression on its face.

The kid began to yell blue murder, but his mum had a chicken leg in her mouth and was busy with the bargain clothes. She didn't pay any attention to her offspring. I was watching this incident with affection and with sadness thrown in for good measure. Just like Smiles warned me— the sadness of consciousness. Then I widened the scope of my vision. I saw a seething of happy sad incidents all around me. I felt enveloped by the irrational pleasure and sadness of life. I was thinking, *Patience*! I was thinking that Olaf would ring me in the morning.

And then I noticed an agitation spreading in from the edges of the seething crowd. They were all dropping their food. The ones with kids were picking them up. Then everyone began to run.

That time the 100PC goons came through on their rape rampage they were dealing to resistance with sticks and chains. I had a flash, now, of Watcher with the gun miniaturised on his big chest. I wished that he'd been around then and that he might be close by now. Right up the western end of the Place, the junk stalls and food concessions thinned out. There, you found establishments like Gabber's. If you didn't know your way around, these would be hard to find. The woman with the chicken leg in her mouth wouldn't see so much to interest her up there. It was more second-hand information than second-hand clothes.

It was from that end of the Place that some kind of shock wave was pushing into the crowds further down. They began to shove past me. They were trying to run. I saw the woman whose kid's sausage had been pinched by the gentle dog shoved back against the edge of the clothing stall. Her mouth was open but you couldn't hear her because everyone else was yelling as well.

Then the stall collapsed. The woman's long black legs flew in the air. I saw the trundler on its side with no kid in it. A few other people were down on the ground there too. The merchandise had fallen over them—I hoped the kid was safe under the collapsed table. But there was nothing I could do. I was being shoved along by the crowd. I'd learned long ago that the best way to get knocked down and stamped on was to resist the flow. So I rode the current out to the edges of the Place where the pressure thinned out. People began to move away faster.

I found a service doorway deep enough to get me out of the mob. I jammed myself in there with my shoulder to the street. Some bales of cheap Japanese manga comics had been dumped there. The crowds went trampling and yelling past. Smiles reckoned I was showing signs of wear and tear. I had my new schedule to maintain, and I didn't want to start racing a hysterical crowd.

I heard explosions up the western end of the Place, on the fringes of the Barbary Coast. It was clear that my danger was the crowd, not whatever was going on to the west. Some of the people running past had blood on them, but that wasn't from the action. It was from the crowd. Quite a lot of that red stuff might have been sauce from the food that got chucked around during the panic. One thing I knew for free. The explosions sounded like phosphorus incendiary bombs. It'd been a few years since I'd heard anything like them, but I hadn't forgotten what they sounded like. Sure enough, some big billows of smoke blew past. Some of it was yellow and some of it was turquoise. That was familiar too. I remembered how any fire that got loose in the Place would go through and clean everything out. I'd seen it happen years ago. I hadn't forgotten.

The crowd had thinned out. Choppers were taking off from the tower blocks. It wouldn't be long before the fire drills in those buildings had employees charging out on to the street as well. Lines of people did leave the buildings and scamper off. But not many. This began to interest me. Bad as it was for the woman whose kid's sausage had been pinched by the dog, it was hardly the Water War riots or the Thirty Year Terror, let alone a 100PC rampage. From the higher buildings they'd have had a view of what was happening down there. Not much, perhaps. Some fire-service choppers came over. There was a lot of shouting through loud-hailers and a few sirens. Little Frank knew stagecraft when he saw it. I knew how to tell this particular difference. I had a strong urge to get up there and see what had happened. Years ago the Binh Xuyen pulled a stunt that sounded like this one. It involved Little Frank that time. Now whatever was going on should've been none of my business. But I couldn't shake the feeling that Place business was still Little Frank's business. I thought of the people I knew up there, especially Gabber. I was scared for them. For that matter, what had happened to the Chinese Opera?

I was sitting down in the doorway. I didn't remember doing that. I had my head between my knees. I was staring at the cheaply inked cover of a manga rag. There was a hero with blades growing out of his forearms rescuing a puppy from a car accident in St Moritz, Switzerland. It didn't make sense. The coloured smoke had blown away. The street was pretty much deserted and the bull-horns had called it a day. A few people were shouting in the shambles of the market. They were busy putting out small fires among the food stalls. There was a stink of burned plastic, but no looters.

I saw one or two people propped up in hidey-holes and a few tottering about looking shocked. On the other hand a big Pacific Island woman was calmly packing up her gear, tut-tutting to herself. She was folding brightly coloured hats and bags as though this was just the end of another day. A couple of Bengali DVD peddlers were comparing notes in excited voices and sharing drinks from a thermos. There was a gas-fired hangi that doled out steamed vegetables and chicken. The family that ran it was lifting the cooker's big lid off a freshly steaming basket. They looked pretty calm.

As I watched, they sold a hangi feed to the big black watcher. He wasn't looking at me and I wouldn't have seen him if the crowd hadn't thinned out. He made his lips into a magnificent tube and blew steam off his snack. I didn't doubt that he was on duty, though he was ignoring me crouched in the doorway.

The paramedics arrived at the bottom end of the Place. I wanted to get up west, but I couldn't remember sitting down. Some time had passed that I didn't have tabs on. I thought, Take it easy, Frank. I was skipping my dose tonight. I was going over my line. Maybe it was going to be like this. Maybe chunks of time fell out of your mind, along with the chunks of memory that fell in.

My hat had gone, one of my trademarks, a good black fedora. Or had it been my summer Panama? I couldn't remember. I felt naked without it. My dove-grey suit jacket was torn, the second suit in as many days. There was dirt on my pants. How could Little Frank walk through Courtenay Place like this? Like some deadshit? Then I remembered the morning Hokkaido changed *Little Frank* to *Cao Cao San*. Though I'd been deadshit naked all morning on the futon, I suddenly felt so. I put my pants on and stuck my head up out of the cabin. Sun, glare, gulls, sea. How could I have explained to Hokkaido how much had changed? How could the owner of the *Why Not?* have told me the same thing? Did he feel free too? When he drove away in my ute, knowing what he'd left behind wasn't the *Why Not?* any more?

'What's up, Frank?' Hokkaido gripped my ankle.

'Nothing,' I said. 'It's great. What's it mean? *Cao Cao San?*'

A paramedic found me. She told me to go home and have a cup of tea. I was speechless. She must have thought I was senile. It was like I'd had my name changed. I felt like a deserter who'd torn off his uniform and run across no man's land towards freedom. No, I felt the way I did the morning I pointed the *Little Frank* through the Chaffers Passage break in Barrett's Reef. I'd spent my parole after Witako fixing the boat—up to a point. She had no GPS and a diesel that conked out. I watched the luff in her mainsail quivering. The same tremor was in my brain at the thought of cutting across the Karori Rip and out into the blue. My only insignia was the boat. I was impatient for my consequences. I felt scared, naked and alive.

Until I got right up to Gabber's.

There were bodies still being dealt to on the ground. Medics were holding perfusion bottles above a few. Others had blankets pulled over them. The riot police had a cordon. Gabber's place was gone. So were the outfits next to it. Where they'd been was gutted and the stalls had collapsed. Heaps of charred junk were lying about, and the place was awash with water and foam. Cops and militia everywhere.

What had Gabber done? Nothing close to him could have brought this down—a hole-in-the-wall blood agency, a little scanning shop, a wok stir-fry, a computer-sex agency. This kind of cheap show wasn't the style of the transnationals he hacked. They'd have hidden what Gabber did in the risk-management sections of their annual reports. I was looking at corny stuff. It had the appearance of Binh Xuyen enforcers before they moved into health commodities and wellness R&D. Before they rebranded.

This event had cheap special effects. It had coloured smoke. It had yellow and turquoise smoke—Binh Xuyen colours. It had taken out some wireless sex and blown up the wok's gas bottle. The authorities got there so fast they must have been told in advance. It had a few dead bodies, some short-lived terror. It was stage-managed. It was opera.

I looked around for Watcher and didn't see him. There were plenty of other old deadshits hanging around. I ducked through to the Barbary Coast and headed up Cuba. I clamped my teeth together to stop yelling curses. Tears and snot ran down my face.

Heigh ho heigh ho it's off to work we go. Mack's door opened before I'd rung the bell.

'Holy Mary,' yelled Mack, grabbing me. 'I saw you coming, Frank. Look at you, baby, my god, what's *happened*?'

'Gabber,' I wept. 'I think they've skittled Gabber.'

And then everything caught up with me. I was sitting on Mack's ornate sofa, huddled up like the galah Boy who was looking stunned and ruffled on the floor of his cage.

'Mack, I think they've done Gabber.'

Mack's big muddy eyes were on full alert. '*They*, Frank?' Then she got up and poured us scotches. I heard them being poured and smelled the one she put in my hand. Her big heavy arm went back around my shoulders. I had my eyes shut because I was crying. I was ashamed. I was scared for Gabber. I was scared that what had happened to him was one of my consequences. God knows what he'd tried to ferret out for me. I was ashamed because I didn't know how to put my riddles together. Because of my ignorance. I re-heard Gabber's long sigh in the darkness the last time I left him.

'*Turandot*,' I said. The old Egyptian's Chinese Opera joke.

'Frank?' Mack's whisky voice, telling me I wasn't making sense again. 'Your *suit*, Frank. You've been in some gang thing.'

I kept my eyes shut and rattled the rim of my whisky glass with my teeth. Mack's breath heaved in and out. My first swallow sank like acid into the pit of my stomach. The second one went down slowly, trailing heat.

Mack heaved in enough breath to power what she was going to say. 'Remember, years ago, you helped me out, Frank?' Mack's big arm pulled me in close. 'You told me about this old doctor who'd rescued your girlfriend. You told me you were paying him back.' She gave me a squeeze. 'Well, now it's my turn, you old bugger. I'm paying you back.' Mack pulled my head on to her big chest. 'Don't be proud, Little Frank,' she said. 'Everybody knows.'

I sat up and opened my eyes. Boy was giving the bars of his cage a hiding. 'Knows what, Mack?' I asked.

'Oh, Frank,' sighed Mack. 'To give you a wide berth, mate. Just to be on the safe side.'

'I haven't noticed anything for bloody years.'

I waited for Mack to continue.

'Okay, Frank, you tell me. Why would the bad guys have it in for your mate Gabber, when . . .'

I finished it for her. 'When I've got an arrangement, Mack? With my old enemies? Is that what people think?'

'People think you do stuff for the Pirates,' said Mack. 'That's how you get quality treatment, Frank. Why you're a flash little bugger.'

Boy was committing unspeakable crimes with his piece of cuttlefish and his mirror. The question Mack had never asked all these years was, Are you doing stuff for them? The answer was, I didn't know if I knew.

'So why would the buggers have it in for you or your mates?' demanded Mack.

'I don't know,' I said. I didn't know what the arrangement was—the one that began in the piney air in the back of Tamar's limo.

Mack got up and let Boy gnash at her finger to settle him down. Her silence was telling me not to shit in my nest.

I should go, I thought. Don't make Mack another consequence. I tried to stand up but felt giddy. When I opened my eyes again, Mack's big pored face was there. Her eyes were full of tears. 'Bloody hell, Frank,' she said. 'What the fuck are we going to do?'

I was letting the 'we' rattle around in my head while Mack went out on the landing. Then I heard her shut the door and shoot assorted deadlocks on it. She dropped a chain across. The security system sang, 'Good night, sleep tight.' Then Mack came back. She looked old and matronly in her trusty peignoir. She brought the bottle of scotch with her and filled up my glass. Then she filled one for herself and took a big mouthful.

'Okay,' she rasped. 'Enough beating about the bush. I've got the night off. Go for it, Frank.'

I told Mack everything I knew about the Binh Xuyen. She probably knew already, but it was a way of telling myself. It was a way of looking for an answer to the question, Why poor old Gabber?

They were very old. Their modern story started among the islands of the Mekong River delta. In the mid twentieth century they moved into Saigon-Cholon with opium and politics. When the immune system epidemics broke out, the Binh Xuyen bought up medical research. They had interests in blood. They got into slave-trade organs and the immunology programmes that developed from AIDS. They got into stem-cell harvesting. They had a luxury transplant hospital chain in India, Bangladesh and the Balkans.

Mack was fidgeting. 'Patience,' I said. I pushed the word ahead of my thoughts, into what I knew. The Binh Xuyen saw that when the immune system packed up, all death was due to disease.

Mack got up and put a cloth over Boy's cage.

They bankrolled religious revivals that wouldn't touch donor blood. The ones that committed genocides during the World Riots and the Thirty Year Terror. Their counter-investment stimulated deregulated research. By the time I got involved, centenarians had been off the front page long enough for people to have forgotten what they were.

'Gabber,' I said. I was getting to the part with yellow and turquoise smoke. I began to cry again.

'"The heart and the mind, what an enigma", Charlie Chaplin, *Limelight*,' slurred Mack. 'You want to have a tangi over Gabber, you want to tell me about your Pirates, or you want to tell Mack what's happening?'

Patience.

I continued methodically, laying a memory track to the present. The Binh Xuyen were right there when the first GTX got under the radar. The necessaries included organs, both donor and artificial. And chimeras. That was when we began to niggle, the Pirates and me.

Little Frank's memories were lining up nicely. There were some earlier ones I didn't want. I didn't tell Mack about the kid standing at the squidder's rail that time Hokkaido and I came alongside in the swell just down horizon from the white line of surf. On my thirtieth birthday. It was when Hokkaido began to turn and go—when she began to make me a consequence of her leaving.

'Nobody's perfect,' said Mack. I guessed I wasn't telling her anything she didn't know. 'Everybody knows you were into weird shit.'

A beat. *Patience.* I asked Mack's question for her. 'So how come we're best mates now? Me and the Pirates?'

She answered it for me. 'Because you're into weird shit together?'

But that wasn't it. I was on a track. It had fire-breathing dragons on it, and yellow and turquoise smoke. 'Not so sure about that,' I said. The track had video games at the back of Geek's shop on it. It had the smell of my mother's neck, which was both cigarette-smoky and sweet. It had firecracker wrappers. Just now, the road wet with smoke-quenching foam by Gabber's place. The yellow and turquoise smoke. The bodies under blankets. 'Not so sure about best mates,' I said. I also had in mind a red Guan Gong mask, a smile with the mucousy slickness of entrails.

I told Mack about the dragons and the yellow and turquoise smoke. I knew these were Binh Xuyen colours. So what?

'So what' was the dragon that appeared on Gabber's screen, not long after I blew the Chou-mask goon's head off. Trickles of turquoise and yellow smoke dribbled from its nostrils. '*Unleashing the dragon,*' said Gabber with mock awe. 'Not bad, but showy, like you'd expect.' He was scanning the columns of characters on his screen.

'So what's it say, Gabber?'

'What, you think I'm reading supermarket specials?' Gabber's face was greenish with reflected light. 'You read the yellow across and the blue-green down. One's your life in

129

this world, the other's your chance in the next. The anagram says something like, Break rules in this life and forfeit lives to come.'

'Whose rules?'

Gabber sighed deeply. 'These guys had a hospital in Cairo,' he told me. 'It was better than a hotel. The only fellaheen that went in there came back out minus kidneys and eyeballs, Allàhu akbar, rest their souls in peace.' He pointed his remote at the screen with the Binh Xuyen dragon. The dragon disappeared and Gabber's face was reflected there. 'In the old days, Frank, it was believed they could wipe out your reincarnation cycle. They could fly, become invisible, turn into animals, invade dreams. They had the Delta peasants shitting themselves. A little flash of Binh Xuyen, and zap! Everybody's playing by *their* rules. So what's new, effendi? People still get burned by the dragon.'

'People still get burned by the dragon,' I said to Mack. 'These days, you don't have to be a superstitious peasant to believe.'

'Believe what?' Mack had only one eye open and that one looked unconscious. But then the other eye opened. She was having trouble focusing. It wasn't just the whisky. The last thing she needed was trouble.

For the second time that evening I decided to put aside the memory of Hokkaido pointing her cell phone at the kid standing by the heaving rail of the rusty squidder rising up and down next to the *Cao Cao San* on the swell. The squidder crew had just biffed the consignment over on the end of a cord. Now there was a lot of yelling going on as they lowered a ladder down the rusting flank of the boat. I was having enough trouble keeping the yacht in position. 'What's this?' demanded Hokkaido, looking hostile. I shrugged. We were collecting what we'd been sent. The kid came down the ladder hanging on to one of the squidders. She had an old, bleached lifejacket on. They weren't wasting new equipment on her. We got her on board. She threw up all over me in the cockpit, and then fainted.

My memory of Hokkaido taking the kid and leaving me—this memory stared at me from the edge of my thoughts as I told Mack the story of my outfit getting burned by the dragon. The two memories wanted to be together—the burning of my outfit and the kid's sick, white face. The sick kid marked the moment my life turned into the street where I'd meet the dragon.

The day I got burned I was walking down a narrow street off Barbary. I had an outlet there. It was located among the loading bays and the derelict back sections of buildings jammed with squatters with their half-mad dogs and desperate vege gardens. There were sweat shops on the first floors and hole-in-the-wall bodegas at street level.

I knew the rules. If you want to buy originals, shop uptown. If you want good copies, shop down. If you want used originals, try ground-level mid-town. But for used copies, go underground. I'd always believed in the basic rules of territory. If any of the parties to a transaction was confused about these rules, it soon showed. It's true, I had a strong inclination to go uptown. But I wasn't there at this time. And so I moved forward on a folded territory. As far as I was concerned, it was just where I was. As far as the Pirates were concerned, it was where I had to stay. And there we differed.

'The past—what a mess. But ah—the future!'

That was later.

Patience.

Put yourself under a hat like mine, there was nowhere to hide. Many old warehouse doorways and loading bays crowded this street. I was used to them being full of litter, stinking like toilets and inhabited by deadshits. Sure enough, there they were—red faced and snoring, their piss running in deltas from under them, their bottles rolled away among the waste paper and hypos. Thousands of hard-luck stories surged back and forth through the towns, camps, caravan parks, squattable buildings and out in the industrial satellites. I didn't see why I should feel sorry for any one group.

But the deadshits—that was one prejudice I'd admit. There was one down there where I was heading, a huge man with his shitty trousers around his thighs who wore a kid's propeller hat on his head. That day, Propeller Head watched me as I went by. He didn't give me his usual line of roared abuse and laughter. Rusty steel shutters had been rolled down over the loading bays. There were a couple of trucks that looked like the Sanitation Department. The Sanitation Department had long ago stopped bothering about this street. Sure enough, these were Pirate trucks. My outlet was in a basement. I knew the rules. The trucks were parked on either side of it, about a building's width distant. I could see that the 'Sanitation Department' had already entered the place. They'd got Crane, my minder, in the nearest truck. He was sitting in the cab, looking straight ahead at nothing in particular and certainly not at me. Crane was a fairly evil bugger. He had to be for his job. Even so, the 'Sanitation Department' had scared him into sitting still. It was Crane who'd phoned and told me he needed to talk to me. He'd arranged the time of the appointment, which was now.

Two men in overalls and masks came up out of my shop. A couple more climbed out of the second truck. I stood there in the middle of the street with my hands in my pockets. There was a muffled thump under the ground. I felt it through the soles of my shoes and in my chest. Right on the dot of Crane's appointment. Always punctual, Little Frank. Several panes of window glass fell into the street. Behind me, Propeller Head began to roar. Thick smoke gushed from the doorway of my shop. It was yellow and turquoise.

The jokers in overalls strode towards me. I didn't react. They ignored me, anyway, just as Crane did. They went past me in the direction of Propeller Head. I stood there with my hands in my pockets, looking at the coloured smoke.

I took a swallow of Mack's scotch. 'I'm sorry,' I said.

'I beg your pardon?' said Mack blearily.

'Sorry, Mack,' I said. 'Just give me a minute.'

I went to her toilet and pretended to have a piss. The old

guy looking at me from the mirror was red eyed. I threw cold water over his head. The memory of Hokkaido and the white-faced kid had moved in close again. Images of them stuttered in my mind. Hokkaido taught me that I could like the wine I'd hated the night I traded the *Why Not?*. But not, I told the Little Frank patting his chilly face in Mack's bathroom mirror, what to do about the fact that I no longer got to choose what I liked. Whose rule was it that I no longer got to choose anything? Hokkaido taught me that we both liked little and fresh food. But not how to feel about the fresh lunches neither of us chose. She taught me that we despised the drugs that made our clients stupid. But not, I told the man in the mirror who looked just like me, to hate the drug that was the cause of me sitting weeping on a sofa in the galah-shit-scented interior of Mack's flat.

Mack was looking at me with one eye shut.

And then, behind me, I heard Propeller Head's roars turn into a yell. I saw Crane's head in the truck cab turn my way. I realised he was looking past me. That made me turn too. I was just in time to see Propeller Head go up in flames. The 'Sanitation Department' guys had doused him in something and lit him. He ran crazily into the middle of the street, waving his arms. At first he made a lot of noise. But after he'd run in circles a couple of times he fell down and was silent, though his body went on thrashing about for a while.

Two or three other deadshits made a run for it out of their doorways. They went stampeding up the street. One of them had a loose shoe and she kicked it off, left it behind and ran on all lopsided. Several other wrecks crawled right into their coats and hid back in corners. Propeller Head went on burning quietly, with a frying sound. He was completely black under the flames, a lumpy silhouette.

The 'Sanitation Department' guys were walking back towards me. Behind me, the trucks started up. The men in sanitary masks ignored me. I couldn't take my eyes off

Propeller Head. People were running into the street. I heard the first fire siren. The fire was already spreading. When I left it was because the crowd took me with it.

'I had nightmares about that burning dero for years, Mack,' I said. Mack was snoring quietly but she was awake.

Was that the end of the story? There was another ending I already knew, and one I didn't know yet. The one I knew was Hokkaido leaving me. 9/11. It was an ending that came before the burning of Propeller Head. Maybe, if she hadn't had to leave me, Propeller Head wouldn't have had to burn. What else did she teach me? When it's finished it's over. When you leave you've gone. These are rules too.

The ending I didn't know yet was going to unfold from tomorrow. This was when Olaf would report on the 'special treatment' Mack and the rest of the street were so sure I was getting.

'Well, you would,' said Mack, as if trying to wind the evening down.

'Would what, Mack?'

'Would remember that burning dero.'

'It was the frying sound,' I said maliciously.

'What's all this dragon shit?' Mack suddenly shouted. 'All this Gabber crap, Frank?' There were blisters of sweat across her forehead. It began to track down her cheeks through the old make-up. There were angry, drunk veins in her muddy eyeballs. Her big fists were bunched up. I saw what the silly bugger in the sports bar ran away from the day she broke his neck in the Cuba Street fountain. 'You've been listening to too much Gabber!' Mack yelled. 'Look what the bastard's done to you, Frank. He's been knitting your brain!'

'But Mack,' I protested. 'Gabber hasn't done anything to me. They've done something to him.'

'They?' screamed Mack. 'You got done over by some protection scheme!' she yelled. 'You pissed someone off. So they did you. That's *normal*, Frank. And Gabber's pissed someone off too, Frank, and they've done him. Normal, Frank. Normal, normal, normal! Have you gone soft in the head?' She got up and wiped her face down with a make-up towel. 'God help us,' she bellowed from inside the towel. 'Sheikettes, coloured smoke, fucking dragons, Frank? You've been watching too much of that Chinese Opera, baby.' She came out from under the towel. Her face was clean and old. 'Coloured smoke, Frank?'

She left it at that and went to make me a sandwich. I sat there assembling my memory of the *Little Frank* before she became *Cao Cao San*. The *Little Frank* was in the arm of an estuary across from Raglan township. The arm's murky, rock-oystery water, teal grey with mud, reached around scrubby headlands into hidden inlets. A cell mate at Witako prison had boasted about the place. I could buy weed from his family and sail it around the coast to where rich yachties liked to throw their money away in the crowded summer-cruising moorings. And that was where you could pluck outboard motors off the backs of carelessly tethered dinghies while their owners were stoned.

The innocence of all that! And then the *Cao Cao San*, which had been the *Little Frank* and before that the *Why Not?*, sailed out with Hokkaido pointing into the breeze like a tern. A shift began in my life that day. I might otherwise have settled into the kind of outboard-motor-hocking existence that would have ended a century ago. Nothing more exciting in it than a couple more spells in the jug. It was Hokkaido who made me lift my sights. It would be Hokkaido who told me I'd pointed them in the wrong direction that day the kid came down the side of the rusty squidder.

I ate my chicken schnitzel sandwich like a good old chap. I heard myself sounding like a complaining old fart when Mack tried to lend me a hat. Night had fallen outside and I slipped out into it from Mack's apartment building. I looked as unlike Little Frank as I ever had. No hat or cane, and I was wearing a cheap raincoat Mack had found me. She'd turned the sleeves back. It came almost to my ankles. She held me close. Then she gave me a little shake, making my head wobble. Then she pushed me away. She was afraid for me, but she was more afraid for herself. She wanted everything to return to Go.

I looked around to see if I could spot anyone watching me. I didn't see anyone and was grateful for my raincoat. There was a famous pastry shop near Mack's, a fixed point in the surging tides of change through the quarter. It'd been there for donkey's years. The building had been replaced more than once, but the cake shop had always hung on to the ground-floor retail space. I'd often gone in there for a coffee and a custard slice. It was one of the places that refused to let me pay. The thought of my vanity made me pause outside the pastry shop's window.

There were the usual racks of tarts, novelties, pies and cake decorations, all on patterned paper doilies and enhanced with dustings of icing sugar, candied fruit and multi-coloured hundreds-and-thousands. There were little bride-and-groom sets, happy birthday numbers and candle holders, lucky horseshoes and keys. The place was like a religious shrine. It resembled the quasi-religious bodegas with their idols and votive merchandise. And next to a sandwich rack was the shop's own god. He was a mechanical chef-doll in a tall white hat who'd nodded ceaselessly and waved a wooden spoon for all the years of my life as Little Frank the vizier of the Place. For all the years the shop owners wouldn't allow me to pay for my treat. All the years I'd imagined my famous Whitey smile was sowing blessings not fear.

The little chef god had been there for ever, yet I'd never wondered how many of him there'd been. I'd never wondered how many times the owners must've had to make another mechanism, another hat, another spoon. I stood there watching the little chef nod and grin and beat the air with his spoon. I saw the ghost of my reflection floating in front of the little chef in the plate-glass window. I leaned my forehead against its cool surface as if making my genuflection at a holy icon. I thanked him for always being there for me.

And then something bulked very large in the cake-shop interior. The quality of light changed before my pious eyes, as though a shadow had fallen against me from inside the shop. This old deadshit praying weirdly in front of the cake-shop window looked up. Inside the shop was Half Ton Jack. He was standing close to the window on the inside—as close as he could get with the display area between him and me. He had a mighty bag in one hand, his supper no doubt. He was looking at me without surprise. It was clear that he'd been waiting for me on my route from Mack's back past the cake shop to the Place and the Chinese Opera.

Half Ton Jack was studying me. And then he took one step sideways behind the little nodding chef, opened the cake-shop door and was next to me. I'd forgotten how big he was. I was looking at the hard, upholstered swell of his body where his huge chest turned into his huge belly. He was a third again as tall as me. There was an old digestive stink on him. His body inflated and sank very slowly as he breathed. When I raised my eyes all the way to look at his face, I saw that it had on it what would pass for a smile.

'"When the blue comes back",' quoted Half Ton, grinning. The grin pushed his cheeks up and made his eyes close. 'The big shot,' he said. 'The poet. "When the blue comes back", right?' Behind him in the cake-shop window the little chef was conducting away with his wooden spoon and nodding. Half Ton's whole body was nodding too, with laughter. 'Oh boy,' he chuckled. 'Is there something you want to help me with today?'

Back when I was still wearing a flash hat I might have disapproved of Half Ton Jack taking the piss out of me. But things had changed.

'You going to buy me a birthday cake, Junior?' crooned Half Ton. When I looked away from the little chef and at Half Ton's face, I saw that his eyes were no longer shut, which made it seem as though he wasn't laughing at all. 'You going to buy me a birthday present? "When the blue comes back"? Big shot? Hey?'

'It's your birthday?' I asked, smiling up at him. 'Many happy returns.' I could have been offended at being taken for some shit-house dealer near the hospital. But how to read Half Ton Jack now? He might as well have come straight out and told me he knew what my business was. That might've been a part of it, but it wasn't all. We watched the little chef for a while.

'So what brings you down here?' I asked, to move things along. 'Got the night off?'

'They're doing *The Three Kingdoms*,' said Half Ton. He opened his bag and took out an éclair. 'It's long,' he added, taking the cake whole into his mouth. For a moment I thought he meant the éclair. Then I realised he was talking about the opera. 'That Cao Cao,' mumbled Half Ton past his mouthful of mashed vanilla batter, chocolate and cream. 'What a creep.' He finished chewing and swallowed. Then, as if coming to his polite senses, he offered me the open bag. 'Sorry, Junior,' he said.

'I'm trying to give them up,' I said. I had the sensation we were both talking in codes. 'Were you waiting for me?'

'Creep,' said Half Ton again, getting another éclair out of his bag. He might have been referring to the devious Cao Cao white-face character in *The Three Kingdoms* or to me. But as he put the cake into his mouth with one hand, he was knocking the other, the one that held the bag of supper, against the great furnishing of his chest. And then I got it. Half Ton Jack was a Creeper. Not chance but intervention had made him what he was.

'I'm sorry,' I said. 'I'm not quite myself.' I didn't mean it as a joke, but the moment I'd said it I began to laugh. To my astonishment, Half Ton did too. The second éclair went down ever quicker than the first. He repeated my *bon mot* in a thick, chocolate-furred voice.

'"Not quite myself",' chortled Half Ton. '"When the blue comes back". You're a funny guy.' Then he stopped chuckling. The tonal shift was impressive. His face reset in that professional expression that made him a security asset. 'You okay, Junior?' he asked. Before I could find an answer, he went on, 'That was a bad business, today, over in the

Place.' He waited for me to come back into the conversation, but not for long. He had a list of things to say. He was working through them with the diligent implacability of a big man who had no concept of obstacles. 'I'm a Creep,' said Half Ton. 'I don't appreciate what they done.' He didn't wait for me to ask about 'they', and he spoke the word as if he didn't expect me to. He was pausing not for me to ask that question, but because the next thing he had to say was going to complete a total message. Little Frank saw him decide on it. 'What they done to your mate,' said the huge man.

He paused again for about two beats of the little chef's wooden spoon. Then he thrust the bag of éclairs at me. 'Take this,' he ordered. I didn't protest that I still didn't fancy cake. I couldn't speak over the sound of my roaring heart. I couldn't match Half Ton's implacable purpose. I clutched the paper bag to my oversize raincoat while he fished in the pocket of his tracksuit top. He brought out a memory stick. It was the sort you could buy in magazine kiosks along with phone chips and power cells. I recognised it as a stock-in-trade of Gabber's low-cost style. Half Ton was holding the little thing delicately between the thumb and forefinger of a huge hand. He reached out with the other and took his bag of éclairs back. Then he handed me the memory stick, as if swapping it for his treats. 'He came to the Opera,' said Half Ton, impatient for me to take the morsel that shone between his immense sausage fingers like one of the baubles in the little chef's window. 'He was in a hurry. He said, Give this to Little Frank when he comes in.' Half Ton did a passable impersonation of Gabber's quick chatter.

'You saw him? He was okay?' I was babbling.

'He came to the Opera,' said Half Ton very slowly, as though he was talking to a not-too-bright child. 'He thought you might come there. He gave me this. For you.' He pushed the stick against my chest, and I took it and held it in my closed hand. 'I listened to it,' said Half Ton. 'You don't mind? It's just music.' I still hadn't spoken and he wasn't going to wait for me. He leaned down and spoke very carefully close to my face. 'Maybe you can help me,' he said. 'Maybe I can help you make the blue come back. Maybe, if you help yourself, you can help me too.' He took my hand with the silicon stick in it and pressed it against his upper body. I felt with a shock how what should have been the soft flesh of a sumo body was hard, not human. 'I know what you do, Junior,' he said. 'I know who you are.' He let my hand go and held the shiny shovel of his palm out. 'Your phone,' he said. I fished it out and gave it to him. 'Cao Cao,' he said to it. Then he entered his number on the keypad. Then, methodically, he handed it back. 'Don't forget, I'm Cao Cao,' he said. His purposefulness moved steadily ahead. 'You call me. Call Cao Cao. You're Blue Back, okay? Blue Back calls Cao Cao. Don't forget.'

'What about . . .?' I began.

'Your mate's gone,' said Half Ton. He was beginning to leave. The big rhythm of his plan was shifting his weight back towards his ticket window at the Opera. 'That Madame Hee,' hurried Half Ton. 'You be careful.' He pushed his face in close. 'You watch out, Blue Back.' His vanilla and chocolate breath went in and out. 'She's something new.'

My mouth opened but nothing came out.

'You call me, Blue Back,' said Half Ton. 'You call Cao Cao any time.'He squeezed my hand with Gabber's memory stick in it. Then he said loudly, for everyone to hear, so that his zoo breath flowed around me and took away even the air I had in my lungs, 'And don't forget—right now we're doing *The Three Kingdoms*. Like I told you. A classic. With Cao Cao. You should take the time.'

And then he joined the torrent of people who had been pushing past us while we stood on the pavement there in Cuba. He body-surfed away with his head and shoulders above the crowd. He left me standing outside the cake shop while my heartbeats and the little chef's wooden spoon got back into synch. While my tears for Gabber ran off my chin on to the cheap plastic raincoat Mack had loaned me.

*

I didn't sleep much that night. I listened to Gabber's message via Half Ton Jack. It was a recording of *Turandot* by Puccini. I looked it up on the net. As well as the synopsis I read the key arias in translation. There were pictures of Puccini as well as of someone called Franco Alfano. I learned that Franco Alfano polished off *Turandot* after Puccini's untimely death. I lay awake thinking about what to do. I hadn't thought like this for a long time. It was hard work.

At first light, I threw open my double-glazed bedroom windows as I would normally have done the day after Expectations. I squirted a quantity of Glade around the room as per usual. The can's label alleged that its contents were perfumed with carnations. They weren't. I took the ruins of my beautiful teal-grey silk and wool mix suit out to the incinerator. Having thought about it during the night, I took an unused diaper out there too. I didn't doubt that the well-briefed Mrs Flitch's inventories of household supplies included this item. It seemed like a good idea, right now, to avoid anomalies in my behaviour. I torched the pile using a dose of Lucifer. I threw some of the Tongan gardener's hedge trimmings in for good measure. I wished I'd taken the trouble to find out the man's name. I suspected that he burned the electrocuted cats in the incinerator. The fragments of charred bone I sometimes saw there didn't resemble the remains of any meal I'd eaten.

I shaved calmly and took my shower. I remembered to freshen my breath with Airwaves. When the new Mrs Flitch appeared with my coffee, I'd be there as usual, bright eyed and bushy tailed, sweeter than a morning in spring. Nothing would be said about the remains of my suit. It would be easy for her to assume I'd had a wee accident.

I was waiting for Olaf the nineteenth-century beach trader to phone in his report but I didn't expect him to do this until later in the morning. During the night I'd thought about Cao Cao. My memory of Hokkaido renaming the *Little Frank* had docked with Half Ton Jack and the villain of the *Romance of the Three Kingdoms*. Cao Cao's gift, Hokkaido told me,

141

was to mistrust strength, including his own. He put his trust in strategy, including that of others. A soothsayer once told him he'd be at best a capable minister in peaceful times but an unscrupulous hero in chaotic ones. His reputation was for craftiness, cruelty and suspicion. Hokkaido said the word 'crafty' implied the kind of bad rap you'd get from those you'd outwitted. Cao Cao's great gift was to think ahead. He thought across the present and moved boldly and unexpectedly. The one time Cao Cao trusted his own force and confined his thinking to the present, he was defeated at the Battle of Red Cliffs. Most of his troops were burned alive. He rewarded loyalty but didn't favour cronies. As a poet, he had a strong sense of mortality.

It was a good name for a yacht. It said something like, Save yourself from the shipwrecks of the present by avoiding the reefs of the future. Back then, I'd liked it because Hokkaido did. Agreeing to it gave me the experience of saying yes to something that someone else, not me, wanted. There was a new kind of pleasure in this. It also felt good that this pleasure was joined to a name that had to do with a successful warlord. The kid in Little Frank liked that.

But mostly the name joined me to the little woman who'd made me look across my dopey present at the possibility of a greater future. She made me look past my strengths, such as Whitey. I looked past the present where the *Little Frank* was collecting barnacles in a muddy backwater. Where resinous heads of weed at summer's end were the only viable currency.

The grit of wakefulness was collecting under my eyelids as I lay in the dark, thinking. What had I been doing all these years since stepping back out of Tamar's piney limo? 'But ah—the future!' I lived in a luxurious present into which my future was decanted as household products. My time was a schedule without craft or strategy. It had no sense of mortality in it to keep it real.

'Ten eighty one.' In the top drawer of my bureau, in an archive envelope, were three objects. They shared the envelope with a sachet of thymol crystals to combat humidity. To know they were there, I still had to open the drawer from time to time, though not the envelope. That morning, I opened the envelope for the first time in longer than I could remember.

The 2000AD comic was brown and brittle. I didn't disturb it. I didn't turn to the page with Halo Jones and General Cannibal surveying the ruined planet. I didn't need to go that far in to remember it. The second item, a photo of the *Little Frank* on her mooring at Evans Bay, was in reasonable shape, having lived in the dark. Hokkaido wasn't in the photo because it was taken before the boat's name got changed. Remittances to the 1081 KidSaver had stopped about the time I left prison. I'd kept successive versions of my lucky account alive, though the pass book was a relic. This was the third item. I held the light, dry relic in my hand. Now was the time for craftiness, not superstition.

I'd just sunk my teeth into my wholegrain roll, confident they could deal with the vicious seeds in it, when my cell phone said, 'Frank.' I sat there with my teeth impaled in the bread and then finished my bite, not wanting to look too keen in front of Mrs Flitch. I chewed calmly as I put the phone to my ear and strolled out to the patio.

'Olaf,' I said, my greeting thickened by bread pulp.

'My name isn't fucking Olaf,' he said in a tinny voice, as though holding his own phone at arm's length.

'I'm sorry,' I apologised. 'We weren't really introduced.'

'How much?' said Whatshisname bluntly.

'How much what?' asked Little Frank. This was my future we were talking about. The guy had to want to tell me the truth.

The man I thought of as Olaf sighed. 'Listen,' he said. He moved his phone closer. I could hear his breath, the sound of a wet swallow. 'I don't know what you do for laughs, but this isn't funny.'

'I don't know what I do for laughs either,' I replied honestly. 'I've forgotten.'

'You said you'd value my opinion.' Olaf was beginning to sound impatient. 'How much will you value it?'

'How much should I value it?' I asked him. 'What's it worth?' I thought my side of the conversation must be sounding crafty to anyone listening, for example the new Mrs Flitch. I could see her out of the corner of my eye in the breakfast room. She was moving the butter out of direct sunlight.

The man named a figure. I didn't even bother to think about it. It sounded like the cost of a plane ticket for a cornea transplant in Kuala Lumpur or a good recycled artificial larynx without too much buzz in it. Now he'd be able to see or sing.

'Fine,' I said. My heart was galloping. 'How do you want it?' I showed my phone lens my cornea and repeated the man's account number after him. The promise of clear vision in KL or a lovely new singing voice warmed Olaf's response when he said, 'Thanks,' as the transfer registered at his end.

This had been a transaction, not a good deed. My impatience may have showed when I asked the winner-takes-all question.

'So how was it?'

Things moved fast then. There was no time to lose. I activated the liquidation of my stock and moved the whole lot into the 1081 cash account. It was still called KidSaver. I enjoyed confirming that when the broker asked me to. I collected Gabber's memory stick from my bedroom. I hit the taxi fast-dial on my phone and said, 'Ready now.' When it called me back I went straight to the front door. As I closed it, I saw 'Mrs Flitch' in the hallway. She was on the phone. The way she was looking at me said I was the subject of her call. I wasn't surprised when Dr Smiles found unscheduled time to meet me.

*

Smiles was watching me. Her forgiving expression had cost her a week's specialist fees with bonuses. We sat in the warm, flower-scented, water-soothed solarium. Her well-preserved body, as we used to say before the term became literal, was alert in a cane chair. The chair was next to a big planter of tropical flowers with long stems and aggressive bits. The forgiving expression suited her because its artificiality had been pushed to the limit. With Smiles, that was a long way down the track. I could see around the edge of her saintly smile. I could see where the smile stopped and murder began. Like the nasty plant beside her, Smiles was a very evolved product. I was getting the measure of how much her evolution owed to me. She was observing me taking this measure.

Dr Smiles and I were listening to Gabber's recording of *Turandot* by Puccini. Across the other side of the solarium some basketcases were nodding and weaving to the music. The doctor was finding it less therapeutic. She could see what the lost causes couldn't. She could see that the pliancy had gone from Little Frank's manner. No doubt I had my reasons for making her listen to an opera in Italian. No doubt I knew something that the opera was telling her. But she didn't know what it was. She didn't know what the opera was telling her and she didn't know what I knew. She badly wanted to know both these things. I could tell she was wrestling with the desire to stretch out a poisonous tendril and stun me into confession. She was humming along to snatches of it like a bone saw.

What did I know?

I knew that Gabber had sent *Turandot* to me with extreme urgency. I knew that *Turandot* was Puccini's 'Chinese Opera'. I knew the story of *Turandot* involved solving riddles or getting your head chopped off. In the end, love conquers all. I knew that Puccini keeled over in 1924. The last bits were polished off by a hack called Franco Alfano. I'd known Gabber for a long time. I knew his style. It wasn't a stretch to guess that, like my namesake Señor Alfano, I had a final act to finish.

I knew Gabber didn't like Chinese Opera. He'd told me. I knew he'd gone there this time. Half Ton Jack told me. I knew Gabber knew about my interest in Madame Hee. I'd told him.

I knew Gabber had been dealt to by the Pirates. I'd seen the brand. I'd snuffled up the yellow and turquoise smoke. I'd remembered the sound of the frying deadshit.

I knew my riddles had something to do with Madame Hee. I knew that Half Ton Jack was a Creeper. I knew he'd betray his masters.

I knew that Madame Hee was important. Half Ton told me so. I knew there was a 'new thing' out there. Dr Smiles told me so. I knew that Madame Hee was 'something new'. Half Ton told me.

I knew I was being watched. I knew I had a deal with the Binh Xuyen. I was seen as their man. I couldn't remember the deal. I could only go back as far as Tamar's slimy liver lips under the red Guan Gong mask. I knew my medication was what blocked my ability to imagine the deal.

I knew I had to Time Out and maybe die in order to remember the Binh Xuyen deal. I'd seen this in the cosmetic sheen of Smiles's anxiety. I was seeing it again as Smiles hummed along to Puccini's Chinese Opera.

Little Frank had been hard at it. The due diligence.

As of this morning, my diligence knew that the domestic component of my medication, the one I'd self-administered for sixty years, was, in the words of Olaf, 'complete shit'. I knew that this 'complete shit' didn't block my ability to remember my MOU, my deal with those who'd secured my retirement.

So I knew that what Dr Smiles put into the trapdoor of skin on my arm *was* what was blocked my ability to remember my MOU with the Binh Xuyen. It was what locked me in a present between the toxic shine of rage in the doctor's patient smile, and that moist, liver-slick smile in the back of the limo. That refreshing siss of breath. 'But ah—the future!'

Smiles's patience was impressive. It was also finite. So was the therapeutic value of the opera. The basketcases were getting sick of it. For Little Frank, the listening time was productive. My knowledge and rage advanced together.

I knew that what had locked me up in this smiling present was also what had made me strut around as the coloured-smoke wind-up bogeyman doing I didn't know what for the better part of sixty years. Going down to Pirate HQ at the Chinese Opera. Fixating on Madame Hee.

I kept my lips pursed in an expression of connoisseurship. I hoped it was making Smiles angry. I myself hadn't felt anger for sixty years. On the other side of the solarium the bored basketcases had begun to hoot over the top of the opera. A chopper went overhead. I saw the poison node under Smiles's floral complexion flinch as if with a thought. I willed her to lose her grip.

Little Frank was keeping his own grip with a silent chant. *Finish the job, Franco. Solve the riddles. Redeem the Princess. Love conquers all. Ten eighty one.* I was pushing my chant against the sound of Smiles humming along. Her humming that sounded like a patient doctor humouring her deluded patient. Her patience that said I might as well join the basketcase chorus. Or the conspiracy freaks who wrote letters to the paper about funny stuff in the water.

Answer correctly, or die!

My hobby now included on-line pictures of Puccini swaggering about with a cigar and a fur collar. Guess what he'd called his white steam yacht? The *Cao Cao San*! So this was this how we lived, near the end, our bewildered fingers following the lines of a script?

I reached across and took Gabber's memory stick from Smiles's notebook.

'But we were just coming to the good bit, Frank,' purred Smiles. Another helicopter smashed at the air above the solarium. Dr Smiles cocked her head at it. 'Frank, honey,' she beamed. 'Life goes on, you see, even if art has to stop.' I was measuring my rage against the doctor's self-control. I was measuring my knowledge against the doctor's patience. 'Is that all, sweetheart?' asked Smiles. Her pager played a little tune. 'Because I really must get back to work.' She snapped her notebook shut. 'Want to come along? A bit of theatre, Frank,' she added wittily. She'd stood up and was looking critically down at herself—at the beautifully cut suit and crisp white cover-coat, the handstitched shoes, the perfect fob-watch. 'Your old friend Gabber was always apt to err on the obscure side, wouldn't you say, Frank?'

'You knew Gabber?' I asked, knowing she didn't.

'But you're always talking about him,' she cried enthusiastically.

Gabber's recording was lying there, in the toxic shadow of Smiles's venomous longing to get to the bottom of what Little Frank was doing. 'Fuck it, Smiles,' I said, adding grief to my anger. 'That stuff you've had me sticking up my arse—it was always rubbish, wasn't it?'

We were walking fast towards the get-serious part of the doctor's domain. She didn't falter. 'It's irrelevant,' she said.

'You're telling me the stuff wasn't necessary?'

'Did I say that?' demanded Smiles. Her shoes were squealing on the linoleum.

'You said it was irrelevant,' I challenged her.

'I said,' defended the doctor, almost stamping her foot as she went screeching her shoes along the corridor, 'that it was irrelevant whether it was rubbish or not.'

I grabbed her arm. She looked at my hand on her crisp white coat. She was thinking about hitting me. I said, 'You're going to tell me that my part of this performance has mattered for sixty years. But it's been you who's blocked me, Smiles. You've blocked the deal that's made you rich. That's kept me comfortable. I'm still Little Frank, Smiles, and you can't fool me.'

'And that fucking opera?' spat Smiles. Her cosmetic face shone with a film of moisture. Her lips were slick with venom. 'That you've made me listen to for the last hour and a bit? You really think I'd believe there's a secret code in there somewhere that only fucking Little Frank can hear?' Smiles's nostrils were edged with white cartilage. There was a rim of dry white froth at the corners of her mouth. She was giving off an acrid smell, like anal sweat. It cut through the camouflage of her expensive perfume. 'Well, here's the good news,' said Smiles. She looked like a staring horned toad with toxins gleaming on its pallid skin. 'You can miss sticking this one up your withered little pucker, Frank, and it won't make a blind bit of difference. And you can miss the next one and the one after that, too, and the worst that will happen will be that you lose a sense of participation, is what we say in the trade, in your own situation. Congratulations for only taking sixty years to work it out, Frank. It must make you feel a whole lot better about your reputation in the town, Frank. For not getting anything put over you, Little Frank, you horrible little fuck.'

'And the bad news, Smiles?' I asked, delighted by her bluster.

'Watch me,' said Smiles. 'Clean yourself up first.'

She pretty much threw me into the scrub-up. I looked at the shower-rose with mistrust. But I was triumphing at making the doctor crack. The only way forward was straight ahead. I gave myself a good blasting with the hot water, scrubbed up with some green goo from a dispenser and dried myself with a towel that had an antiseptic smell. Little Frank looked at the reflection in the scrub-up mirror of a skinny, bow-legged little runt with a high, bony rooster chest fluffed with white hair. The white hair on his head was sticking up in a cockscomb. He surprised me by doing a crowing little dance routine, with elbows stuck out. There was a vacuum-sealed pack of clothes in the changing room. I put them on. My own clothes I'd hung in a locker. They were like an effigy of the little guy dancing. I'd taken Gabber's memory stick and my phone with me to the shower stall. If I'd had a gun I'd have taken that too. The underwear in the clothes pack had that hint of formaldehyde that goes with brand-new institutional issue. The new white cotton shirt and pants smelled of preservative as well. I embalmed myself in them. I put on a pair of white slippers. There was an inside pocket in the shirt. I dropped my phone and Gabber's chip into it. The phone had Half Ton loaded. It was clocking the ongoing transfer of funds to 1081 KidSaver. Crafty Little Frank was hanging on to it.

This wasn't the first time I'd gone to theatre. But it was the first time Little Frank had done so since waking up angry. I was standing there like a cross between a monk and a lavatory attendant when the door opened and Smiles came in. She was dressed all in white as well. She took my breath away. She'd become one giant smile, shining. You had to turn your eyes away from her brightness. As well, she was wearing a white Stetson hat. It was the kind country singers wear in sleaze bars along with buttock and crotch windows in their Levis. The hat was so wrong it made her look insanely confident.

'White suits you, Frank,' she said.

'Smiles, the hat,' I began. Then I remembered I'd seen this routine before. But now it could shock me. Her power was like a bank of klieg lights.

We donned masks and entered the wet section. I took my place with medical students on the observation deck. My breath was vibrating through me like charged-up air through a subway tunnel all lit up with blue flashes and gusts of ozone.

The doctor, in her white country music hat, turned and looked up at us. I was sure she was smiling at me. I could see her eyes going over the parts of me that she could see. I stood there and made that blank trader look cover my entire body. Then Smiles looked away, because they were bringing in a gurney.

The equipment Smiles was using involved a laser that sealed what it cut. The doctor unzipped the flesh of the bodies. Cages of bones were whizzed through with a little saw. Enough blood got around to justify Smiles calling the place the wet section. But there was nothing to it, really. Except that Smiles twice changed her hat. She came back in with a clean apron and a white version of a seaman's cap. Another time it was a pillbox. A titter of applause went around the observation platform. But the hats made my blood run cold. We'd been in business together a long time. Her performance was saying, 'You think you know something secret? Here, try something that's not, you little crook.' Then another gurney came in. Smiles had the pillbox on. When they took the cover off the body, I saw that it was Mack. Smiles turned and looked up at the observation platform. I was standing there with death tearing through me and, now, a great icicle driven through the pit of my stomach. Smiles turned back to the big, fawn-coloured body with breasts fallen sideways and the squat hips of a man. The band of Smiles's pillbox was dark with sweat, and the back of her theatre gown was wet as well. I saw her shoulder blades lift inside the damp white cloth with the motion of hefting equipment. Before Smiles could unzip Mack I went out the door of the theatre like a ghost through a brick wall.

I paced myself through the corridors. Smiles had provided me with a costume. I carried Mack's terror. I added it to the weight of my knowledge. My knowledge was a mighty club. I was carrying it towards the blow I'd strike with it.

My route wouldn't be green and white. It wouldn't be marked with the red stripe that delivered Little Frank to his watchers. I thought of the chimney that was visible from the solarium. I oriented myself towards that side of the building until I saw its fuming shaft through the window of a stairwell. I descended using stairs whose landings were jammed with empty plastic containers and cardboard boxes spilling rolls of mouldy toilet paper. The windows were filthy as I approached ground level. Their steel frames had rusted and begun to rot the crumbling concrete of the walls.

At ground level I stepped into a scummy puddle with a rim of rust. The fire-exit bar across the door had seized, but Little Frank smashed it up using a section of metal shelving. I stepped outside into air that was neither fresh nor institutional. It had a sick smell of leaching waste, rendered vomit and festering blood. That was when Little Frank sank to his knees and emitted a great, bellowing roar of rage and grief. I ejected this yell from the pit of my guts along with a fountain of burning bile. I'd been weeping internally for sixty years. I hurled my reservoir of poisonous salt into the filthy yard of the hospital's incinerator.

When I stood up, my legs were trembling but they moved me towards the far side of the yard. There was a space where one wall didn't abut with another. A triangular gleam of daylight entered there and marked the surface of the yard. The knowledge of what I had to do next was also simply lit.

The walls of the yard consisted of concrete alcoves, as though vehicles had once been stored there. I stepped aside into one, out of sight of the hospital windows, and took the phone from my inner pocket.

'Half Ton.' Then I remembered. 'Cao Cao,' I said. 'This is Little Frank.' Then I remembered again. 'This is Blue Back. You can help me.'

There was something else in the alcove with me. I heard it breathing. I couldn't see anything in the dark, but there was a stink like battery chickens.

'Blue Back is calling Cao Cao,' said my phone.

'Blue Back is calling Cao Cao,' repeated whatever was there with me. Its voice formed the hard 'b', the throat-shutting 'c' and the echoing 'ao ao' separately and with difficulty. It was a poor little Creeper, I saw, in a nest of rags and paper at the back of the alcove. 'You can help me,' mimicked the Creeper. She had the great, ladle bottom lip of the woman who'd approached me outside the hospital the day I'd met Olaf, but no arms or legs that I could see. Her tiny body was covered in spiky hair that was more like feathers. The roots of hair had grown into thick, embedded sheaths. There were protrusions like wee purple breasts on her chest when she levered herself up. Her arms and legs were about a quarter the length of ordinary ones.

'No, I can't,' I said.

'Can't what?' said Half Ton's thick voice on my phone. His face loomed on its screen.

'I was talking to someone else,' I told him. A dozen or so Creepers had come out of alcoves along the walls. They were noticing me. 'What would be excellent,' I said to Half Ton, 'would be if you could come and get me.'

There was a pause at Half Ton's end. 'Who were you talking to?' he asked. Even on the phone, I could hear his voice surfing on the great motion of his breath.

'A Creeper,' I said. 'I'm at the hospital, out the back. There's a few living here.'

'I know,' said the big, slow-breathing voice. 'Near the crematorium. I see you.'

'Is that what it is?' I had the feeling we needed to go gently through this negotiation.

'They get stuff,' sighed Half Ton.

I didn't ask what stuff they got from the crematorium. I was looking at the poor wee chicken thing who'd settled back down in her bed. I was trying not to think of Mack's big beige body being unzipped by the woman in the white pillbox hat.

'I need you to come and get me,' suggested Little Frank, with a bit more urgency. 'Can you do that?'

'White transport.' Half Ton seemed to be measuring the time to the hospital crematorium in breaths. 'Fifteen minutes,' he said.

'Cao Cao closes,' said my phone, and I shut it.

'Cao Cao closes,' said the wee Creeper.

I went over to her nest and sat down on a plastic crate. Her smell was bad, but I didn't mind it. I picked up her hand. It was a real hand, but miniature, light and almost boneless. It was warm like any other hand but the back was covered with a scratchy layer of minute feathers. I stroked them the right way, along the back of her hand and on to the little fingers. That way they felt soft.

She may have been asleep when I heard a vehicle come into the yard. It was a white transport. The other Creepers knew it. Half Ton was talking to them as I opened the passenger door and got quickly in. I had a sensation like static electricity in my fingers from stroking the little feathered mitt back in there. I hoped no one had seen me from the hospital windows.

The vehicle sank when Half Ton got in. Its whine of dynamo was like a complaint as he backed up and drove from the crematorium yard.

'I come here,' he said. 'I help them.'

That was it. We drove out of an anonymous utilities area with security fences and attempts at landscaping. There were berms, flower beds and the occasional palm tree. Rubbish was blowing around. The fences were festooned with trapped plastic bags. The world of the Creepers' yard seemed implausible.

'Lucky for me,' I said. I was remembering the little silky hand and the sour stink of filthy quills.

'And they help me,' continued Half Ton. His remorseless rhythm was one phrase followed by about six big slow heaves of breath. 'And we both help them,' he seemed to finish, but then added, 'Binh Xuyen.' He turned and looked at me. 'You know them,' he stated for a fact. 'And the Binh Xuyen help us,' he did, then, finish.

So there I had it. Half Ton recruited Creepers to do whatever Creepers could do for the Binh Xuyen in return for whatever it was the Binh Xuyen could do for Creepers. The arrangement hadn't been a lot of help to the little chicken thing.

'Where do we have to go, Junior?' asked Half Ton. His voice was so slow now that the question heaved around inside the van like an enquiry about the ultimate meaning of the universe.

'Wanganui,' I told him. 'Can you do that?'

'What's in Wanganui?' He didn't say no.

'A friend.' I believed this would be true. 'Her name's Hokkaido,' sobbed Little Frank. I had to lock my teeth together to stop the hope that geysered up past my rage and sadness. But then I vomited again, out the transport window. 'I'm going to die,' I said, when I could.

154

'I know,' sighed Half Ton. He handed me a dirty towel smelling of greasepaint. It was getting dark. He drove past the end of Courtenay Place where Little Frank had woken up all those weeks ago and then, as I began to fall asleep, around the glittering harbour to the western motorway.

Part Two

THE RIVER

What had happened, what was happening and what might happen were shuffling across the whited-out spaces of my mind in no particular order.

'Came back real fast.' Half Ton's voice out there on the moonlit plateau. 'Says go to the Phaedo. Like you said.' There was a little street map on the transport's GPS screen. 'They expecting you?'

I couldn't see how.

I was reconstructing my path to the Phaedo Peace House. Beyond the window of my bedroom at the Phaedo, and a time ago that I couldn't measure, Half Ton and I crossed the empty plateau to Wanganui. I remembered how back then we were powered by the deep, monotonous thrum of Half Ton's rendition of how many had died for him. *Quanti ho visto morire per me!* He liked Turandot's remorseful aria, and I remembered how, when the Phaedo responded 'real fast' with the street map on Half Ton's GPS screen, the ghost of another merciful establishment from an unmerciful past returned to the muddy estuary of Little Frank's mind.

Now the same memory was slapping like an incoming tide at the edges of my vision where, from my bed, I could see a briar rose twined thickly into a wattle tree outside my window at the Phaedo Peace House. It was late summer and the wattle flowers had long ago turned into wrinkled seed pods. Little Frank had enough verve left to get amusement out of that. The briar rose was persisting with successions of flowers, but its dead flowerheads were cluttering up the foliage. Birds were zooming in and out, especially first thing in the morning and in the early evening. My favourite pastime was to lie on my bed at these times and watch the birds. Their intelligence was all in their bright, quick movements, their attentive eyes and their rowdy manners. I was getting fond of them.

The tangled branches and foliage of the wattle and the briar rose looked like those barricades people wake up behind in fairy stories. Dust hung in the shafts of sunlight at the back of Uncle Geek's place where the second-hand kids' books were. It was there, where a funny sickish smell came off the old brown paper, that Rapunzel waited behind her fence of thorns, where unawake palaces were overgrown with dark forests. I liked the bit where Snow White suddenly coughed out a chunk of apple.

'Come on, boy. Your mum's here. Finally.'

'Come on, Frankie, get your nose out of that.' Or, more often, the video games—the scarlet and gold dragon boat. Prising my fingers off the controls.

The plateau was bleached by moonlight. Half Ton's voice had a washed-out sound as well, or else Little Frank's consciousness was too dimmed to hear or see more than pale ghosts of what was going on. Half Ton was talking to his phone. He was telling it to find Hokkaido in Wanganui. He was telling it the only clue I had: Phaedo. Even so, I got a pale shock when I heard him repeat after his phone, 'Phaedo?' That was the name of Dr Jack's outfit back at Raglan all those years ago when Hokkaido and I first met. When Little Frank first began to learn about the difference consequences made to your life.

'Came back real fast—mean anything to you? Phaedo?' There was a red dot on the van's GPS map. Half Ton's voice changed when he talked to me, rather than to the phone. With me, he was measuring what he'd found out about Little Frank against the little wreck sitting beside him. The pale night hills with streaks of mist in the gulleys streamed past the windows of his transport. 'You've been asleep,' said Half

Ton, sounding kind. He made the simple statement resonate like something more significant.

'That's right,' said Little Frank primly.

'That's right what?' Half Ton wanted to know. 'Phaedo or asleep?'

'Both,' I said. I should've said, All three. Meaning I'd been asleep for half my life as well.

'Who's Phaedo?' Half Ton asked. 'Came back real quick. They expecting you?' He wasn't making conversation, he was just astonished. He pointed a sausage finger at the bluish map on the GPS screen.

A great many years ago, Hokkaido explained about the death of Socrates from drinking hemlock—how the account of this assisted mortality was conveyed by Plato through the character of Socrates' friend, Phaedo. The Phaedo with beautiful hair. Dr Jack had told her the story to explain the name of his euthanasia outfit at Raglan. Socrates went numb from the feet up and his consciousness was free to contemplate eternity without physical distractions. Young Frank thought that was ridiculous back then. Right now old Frank was having second thoughts.

It'd been half a lifetime since I'd been conscious of anything like the wattle tree with the rose all over it. Back in Wellington, my own garden had been familiar to me for years. It was designed for maximum privacy and no work, there was nothing spectacular about it—a few big planters, a couple of hedges the Tongan guy came to cut and retrieve the stiffly grinning electrocuted cats from, and several clumps of flax as windbreaks around my little terrace. I'd never been a gardener. After Hokkaido and the *Cao Cao San*, nature for me had flowered in concrete and asphalt. Later, in the Petri dishes of Smiles's lab. I had a patch in one corner of my home garden. Here, Little Frank liked to try excelling at tomatoes. But that was it. My garden said something about what I'd done with my life—me, Little Frank. No one got in there through my fence of thorns to disturb my beauty sleep. No apple-ejecting cough. Until now.

Next, Half Ton asked what I was humming. Maybe he was being kind again, but it didn't sound like conversation. What did he want?

'Hell's teeth, Ton,' I said.

'That's what the tune is?'

'I mean, what's it matter?'

'I was just asking,' said Half Ton soothingly. 'You do it all the time.'

'Do what?'

'You hum, Frank,' said Half Ton. 'You've got all this stuff happening in your head.'

You can understand why I liked to sit out there on that terrace where the late-summer sun came in. I'd be gloating a bit on my tomato crop and looking forward to taking one in at lunch time the next day for Mrs Flitch to cut up and serve with leaves of basil and some fresh mozzarella cheese. Quite often, I'd identify the tomato of my choice the evening before. I'd visit it a couple of times during the morning, before clipping it at the last minute after it'd had a decent blast of sunshine. I amused myself with the thought that I was the Kidney Ravi of tomatoes.

'So, what is it, the hum?'

The thing with Half Ton, once he'd started you couldn't stop him. I had to keep him quiet somehow. How was I supposed to think?

'It's a tune from an opera called *Turandot* by a composer called Puccini,' I said. 'I doubt if you know it.'

'You're forgetting,' said Half Ton. His face turned towards me like a moonlit satellite dish.

'No, I'm not,' I argued back. 'I'm remembering.'

Half Ton sighed. In that sigh I heard the nippy sound of Little Frank's ill-tempered voice. Then I also remembered that it was Half Ton who'd given me the memory stick with Gabber's last message on it. 'Sorry,' I said. 'You're right. You listened to it. The Chinese opera.'

'The Chinese opera,' repeated Half Ton, as if that explained something.

He went back to driving across the moon-sickened plateau. When he hummed the phrase, '*Quanti ho visto morire per me!*' the air inside his transport thudded as though with a bass subwoofer. I felt his hum against the membranes of my eardrums, or whatever was doing that job in there now. I felt it inside my head where the memory of Dr Jack's Phaedo house was vibrating like cicadas in the summer heat above the silty estuary where the *Cao Cao San* waited, only she wasn't called that yet.

'Do you mind?' I said. 'I'm trying to think.'

'Little Frank,' murmured Half Ton, as though he was saying, Yes sir!

That sickish smell of hot video monitors in the dust-shafted back of Geek's place was always followed by the smell of my mother's neck. That's where I'd put my nose when she picked me up.

'You're a mouse.'

'No I'm not!'

'With a wet nose! A rat!'

'I'm not. I'm a frog!'

'Ugh!' She pretended to shake me off. 'A horrible wet little froggie!'

Geek smelled of cigarettes. Sometimes of Dettol. Sometimes he let rip these massive farts that followed him around inside his pants. But I never smelled his neck close up. His breath had a kind of yellow smell, like his teeth. It was a mixture of cigarettes and what he looked like—tired, usually, so that his hair didn't have much life and his eyelids hung down. There was another smell I knew well. It was the explosive stink of fireworks at Guy Fawkes. It had something in common with Geek's farts. It used to hang around the mouldy Council rubbish bins on Lyall Bay Parade when we let off Double Happys in them. It used to float back over the fence by Mr Chan's greengrocer shop when we biffed crackers into the yard where his ancient mother was stacking cabbage crates. I associated the smell of brimstone and cabbage with her squealing, blood-curdling curses.

When I walked home from Mack's with Gabber's recording in my torn pocket and the memory of Half Ton's hard chest in the palm of my hand, I was feeling pretty calm. All the floating restaurants and the casino were flashing. The casino had laser tracers zapping out from it. Because it was a beautiful late- summer evening, there was a big crowd out around Oriental Bay. There were parties going on along the sea wall; smoke was drifting about from the grills and wok barrows, and even the fortified bay-front apartments looked gay.

There was an old apartment tower block that had survived redevelopment. It was down the north-eastern end of the Parade. It had pretend plaster scrollwork under the windows—wreaths and loops that seemed to spell out MOM. It had always been a bit of a joke with me, to refer to the old pile as 'Mum's Place'. Like the crumbling Gateways apartments, it gave the neighbourhood a bad name. The night I walked home from Mack's, someone was having a party on the rooftop of Mum's Place. There were coloured lanterns strung along the old balustrades. I could hear loud, thudding Asian house music. A lit-up dirigible in the form of a dragon was wobbling overhead, tethered to the roof-garden railing. Across the glittering water, beyond the floating restaurants, I could see the long streaks of car-lights on the speed-link. I knew already that that was where I wanted to be. Once I'd sorted my business out with Dr Smiles. Once I'd heard from Olaf.

I was travelling into the centre of my universe, not out and away. Its terminal centre would have a name like Phaedo. The smell of limes that Hokkaido's hair produced all by itself had always told me she knew more about being alive than Little Frank would ever learn. I was still wearing the hospital whites. Full moonlight was bleaching out distance on the high plateau. At one moment I found Half Ton and I were parked by the roadside. Little Frank was coming out of a kind of mental white-out. The white-out was trying to erase a bad dream. The van radio's Lyric Semester all-nighter was playing some old Merle Haggard song, and Half Ton was shaking me.

'I think you're having a bad dream, Little Frank,' he said.

'You can say that again.'

'You were talking.'

I got out and had a long, effortful piss into the grass by the road. It felt amazing—like I was being emptied of time. I felt the pressure of all the days I'd been wandering about on my quest flow sluggishly out and steam in the moonlight. A truck with a trailer attached went whining past and blew its klaxon at me. Too right, I thought. You bet your life. Thanks. The truck's headlights went up the next hill and disappeared. There was a paddock of rustling, dry maize stalks through the fence, and I even wanted to wade into them and just lie down there in my white antiseptic pants and shirt. But I thought, No, get cracking. Finish what you start. Geek used to say that.

'What say you turn it off, Ton?'

'Sorry,' said the slow, axle-greased voice of my saviour. 'I put it on when you were asleep.' He turned the radio off. His breath went in and out a half dozen times. 'You were talking like a little boy.'

'I was what?'

'Like a little boy.' Half Ton's slow huffs may have been laughter, but Little Frank didn't jump to the conclusion that anything was funny. 'Your voice,' said Half Ton. 'Like a kid's.'

It didn't seem much later that I was looking out a big old sash window at the briar twined into the wattle. There were other old trees in the grounds of the Phaedo Peace House. At night I'd imagine I could hear the sound of magnolia blooms thudding to the ground—like baby tree-sloths or something, I thought, dreaming and losing their grip somewhere in forests where there were still tree- sloths, where there were still forests.

But wait.

This was where my careful reconstruction of that trip had arrived. The realisation came to me quietly. The sounds of tree-sloths in forests had to be imagined, because my window was double glazed and sealed shut. I was imagining the sound of falling magnolia blooms and also the tree-sloths. They seemed quite real, like the smell of the tomatoes I'd left behind at the outer edge of my life, where I couldn't imagine anything. Like the smell of limes I was still waiting to encounter at its centre, where my imagination would come back to life for a little while—for long enough.

I thought of the deep hum with which Half Ton filled the interior of his transport. *Quanti ho visto.* The Chinese opera. I thought of the sound of his hum as having the quality of moonlight, the white face of cruelty and treachery. I'd wanted Half Ton to shut up, wanted to hear myself think, wanted to know where in time I was, wanted to keep it simple, wanted to finish what I'd started. But it was my memory of the big guy's copy of my own hum that reminded me of my old powers as I lay on my bed in the Phaedo Peace House and waited for Hokkaido to show up. Waited to see if she would. Cruelty and treachery would be on her mind when that happened.

'Cao Cao,' said Half Ton's phone.

'Talk,' he said, dropping the heavy word into moonlight. There was more going on with Half Ton than I knew. My hearing aid picked up the tiny scratches of voice in his ear-piece. Then his huge body went rigid. The white van swerved and straightened. His musical hum as we drove was deep and melodious, but the sound that came out of him at that moment was dissonant, like a bass screech of metal on metal.

'What's up?' I wanted to know. But he just drove. When I put out a hand to shake his arm, he threw me off and returned his hand to the steering wheel. For a moment, his face loomed towards me—moonlight flickered across it as we drove through trees. I saw huge tears tracking from the folds of fat around his eyes.

'They burned the yard,' he said. 'All of it.' He was looking straight at me. 'All of them.'

At first, I spent a lot of time by the window of my bedroom. There were only half a dozen other inmates at the Phaedo Peace House. All of them were Timing Out. The Peace House was a five-star hospital that looked like a hotel, or a five-star hotel that looked like a hospital. It hid its luxury behind the worn façade of an old mansion by the river. Its clients, including me, could afford to be well catered for. It reminded me of the Apollo chain that sprouted outlets all over the organ-donor territories of India and Asia during the immunosuppressant heyday of the kidney harvest years. This was when the Binh Xuyen and every other enterprising agency were pumping up the market for cyclosporine. It was said these luxury hotel hospitals were the refuges of choice for Pirates and others evading the attention of law-enforcement agencies. This was later true of the establishment over which Smiles presided back in Wellington—and especially of the zone whose serenity was hidden behind the less serene one painted green and white and provided with a red, exit-finding stripe on the floor in case you had to crawl out. Helicopters didn't need red stripes to find their way in and out of the serene zone. The clients who got out of the helicopters didn't always look to be in need of a tune-up. The same was true of the cargo Smiles referred to as 'cadaveric'. But that was a different story.

'There have been four great ages.' The doctrine-according-to-Smiles had the first 'messy' age down as blood transfusion. Blood typing created a mix-and-match market and a boom in test kits. This was before my time as a trader, though the blood-bank vamps stuck around. The second was the 'heroic' age of tissue-matched organ transplants. Its supply-and-demand, Smiles purred, was regulated 'by love and loyalty'. Little Frank was ignorant of these family heroics whose popular stories involved giving loved kin your important bits. This was the age when I had Hokkaido. I didn't think there was anything more to want. I'd given her my heart and I didn't want it back.

The third age was the commercially positive one of immunosuppressants. The world was divided into those who bred and donated organs, and those who could afford to harvest and receive them. This was where I began to apply my skills to the business of life and death. It was also after I'd lost Hokkaido. It was the age of brain death, of cadavers, of exposés and outrage. It was the age of opportunity.

Little Frank wasn't laughing when he joked that he had Hokkaido in the romantic age of tissue-matching and lost her when compatibility stopped mattering. I was wondering when she'd show up again. How long would that take? The little heart I'd reclaimed in the end was clenched around this question. I woke up with it clenched, morning after morning, in the Phaedo Peace House.

And then, after a time of darkness and confusion, came the 'great age'. Behind the sealed visor of her lab suit, Dr Smiles was radiant with satisfaction. A woman I knew only as Sukthi was more modestly smiling beside her. Even so, Sukthi's teeth were so white their reflection seemed to jar the light inside her visor—but with a brightness of warm pride, unlike Smiles's chilly power-surge. Smiles's voice reached me inside my helmet, tinny with amplification. Obviously thrilled, she said, 'Embryos hitting the lid like hot popcorn.'

Smiles, Sukthi and I were grinning through our masks at a Petrie dish whose surface scum was minutely pulsating. 'Magic,' radiated Smiles. These were stem cells that Sukthi had persuaded to become heart cells. Smiles clapped her white gloves together. Hosts would get the competitive chance to prove they could grow this eager slime into something with commodity value. Something that could be pierced by the arrows of love. It was a healthy, contestable market.

In the grimly speeding transport that was fleeing from Smiles towards the Phaedo Peace House, Half Ton's phone called him again. 'Okay,' he said. The tears had dried like snail trails on his face. He pulled the van over behind trees in a lay-by at the bottom of a long incline. There was a clear view behind us where the road crested the moonlit hill. He pulled me out of the van and shoved me hard into the trees. 'Lie down,' he said. 'Don't fucking move.'

Through branches, I saw the fast car come over the hill. It was on infra-red, no lights. The back door of the transport slammed. There was another slam, like a giant Double Happy in a rubbish bin, as the car passed the lay-by. It knocked the breath out of me and made my hearing aids squeal. The car fireball catapulted into the paddock on the other side of the road.

There was a roadblock before the bridge over the Wanganui River. I watched Half Ton hand over the grenade launcher from the back of his transport. The door slammed again. A Maori guy in a beanie waved us on.

'Maybe you can help me, Blue Back,' droned Half Ton, edging his transport through piles of concrete blocks on to the bridge. 'Find this Phaedo,' he added, as if to say, First things first.

'Ten eighty one,' I said. 'KidSaver.' It was clear we had to sort out who owed what. Little Frank had never felt this tired in his life. 'I'll fix you up,' I said. 'I owe you.'

There were no lights on in the town. I was no help. I fell asleep again as if falling into the moonlit surface of the huge, muddy river.

I woke up around noon. So the bedside clock said. I was wearing pyjamas I'd never seen in my life. They bore the embossed monogram of an ornate goblet. I smelled of soap but had no memory of bathing. It seemed to me I was in a hotel. My bedroom had a well-appointed bathroom opening off it. One of the toothbrushes in it had been used. There was a small, windowless lounge with a light-well skylight that had distant clouds floating across it. Comfortable armchairs and a sofa hinted at a social life I couldn't begin to imagine.

There was a fridge with fresh juices and bottled water, and on a low table there was a bowl of fruit. A bottle of water had been drunk already. There was two of everything I might need: armchairs, glasses, fruit plates, towels and pillows. They gave the eerie impression that someone was missing, rather than the comforting sense that I was actually there myself. There were also fresh flowers in a vase on the desk in the bedroom. They must have arrived while I was asleep. I had no idea how long I'd been asleep.

I drew pale yellow linen curtains and found a double-glazed sash window and a view out to a wattle tree whose seed pods were dry at the end of summer. A briar rose with late-summer-dead flowerheads was twined around the wattle's branches. The window wouldn't open. The scene outside was eerily silent.

The fear I felt reminded me of the time I'd walked through hospital corridors wearing theatre whites and wanting to be outside so much I tossed my guts when I got there. The door to my suite opened, though. I saw a modest corridor with a high ceiling stud and skirting boards of old wood. My suite seemed to be concealed behind this museum-like interior with its smell of beeswax, and its dim coloured light filtered through stained glass in the door at the end of the corridor. How long had I been in the mansion Half Ton found at the far side of the moonlit plateau?

There was no sign of Half Ton, anyway. The hospital whites I remembered from the drive were nowhere to be seen. Nor were any other clothes except the pyjamas monogrammed with a cup of hemlock.

'Ten eighty one.' There were two blue towelling bathrobes hung up in the suite's bathroom. I put one on and walked in my bare feet down the old-fashioned corridor. Two possessions lay on the table in my lounge: my phone and the memory stick from Gabber. These I held in my hand as I walked along the antique runner of carpet with its brass cleats at the sides. I went towards the door of stained glass through which red, emerald and amber light shone. I wasn't surprised to find that the stained glass was a picture of Socrates. He was surrounded by his friends, including, I guessed, Phaedo—the woman whose long hair was the last thing he felt before he lost touch, so to speak. So Hokkaido told me. So Dr Jack told her. I began to reassemble my journey.

There was a moment early in our time when Hokkaido tried to tell me what she thought was good. She thought what Dr Jack was doing was good. She thought it was brave, helping people to die. She thought he'd been brave to rescue her—the people he took her from could harm him. She thought it was good of him to grubstake her in the boarding house at Raglan, even though it would fill up with deadshits like me. She thought it was good of him to let her go when she hooked up with me, whom he considered a deadshit.

She thought it was good of me to help him out with the supplies he needed. That it was brave of me to protect the locals by going offshore for them. She thought I was good to do this when Dr Jack made no secret of the fact he thought I was a deadshit. A deadshit who was unworthy of her.

I told her I pretty much understood why old Socrates would want to feel Phaedo's hair before his lights went out.

'I really like your hair—it always smells like limes.'

And then there's this kid throwing up on me in the cockpit of the *Cao Cao San* while the rusty flank of the drop-off Korean squid boat heaves itself out of reach.

'Say what you fucking well like, Frank, this is not good. This is very, very bad. Don't you dare smile at me. Don't even think about trying to talk me round.'

'Round what?'

She pretty much slept all the way up to Manukau Heads, the kid—a dodgy trip. Hokkaido had to help me sail the boat. Then she took the rubber duck with the kid in it, and the last I saw of them was the outboard's white wake cutting up into Huia Bay. The bushy ranges in the north where they were headed were blue-green and almost covered by misty rain. The duck's wake went in a straight line, across the tops of the whitecaps, just like you'd expect Hokkaido to. It wasn't hesitating or looking left or right. I was meant to drop the kid further round at Big Muddy Creek. I didn't bother going in there to explain myself. I motored back out past Ninepin Rock with a storm jib to steady the boat. Like the people Dr Jack had taken Hokkaido off, the people expecting me further round from Huia were capable of doing harm. I'd rather take my chances with the tides and the onshore wind.

I was in a world like the Opera. It had a view down into the theatre where Smiles executed skilful costume changes involving hats. It had a landscape made ghostly by treacherous moonlight. It had an interior lit by the coloured gels of Socrates' death. It had a theme tune: 'How many have I seen die for me!' It had themes of remorse, fear and hope. It was mostly bullshit. Bullshit and coloured smoke. Little Frank knew this. I knew. I was awake to this. But I was in it.

What was I hoping for when I opened the door with the stained-glass picture of Socrates with Phaedo and the crew? That Hokkaido would be there? Had been 'expecting me'?

'Your hair—the limes.'

'If you smile I'll hit you.'

To be forgiven?

Wake up, Frank. 'Ten eighty one.'

The door opened to a pleasant communal room in which a home entertainment centre screen had a game of cricket on it. I was the only person in the room wearing a blue dressing gown. I turned and left immediately. I probably cursed. One of the inmates, a man with the huge eyes of someone whose body has almost left his consciousness to its own devices, jumped as if startled and looked at Little Frank over the back of his armchair. I felt his glowing, possum eyes follow me down the corridor even after I'd shut the door with the picture of Socrates on it. I slammed the door to my own suite, but the eyes were still there. Stuck to the back of my neck. Like the truck klaxon in the middle of the bleached-out plateau, they were saying, *This* is how fast it's going, your time.

Amped-up whine of a big-haul dynamo. Headlights gone in a split second. Blast of dusty wind and scatter of loose gravel. Red tail-lights disappearing over a hill. Gone. Finished. A white plain with cloud shadows shuffling across it. The dry sound of maize stalks in the roadside paddock. Slam of Half Ton's weapon. That other time, I put up the storm jib and left the yacht's diesel donkey thudding away. The swells were up around the top spreader on the mast. The horizon was lumpy out there when the *Cao Cao San* rode up to the tops of the heave. Down in the troughs it was dark. I sat there with my freezing hand over the tiller and tried to get rid of the memory of the rubber duck's bright, straight-ahead wake zooming away towards the rainy hills.

How many times can you make a wrong turn in one life and not get hold of the idea that time's always going to run out, no matter what you do to slow it down? Back then, I got rebellious. Who did she think she was? Telling me what's good and what's not. Back then, I had plenty of time. So I thought. Now, I knew that time was running out and that what I'd had of it I'd probably wasted.

I remembered what it felt like, the despair, in the troughs with the grey-green water shutting out the sky. I thought, How do I know I can trust Half Ton? What's he mean, 'Maybe you can help me?' I thought, How do I know Hokkaido's alive? How do I know what this place is? When the *Cao Cao San* heaved up on top of the swell and I saw the lumpy horizon with washed-out light coming up into the sky, Little Frank's hope returned. I had to relax my face to ease the ache of the smile on it. I saw the gold and red dragon boat on the video monitor and my mum walking through the dusty light in Geek's second-hand shop.

'Get your nose out of that, froggie boy.'

I saw the luff in the *Little Frank*'s mainsail as she cut through the Chaffers Passage at Barrett's Reef, the time I made my first run. I was yelling with the joy of freedom when cold spray hit me in the face. I saw the stripe of sunshine on Hokkaido's back the day *Little Frank* got renamed *Cao Cao*

San. I saw Madame Hee in *Taking Tiger Mountain* the last time I'd seen her. Then I was back in the dim trough of dark water and Half Ton was stopping himself from hitting me on my bursting chest as I lay on the floor of the Opera.

'When the blue comes back.'

Someone was trying to open my hand, but what I had there was Gabber's memory stick and my phone with Half Ton's code in it. I resisted even before I was really awake.

'Fuck off,' I said. 'Ten eighty one.' But then I let the things go. I knew I had to.

'Come on, Frank,' said the little mole in the uniform that matched my dressing gown. 'Time to get you sorted out.' He made me think of Uncle Geek. Same dead hair, same intelligence flattened by the world's rejects. Same teeth.

The pale yellow curtains were open and the briar-twined tree outside was full of busy birds I couldn't hear through the double glazing. If there was music in the world outside, I couldn't hear it. I had to get out there.

'I want to go out,' spat Little Frank past the thermometer. The twitchy Mole had me sitting up and was taking my blood pressure.

'I hope you like lasagne,' he said, letting the air out of his blood-pressure kit. That and his tired sigh sounded the same. 'With spinach,' he sighed. 'And I put your things back on the dresser. Your phone and stuff.' He was going out the door of my bedroom. 'And I got you the papers,' he said. 'The ones you like.'

Which ones were they?

Life—why do we turn it into the commodity we want to possess more than any other? And why, by the contrary token, do we love death so much?

'Cao Cao,' I said. 'This is Blue Back.' I couldn't help it. 'For Christ's sake, Ton,' bleated Little Frank, shaming himself. 'Where the fuck am I really?' I waited while the phone looked for Half Ton. 'I'm going crazy here,' I told it. 'The food's disgusting,' I added for good measure. Mrs Flitch wouldn't have let the Phaedo's lasagne anywhere near Little Frank. The spinach was shit.

'Cao Cao is not responding,' said my phone. Then it picked up the local signal and began a screen-saver slide show. I watched it. There was nothing better to do. There was the river, of course. The old shot tower on the hill. Then I saw an image of the nearby Ratana church. The phone was answering my question about where I was. It wasn't the answer I needed most, but I was happy to see the image of the white and red Ratana building. It took me back.

I used to be in the smaller towns a lot when I was still a kid trading junk out of old Geek's place and tooling around the country in my ute. I used to turn off country roads and stop outside dilapidated farm sheds that were vibrating with secrets you could see a mile off. They were going to wrack and ruin, most of these outfits. The little towns were inhabited by young ghosts with septic nose-studs and kids they couldn't afford to bring up properly. By useless survivors desperate to sell anything, including, in some locations, the dope that was my cash income. I knew most of the towns within a day's drive of Wellington pretty well. But I had a soft spot for Wanganui. One reason was because it was close to the Maori centre of Ratana. There was a museum there that was also a shrine containing the crutches chucked away by cripples cured by the old prophet, Bill Ratana. I went there a few times, out of curiosity, but also because the place spoke to me about something.

I watched the little slide show of the Wanganui region for a while until it got to the Ratana church again. Then I paused it.

'Blue Back is calling Cao Cao,' I said, looking at the picture. 'Keep trying.'

The place with crutches in it asked questions about what was whole, or new, or different long before drugs that would shift our ideas about magic came on the market. For a throw-away kid brought up in Uncle Geek's second-hand junk shop, those crutches said that within discards the real person, the whole person, survived somehow. I was a mean little fucker. But it was peaceful in the crutch museum. I liked to stop there when I got the chance.

'Cao Cao is not responding.'

'Keep trying.'

Once the immune system epidemics took off, a lot of people's thinking got changed. There was the rush to quack healing. The black-market pharmaceuticals and the blood, organ and tissue brokers. Just as many hopeless cases were flogging off their kidneys and eyeballs and the cadavers of their dear-departeds, not to mention their brain-dead dear-nearly-departeds, as were buying incantations, smouldering herbs and duckings in cold water. There were plenty of spooks on both sides. Years after tooling around the countryside in his ute, Little Frank drove his mature consciousness among them and prospered. Insurance companies ruled the world of the wealthy. The Kidney Ravis of the world knocked on the doors of the organ-rich poor. The Binh Xuyen, in all their guises, also prospered. Their paths and those of Little Frank began to cross. The public façade of the Pirate brand featured the red Guan Gong mask I saw on Tamar's face.

I lay on my bed with my silent phone on my chest and watched the silent birds in the wattle outside. I saw that, in those prosperous years, I was trying to prove to Hokkaido that, since we weren't organ-compatible any more, she could no longer tell me what was good. But if I'd listened, if we were still a match, I mightn't have ended up in the back of Tamar's car in the luxurious atmosphere he could afford to promise me.

But I still couldn't hear the promise that came from between Tamar's purplish liver lips under the Guan Gong mask. His bottle of hissing, pure beverage met those lips. It irrigated the deal he'd just made with Little Frank. But I couldn't hear the words. Only the wet clicks in his throat as the liquid went down it.

'But ah—the future!' said Tamar smoothly.

'Cao Cao is not responding.'

There were all those spooky fads and vamp sects about blood. A lot of high-tech gobbledegook about restructuring evolutionary models. There were evil little wars that were really genocidal quarantines, the rich nations immunising themselves. There was the Thirty Year Terror. There were the World Riots. There were the waves of energy crises. Worst of all, the Water Wars. Whenever it got worse, it got better for me. Whatever was bad was good for the Sheikh of Courtenay Place.

During those years of my mature prosperity I sometimes thought about the crutches in Bill Ratana's museum of faith. I was a whole man. I'd thrown away my crutch called Hokkaido.

I ate fresh fruit from the bowl, using one of the two fruit knives and one of the two dessert plates. I resisted the impulse to talk to the absent companion proposed by the other knife and plate. I washed this repast down with a drink of fresh—it said on the label—juice from one of the two bottles in my fridge. The second-rate lasagne and shit spinach I covered with their stainless-steel lid. There was only one helping, but that was one too many.

I told the phone to try again. I paused on the little picture of the Ratana church. Little Frank was brought up in a junk shop. I was a piece of junk myself. I got over it. No one questioned the usefulness of those clapped-out appliances, those 'worn-again' clothes. But no one imagined they could be different from what they were. Every dog has its day. Flowers fall off trees. Animals die. Appliances blow up. But I was brought up second hand, among second-hand stuff. By the time I was old enough to look after myself, I'd understood that the universe itself was an opportunity shop. Stuff came and went, or it changed and adapted—that's how it worked.

What Little Frank came to mistrust was a certain kind of newness. The kind of newness I didn't trust wanted to pretend it wasn't in the same opportunity-shop universe as the rest of everything. Those crutches cast aside by Bill Ratana were my aid to thought. They were among the things I turned my mind around. It wasn't just that I didn't need Hokkaido to prop me up. My world view was steadied by the idea that even used items have a kind of newness in them. That the so-called new item is likewise packaged by its ability to become used. That everything goes phut in the end anyway.

'Cao Cao is not responding.'

I looked at the little image of the Ratana church. I thought about the Chinese Opera and the 'new thing' there. There's knowledge that Expectationers keep in the museums of their consciousness. While they watch the operas of their lives in the dim comfort of their longevity, this knowledge is there. It breathes in the dark back there in its back row. Sometimes it coughs or rustles a bit, or laughs. Sometimes it goes, 'Woo hoo.' Little Frank was laughing all by himself. Passing the time.

Then my phone made an optimistic noise. The image of the red and white Ratana church zapped off the screen. 'Cao Cao is calling Blue Back.' The screen's video counter was ticking over. 'Please wait Blue Back. Downloading video now.'

'Get a move on,' said Little Frank peevishly. I wanted to get out. I wanted to see Hokkaido. I wanted to know what was going on in the Phaedo. I wanted to know what was so peaceful about it. I wanted to know if the Phaedo I was in was the Phaedo I thought it should be. I wanted to know what Half Ton was up to. I wanted my hat, my cane, a decent suit. I wanted a fresh handkerchief. I wanted a seasonal flower for my buttonhole. I wanted to walk by the big, brown, slow river. I remembered flood timber heaving along past the piles of the bridges. I wanted to hear the happy birds I could see tearing in and out of the wattle and the briar rose.

I wanted to talk to someone like Gabber. Or Mack, whose world view was about as metaphysical as her galah's. I wanted them to be using the second glass, plate, drink and chair in the Phaedo Peace House. I wanted them to be alive. And hungry enough to finish the lasagne with spinach.

'Thank you for waiting, Blue Back,' said my phone.

I heard a ghost of the word 'patience'. I heard the hissing spook of Tamar saying, 'But ah—the future!' I put the phone down on the bed beside me to stop myself from chucking it across the room. I was sick of waiting for everything, sick of my patience. How was Franco Alfano going to get the opera finished? How was I going to finish what I'd started? What was Little Frank to do?

'Video message for Blue Back,' said the phone beside me on the bed.

I picked it up and watched an image fill with crimson light on the little screen. Then I heard the squealy, clattery sound of music from the Chinese Opera. The video moved shakily forward through a portal in the form of a giant dragon. I knew this. It was the entrance to the Chinese Opera. A text scrolled under the screen. The screen was filling with a miniature set in which red banners were massing and unfurling. The text said, 'r u ok. don phon me BX. 1081 ok. cao cao.'

Then Madame Hee entered stage left on the parabola of a great leap. One arm was extended in front of her in a clenched-fist gesture. She had one leg lifted up so high behind I thought she must surely fall. But when she landed her tiny red mouth opened under the Maoist fatigue cap. It made a sound like the white incision of Hokkaido's wake in the murky water of the Manukau. Like the icy gleam of sky at the heaving horizon when the *Cao Cao San* crested. The clatter of discarded crutches. The shriek of a klaxon in moonlight. The squeal of time venting from leaky Expectations. Like the shrill noise of consciousness itself.

I heard Tamar's purple lips say, 'If you're happy with that.'

I heard Little Frank say, 'Yes.' He said, 'Thank you.'

The sequence with Madame Hee kept repeating.

I don't know what the Mole stuck in my arm. When I got my senses back, I was watching cricket on television in the day room.

'How's it going, Frank?' asked the withered bloke with the marsupial eyes.

I had a newspaper on my lap. I'd drawn boxes in red biro around items in the classified section. One of them was a quote from Abraham Lincoln. It read, 'Most folks are as happy as they make up their minds to be.'

'Fuck off,' said Little Frank. Night Vision's eyes dilated a bit and he shrank back into what was left of his body. But I wasn't talking to him. I was talking to Abraham Lincoln.

The other thing I held on my lap was a piece of paper with Half Ton's text copied on to it. *r u ok. don phon me BX. 1081 ok. cao cao.* The careful handwriting was Little Frank's. The piece of paper had been folded and unfolded many times. It was asking if I was okay. I didn't know if I was okay. It was telling me not to phone Half Ton because Binh Xuyen. Because Binh Xuyen what—they'd burned the Creeper yard? Because Half Ton had got me out? They were looking for me? I didn't know. The KidSaver was okay. That I knew. I could see the account on my phone. The text had been folded and unfolded across the memory of *Taking Tiger Mountain by Strategy*. The riddle Franco had to finish involved taking the Opera by strategy. There were resources. I knew that. Half Ton knew that.

Don't call me, I'll call you. Cao Cao will call you. When would Cao Cao call Blue Back? What harm could it do for Blue Back to call Cao Cao? What was he doing?

Nor was I cursing the 'ageless' Asian woman who'd come into the day room at the moment I said 'Fuck off!' to Abraham Lincoln. But the look on her face said she thought I was. Either that or it was the look she'd prepared already. Knowing she was going in there to meet Little Frank. Expecting treachery. A shock registered on her smooth face, a split second, like someone woken by a slap. Then her expression sealed over.

The smile on Little Frank's face and the heart in his panting chest clenched simultaneously. Then the blue came back.

*

'I want to get out,' I said.

She wasn't Hokkaido. She was taller than Hokkaido. She was taller than me. 'You were very anxious to get in when you arrived,' said the woman. She'd muted the wide-awake, hostile look on her face. 'So was the big guy with you.'

Little Frank was going to say, 'I don't remember that,' but he was too proud.

'But you don't remember that, do you, Frank?' she said. She was smart.

'Ageless' is a meaningless word, but I was falling back on it as I studied her face. My guess was very high-quality Expectations with tissue supplements. This was a big investment. It spoke of an elite client base. She was a hundred years old if she was a day, but she'd locked off around fifty. The hair was especially fine—long, and held up in an elegant bun. She was wearing a simple, dark business suit with a plain white shirt buttoned up at the neck. She had the long fingers and torso of a tall woman, and a high, clear brow. Her only adornment was a lapel brooch with the Phaedo logo on it. Mostly what I was looking at was character and wealth. Both were impenetrable. She held my gaze without aggression or deference—I saw years of practice. Like the suite I was sleeping in, her office seemed concealed within the old mansion. She gave the impression of being concealed within herself, an impersonation. Her clothes were neutral but expensive, like the trim body they covered. My instincts were blunted by something functional and automatic about her. Even the anger I first saw on her face was too appropriate to mean anything. The room was functional too. It was almost empty except for the plain chairs and table where we sat. There was a trestle desk with a notebook computer on it.

On the wall behind the desk was a framed photograph of an old villa on a hill with a driveway going up to it. There were cabbage trees planted along the driveway. The villa's deep shadowed veranda had a river-stone balustrade in front of it. There was a second framed photograph next to the one of the villa on the hill. In this one, a big old man with a ponytail and a very small woman were standing side by side on the veranda. His hair was white. Hers I couldn't see, because it was under a softball cap.

'Dr Jack,' I said. Then I stopped. I refolded the piece of paper with Half Ton's text on it. I put it in my dressing-gown pocket with the phone and the memory stick. Then I took them all out again. It was my hands that were passing them back and forth.

'But you remember that all right, don't you, Frank?'

'I'm *peacing* it together.'

She heard my foot on the funny pedal when I said '*peacing*'. Her anger was back. 'That's debatable,' she snapped. She had this gesture—an emphatic fist with her index finger extended. Then she returned to her professional manner. 'I'm sorry,' she said. I thought she meant it, too. 'I guess we have to get to know each other.'

'What is this, a therapy session?'

The distance in time between the Phaedo Peace House in Wanganui and the big man and little woman on the veranda above the estuary at Raglan was so huge it stretched my disappointment thin. My disappointment and grief trembled inside me like the beating scum of heart cells in the Petri dish in Smiles's and Sukthi's lab. I took a sip of the green tea the Mole'd brought us. It tasted of chestnuts. How did I know what chestnuts tasted like? Hokkaido taught me. The space between the little woman on the veranda and the tall 'ageless' one who matched my sip of green tea with one of hers, pushing her lips elegantly forward, was also too wide and thin to bear. The distance was trembling with a million tiny heartbeats. It was going to break.

'That's my mother,' said the woman.

I went into a dark trough. Icy water stung my face.

'Now listen to me,' she said. 'Okay, let me get you a tissue, Frank,' she said.

*

182

I'd sat upright suddenly in Half Ton's transport and cricked my back. Half Ton was shaking me. I was pouring sweat. I stared into the moonlight as though my dream was still showing on some screen there.

'Hurt my back,' I managed to say. 'Pull over, I need a piss.'

'You were talking.'

I got out and pissed next to a paddock of dry, rustling maize. I'd lost track of time. I nearly jumped out of my skin when a trailer truck went past blowing its klaxon. Merle Haggard was singing 'When you begin the beguine' on the van radio.

'What say you turn it off, Ton?'

He turned the radio off. 'You were talking like a little boy.'

'I was what?'

'Like a little boy.' It was hard to tell when Half Ton was laughing, especially if you couldn't see him. 'Your voice,' said Half Ton. 'What was all that about?'

I wasn't going to tell Half Ton I'd been dreaming about a pirate ship. There was a pirate-ship video game at the back of Geek's place. I used to hide it so no one would buy it. No one did. The pirate ship had a swollen shape, pointed at both ends. Lateen mast with a boom across it, and a dhow sail. Curly giltwork along the sides of the boat, cannons and flame throwers sticking out, luxurious canopies for shade with silk pillows under them. Ferocious crew dressed in bloodstained finery stripped off their victims. Pet monkeys with scarlet fezzes in the rigging. Serpents uncoiling out of baskets. A panther with a jewelled collar round its neck pacing to the end of its chain on the poop deck.

I woke up yelling for my mother. I heard myself.

'Like a kid's voice,' said Half Ton. He pulled over so I could have a piss. I pissed away my terror. I pissed out time. The paddock next to me was whispering. The hills were moonlit—white and deceitful. But it was okay.

'Come on, froggie boy.' It was okay. We were going home. We were going to the Phaedo.

*

'It's okay, Frank,' said Hokkaido's daughter. 'I can't remember you either. But my mother said you saved me.' She leaned a bit closer, as if to watch my reaction. 'That's what she told me. All those years ago.'

I sensed a challenge.

'Your mother?' I was gripping the phone and memory stick so hard my hand hurt. My heart was gripping hope so hard it hurt too.

Hokkaido's daughter pointed up at the photograph of the big man and the little woman on the wall. 'That's her,' she said, a bit mechanically.

'No, it's not,' said Little Frank. Hokkaido's daughter lifted her eyebrows at me. 'I mean it's not okay.' I could feel my time sliding away and myself sliding around in it. 'I've got to finish the opera,' I said. I knew what I meant, but it came out wrong.

'I meant, it's okay, you're not really my father,' said Hokkaido's daughter. 'My mother adopted me.' That pause again. 'All that time ago.' She seemed to need to keep saying that. The shadow of wind-stirred leaves fluttered on the table between us in light sliced by venetian blinds. An agitation like the leaves was concealed within her poise.

'Hokkaido.' I said the name aloud to someone else for only the second time I could remember since firing up the *Cao Cao San*'s diesel and going back out past Ninepin Rock with a steadying storm jib into the dark, heaving swell all those years ago. 'Your mother.'

The first time I said the word 'Hokkaido' again was when I told Half Ton where I wanted to go in Wanganui.

'An establishment. Probably called Phaedo. Owner's name should have Hokkaido in it.'

'They might as well have been waiting for you,' he said. 'It came back so fast.' Six heaves of breath. 'Phaedo—mean anything to you?' There was a map on his GPS screen. His silence after that filled with breathing that was a question I

184

didn't answer. 'A friend,' said Half Ton, experimentally. He was trying not to make it sound like a question. Little Frank said nothing. *They might as well have been waiting.* I knew that hope was as deceitful and treacherous as moonlight, but my resistance to it was diminished by recent events. 'Okay, then,' said Half Ton. 'I'll just drive.'

'That's just where her father came from,' said Hokkaido's daughter, in her bare office. 'He came from Hokkaido. Hokkaido in Japan.' She must've seen my look. 'Okay,' she said. 'You can go on calling her that if you want to.'

'If I want to.'

'That's right.' It seemed to me that Hokkaido's daughter was thinking what to do next. 'If you want to.' I knew Little Frank was smiling. Whitey was making my cheeks ache. But I couldn't do anything about that. Couldn't say anything, either. 'So, you can piece this together, right?'

I saw her waiting for my bad joke. But I couldn't push any words past Whitey. The green tea's taste of chestnuts was reminding me of trees. I managed to say, 'Can I go out?'

'If you want to.' Hokkaido's daughter sighed and looked at my dressing gown. Her hair was fastened high on the back of her head with an old-fashioned tortoiseshell comb. I knew my grin was back. 'Might do you good.'

In one hand I held the cup of green chestnutty tea. In the other I gripped both the recording of the Chinese opera finished by Franco Alfano and Little Frank's phone. I also held the folded copy of Half Ton's text. Hokkaido's daughter looked at this hand. She made me see her looking. She made me see the hand for myself. It was the troubled, obsessive hand of a patient hanging on to all that was left. 'Why don't we finish this now?' she said. The angry expression I'd first seen flash on to her face was back. But now I could see that her anger had been waiting for a long time. Or had been asleep for a long tome. This was a patient woman. 'You're right, Little Frank,' said Hokkaido's daughter. 'Your time's running out.' She put her cup down and got back inside herself. 'Isn't it?' We both stood up. Some reunion.

'I want to go out,' said Little Frank. I tried not to look at the photo of her mother on the wall. I tried to see where her anger had gone. 'Please,' I said. 'I just want to go for a walk down by the river.'

'Okay,' said Hokkaido's daughter. Hokkaido's adopted daughter. 'But just so we're clear.'

Back then, I needed Hokkaido on the tiller while I took a couple of reefs in the mainsail. The wind was getting up. I didn't have a safety harness on. The sick kid was in a blanket below. Hokkaido could have tipped me over, easy. One swing of the tiller. But she didn't.

'She didn't,' I said.

'As a matter of fact, she did.'

'Did what?'

'Told me. How you rescued me from those Squids.'

Hokkaido didn't tip me over. But when I opened my hand and let the phone and the memory stick fall on the floor of her daughter's office at the Phaedo Peace House, it was because the truth was, I didn't rescue the sick kid in the blanket. I'd been meant to trade her. She was in the consignment. Hokkaido rescued her from me.

'But then you left her. Us.' That wasn't true either. Her mother left me.

Her daughter didn't move to pick up my things from the floor of her neat office in the Phaedo Peace House. 'Don't forget your things,' said Little Frank's daughter. That's how I had to think of her. My daughter. Her mother had lied about me twice to the kid she'd adopted. For that, I owed them both a truth. I wasn't her real father but I was the next best thing in her mind. Even at her age, this mattered. This was a story that had slept for most of her life. Or had been a dream. I saw it wake up in the world when she thought she heard her father curse her, in the day room of the Phaedo Peace House. I could be as good as the next best thing in the time we had left. I owed them both that much. 'We'll get you some clothes,' she said. Her pause was delicate. 'Your big friend.' Her compact body and arms made a disdainful gesture of largeness.

'You mean Half Ton.' I wondered what else I'd told him, apart from my KidSaver number. When I stood up again after retrieving my phone and the memory stick from the polished wood floor of my daughter's office, she was looking straight at me with a question all set to go. Leaf shadows flickering between us.

'I guess he took care of the business end,' she said. 'Your business affairs.' Little Frank put his items back in his pocket and left them there this time. 'Between us, we're going to have to make this work,' she said. 'Of course, it's your decision.' That pause again. The one that stretched time out. 'She said you'd probably show up one day. My mother did.' I guessed she meant that it was my decision to Time Out. 'What size?' She looked me up and down.

Little Frank tried a joke. I made a coffin shape with my hands above my head. 'Oh, I'd say the economy.'

Then, just for a moment, inside herself, inside her office that was hidden inside the Phaedo Peace House that was hidden inside an old house in a ruined neighbourhood of broken-down mansions overgrown with forgotten gardens full of happy birds I couldn't hear because their songs were kept from me, my daughter smiled. She didn't smile with her neat mouth, but with her eyes. That was something her mother used to do. Not her real mother any more than I was her real father. But all the same.

'I'll get Charlie to measure you up.'

'No synthetics,' said Little Frank primly. 'Italian.' I had Whitey on. It was hurting my face.

'Don't forget your things.'

I got back to my superior accommodation past the reproachful gaze-avoidance of Night Vision wasting away in front of another historic replay of test cricket. I was horrified by the silence of my absurd room and the mute happiness of birds in the late-summer branches outside. I had to get out there where I could hear them. Little Frank who knew Hokkaido was gone for ever had to get out. I didn't know how this worked. Great wedges of time were splitting me open.

'Got to get out of here, Mole. Christ sake. Look at them.'

'Look at what, Frank? Why're you calling me Mole?'

'The birds—what?'

'Why you calling me Mole?'

'You're?'

'Charlie. I'm Charlie. Hold still.' The Mole got a tape-measure round my scrawny neck. 'Stand up, Frank.'

'Say please.'

'Please stand up, Frank. Please.' He ran his tape down what I knew was called my 'inside leg'. I was looking down at the thin, lifeless hair across the crown of his head. It looked as if it would tear loose if you pulled it. A smell of hasty cigarettes came off his clothes, along with a smell like injections. He was agitated all the time, that was his condition.

Uncle Geek pretty much threw the soccer gear at me in my lair at the back of the storage space behind the shop. 'Got to get you out, boy.' His beaver teeth emerged in an encouraging grin. I didn't believe it. I knew he didn't either. He was just doing the right thing. He was 'lumbered with me'. He'd signed me up. He did the same with the Sea Scout clobber. 'Off your arse, boy. Got to get out. Get you out.'

Little Frank was looking at the stale crown of his uncle's head as he got fitted out with escape gear. Soccer shin-pads and clapped-out boots from the seasonal sports bin at the front of the shop, club jumpers with ingrained grass stains, a second-hand Sea Cadet blouson rusting at the eyelets.

'K-k-keep still, Frank.' The Mole's stammer got worse as his hands got steadier. This made him an artiste with the hypos he stuck into patients at the Phaedo Peace House. The more excited he sounded, the more likely it was he was drilling Night Vision.

'Where did Dad go, Uncle Geek?'

'Dunno, son, but I bet it was a long way from your mother.'

'And where did Mum go?'

'Dunno that either, but I bet it was a long way from you.'

Yellow beaver grin, so you never could tell whether Geek was grinning or just showing his teeth. He knew something.

The Mole was blathering on.

'Cut it out, Mole,' I said. 'Don't confuse me.'

'Hold still,' insisted the Mole. He spanned my puny shoulders with his tape.

'They'll do,' said Geek. He'd rescued me a pair of used soccer boots. 'Don't complain. Wear an extra pair of socks.'

The first air to enter Little Frank's nostrils as he stepped out through the back door of the Phaedo Peace House had a wet, mouldering freshness of autumn leaves. I sucked in a mushroomy smell of sodden grass tamped down into old, lawn-rollered clay. I could hear the happy birds. I didn't have to imagine them. They were still making the most of the dry seed heads in the shrubbery. Synchronised squadrons of them flew from bush to bush. They shook the weedy branches with their disputes. Little Frank tilted the brim of his winter fedora up so he could take them in. There, where the old lawn sloped away from the decrepit exterior of the Phaedo Peace House, was the big slow river.

I filled my reliable roosterish lungs with what felt as much like the sound of the world as its air. I felt three things. The first was a happy desire to sing. I swished my cane at an old hydrangea and watched the dead flowerheads topple. I hummed my theme. *Quanti ho visto morire per me!*

The second thing I felt was that I could only get a quarter of a breath in.

Third, a sodden sensation, like sniffing up a blockage of the wet leaves past my freshly trimmed moustache. I stopped with the view of the brown river filling the space under my hat brim and leaned on my cane. I took half a dozen of the quarter-breaths. The space in my chest didn't get any bigger. I could see the polished tips of my new brogues at the base of my view. I could see the backs of my hands on the head of the cane. They were thin and white. The veins there were coloured a fragile mauve, like the old hydrangea flowers I'd just belted off their stems.

Back inside, my hat resting on my knees in the day room, I reminisced about my time as a Sea Cadet in Evans Bay. I convinced Night Vision—his marsupial eyes underwent a spasm of blinking, and he fell asleep. The notion of time running out wasn't theoretical any more. I felt it going and not coming back, like breath. My daughter's hard look said she didn't buy my losing-it routine, unlike Night Vision. She'd be keeping an eye on my 'business affairs'. The ones she thought Half Ton was taking care of. Behind her hard façade, I sensed the agitated flutter of wakeful doubt.

Down by the Wanganui River towards the town were some old warehouses. The lower ones, near the remains of a collapsed roadbridge that had never been rebuilt, were half flooded. A joker there had cranked up a little business ferrying walkers across where the bridge used to be. He had a big flat-bottomed steel punt he'd built a deck on and covered with a canopy of sorts. He powered the thing with an old-fashioned Chinese tube-well diesel, by the sound of it.

'Twenty bucks,' he said, looking at my flash outfit. I gave him five and stepped aboard.

I'd paced myself along the weedy footpaths from the Phaedo. But I needed to find a seat. There was a plank laid across some up-ended crates at one side of the ferry. I parked myself there on my unfolded handkerchief and watched the town bank chug closer.

It was pretty much a Chinatown. What did I see but my old friend the dragon: 'Red Dragon Exterminating Company'. The exterminator's brand dragon was wielding a nozzled hose and a backpack tank. The hose was squirting fire. I was getting used to my leaky mental sievage that immediately delivered an image of Propellor Head frying in the puddle of his own blackened fat. I let them come and go, the flashbacks. I kept a steady course. One foot after the other. One day at a time. One breath at a time. First one target and then the next.

Below magnificent scarlet calligraphy, the He Zhen Snap Button Co. offered 'All Types of Metal Button Operations to Garmet Metal Button Machines & Dies Sales'. The Five Brothers Fat Enterprise Inc. were there. Their billboard was fading on the mildewed brick wall of a warehouse whose foundations were under water. A couple of blocks up from the river was the most I wanted to manage on this foray. The streets were packed with people whose business worked better in small increments. They were busy, cheerful, physical. It was like my old kingdom of Courtenay Place, but marginal and edgy. It was serving a frontier of some kind.

Slow surges of eels stirred the murk of tubs with hoses running in them. There were trussed chooks whose resigned heads rested on the broken footpath. Behind the wet markets were streets of useful junk—horse harnesses, generator spare parts. Stuff that looked to have been bashed out of mild steel, with lumpy welds. A couple more streets back, the herbalists and acupuncturists served the needs of hard-working traders with crook backs. Little Frank made a mental note to avail himself of the services of the Qi Gong Tui Na back rub, foot rub and reflexology. Their price list offered quarter, half and hourly rates. They did acupuncture, herbs. I thought an hour's worth plus some attention to my soggy lungs would be worth a return trip. I liked the look of them better than I liked the twitchy Mole's smell of ampoules.

I needed to be in better shape to make and implement a plan.

This was the other thing that happened to Little Frank as he halted to consider the lack of breath in his lungs while watching the river's thick, effortful flow. Once I'd got over the thrill of being outside with the birdsong, and got the measure of my lung capacity, it was clear that I was Timing Out faster than I was deciding what to do with the rest of my life. Little Frank had an opera to finish. So, I sensed, did Half Ton. So did my daughter. Perhaps we could close together.

*

191

My second meeting with my daughter.

'My lungs,' I began. She waited. I saw the thought forming behind her neat face: How much longer? My next question surprised me as well. 'Your name,' I said. I didn't know her name. She was wearing the same kind of expensively simple suit as last time, a trim grey linen number, a plain string of pearls, the same you-wouldn't-know make-up. But a different antique comb holding up the elegant pile of dark hair. Inside the insideness of her, visible as a stiffening of her neat surface, I saw another thought taking shape. I couldn't blame her for thinking, It's only taken you this long, Little Frank. Of course, it was really me who was thinking this. 'I'm sorry,' I said. 'I've forgotten a lot of what's happened.' She waited. 'There's stuff I need to remember,' I said.

'Stuff.'

I pictured a future time when my lungs wouldn't let me sip even enough air to join Night Vision in the day room. 'I haven't got long,' I said. But she knew that. Her name hung in the silence between us. Little Frank spread his hands apologetically. Sincerity wasn't my long suit but I wanted to try.

Behind my daughter, her mother looked at me from the shadowed veranda of Dr Jack's pull-the-plug outfit above the Raglan estuary. I imagined the *Cao Cao San* swung on her anchor in the thick teal-blue water. I imagined Hokkaido's smooth back with the stripe of sunshine across it. Then I banished the thought. It seemed indecorous, somehow, in the presence of her daughter's careful silence.

'Tell me why you came here,' she said. Like all her sentences, this one cast the shadow of something unsaid.

'Not to avail myself of the services of the Phaedo Peace House,' I said, feeling a bit witty. Her eyes smiled, just. 'There was a bit of strife back in town,' I said. I guessed she knew that, too. I saw her impatience reach a certain point. 'But since I'm here,' I finished.

Dr Jack was looking at me from the wall behind her. The grumble of his voice inside the big tea-coloured torso was calm. Don't trust this one, went the deep vibration, factually.

'Here's what I know,' said the proprietor of the Phaedo Peace House. She'd come to a decision—she did that emphatic thing with a fist and index finger. 'I came from Manila.' Little Frank pricked up his ears. But then she paused. 'Ruth,' she said, as an afterthought. 'Among the foreign corn.' Her smile was nice, with a glint of gold. 'Foreign Corn O'Sullivan.' O'Sullivan was Dr Jack's name, not mine. I remembered that much. 'Dr Jack adopted my mother. After she adopted me.' The smile went away again. 'That made him my grandfather.' The shadow sentence was, 'After the deadshit Frank left us.'

'Here's what I know.' Her expression didn't say whether she thought I knew anything. 'I know you thought my mother might still be alive.' Shadow sentence: 'You didn't know she wasn't.' Little Frank heard the shadow. The mess in my lungs rose, like the tidal bore that used to run up the Raglan Harbour. 'But you're really here because of Tamar. The Dragon.'

Things moved forward very suddenly. Time jerked forward.

'Tamar.' I had just enough breath to repeat the name. What was left hissed out of me.

'But ah—the future!'

The siss of gas from a pure, refreshing beverage. The hiss of time leaking from Little Frank.

Foreign Corn knew something about Tamar.

The careful back-rub at the Qi Gong outfit was warming right through to my lungs. The man who did my feet knew where the places were that unknotted my mind. The warmth of burning herbs, too, was comforting the way a poultice might have been to little Frank before he got big enough to be Little Frank. What was also comforting was the Qi Gong man's silence. It extended the silence I'd chosen after my second meeting with Foreign Corn. My daughter.

After that meeting, I immediately left my daughter's office and walked back through the day room past Night Vision. His eyes clamped shut for fear I might unleash another reminiscence. He'd find out soon enough that he'd had his lot. No need for Little Frank to bore him to death anyway.

After a while I went out. I gave the ferry guy ten dollars and said one word, 'Return.' I gave the Qi Gong man fifty dollars and said, 'One hour.' I said 'Shrimp dumpling,' to the stall-owner at the edge of the wet market. I ate my dumpling soup with rice noodles in silence. I was beginning to be hungry again. I needed cunning Little Frank to be there for me for as long as it would take. He needed to recruit some help.

The next time I went out, the Mole said, 'Need help?' He was quivering with knowledge that accumulated at the borders of death.

At the ferry, the big guy in army fatigues waved me on without paying and made a tough kid stand up so I could sit on the plank bench. Little Frank appraised the extreme economy of the ferry guy's effort. The Qi Gong man saw me come down the steps into his little basement and said, 'Tell you something.' He didn't, as it turned out. But he held my foot in one dry, warm hand and made a gentle stirrup across its instep with the other. Then he tapped me on the diaphragm and spread his palm across my chest.

'Yes,' I said, economically. His index finger drove into something under my big toe. I said 'Yes' again to his raised eyebrows, feeling the knots in my temples slip a little. At the noodle stall, the woman said, 'Ginseng,' when she poured me the cup of tea I hadn't asked for. 'Best pick-me-up for old buggers,' she said.

The next time I made a sortie, I got the Mole to use his own phone to call Half Ton on the Cao Cao number. I told him not to mention Blue Back. We got through. Yes—Half Ton had an opera to finish, not so different from mine.

I asked the ferry guy if he'd trained with boats. He gave me a yes with his eyebrows.

194

'I'm dying,' I told the Qi Gong man.

'So am I,' he answered. It was a joke. At the end of the session, he asked, 'How long?'

'An hour as per usual,' sniffed Little Frank.

'No, mate. How long you need?'

Good question.

When I asked the noodle woman if she had anything stronger, her look said maybe.

'It's not about you, Frank,' said Half Ton on the Mole's phone. 'They'd had enough of us,' said the voice like a rock slide. 'You were just the excuse.' The pause was a full twelve breaths. Each of them would have lasted Little Frank a day. I needed some of their time.

Half Ton's face filled the screen of the phone with its pallid menace. I was waiting for him to respond to the offer he wouldn't hear me make in as many words. The big pale orb moved back, and some fragments of his 'hideaway' appeared around its edges. His word 'hideaway' seemed quaint given the ordinariness of what I could see of it. There was a window with venetian blinds slicing light into bright streaks on a wall. A rack with plates stacked up in it.

'Yes,' said Half Ton's mouth from as far away as his outstretched hand with his phone in it. 'You can help us.' As if that hadn't been what he wanted all along.

'Ten eighty one,' I said.

'Cao Cao closes.'

There'll always be a certain kind of survivor out at the edges of the possible. It was the ones beyond the light of the camp fires that I needed now. The levees on both sides of the river beyond the markets were occupied by campsites. People had been moving through these places for years. The shacks had become elaborate. Most had televisions. A whole border economy was functioning there, like Courtenay Place back in town. But it had greater extremes of enterprise and despair. There was more creative exploitation, more resignation, more brutality. Water, power, shelter, somewhere to shit—these utilities were someone's assets, and if they weren't protected they'd soon be someone else's.

The competitive rackets in the Wanganui riverbank camps were transportation, spare and recycled engine parts and tyres, documents and permits, boat-ride shares, accommodations, pharmaceuticals.

There was a cold place in my mind that the Qi Gong man's fingers edged around at the base of my big toe. A shard of ice in my chest the careful fingers on my instep couldn't melt. The noodle broth that sank to the pit of my stomach didn't reach the rage that burned in Little Frank's bowels. My rage knew it had to return to the place where Tamar's contract had tried to trap me. To the Chinese Opera at the Oaks, at the end of the Place, on the edge of the Barbary Coast, in my home town. Little Frank had to get back there before it was too late.

'How long you need?'

The old fool my daughter was looking at was planning murderous revenge. What she heard were Little Frank's smiling jibes. What she deduced was Timing Out dementia. What she watched were my obscure ten-eighty-one transactions. What she worried about was what was happening to ten eighty one. What she wanted to know was: how much longer?

'Not long,' I said. Because there wasn't any point asking for more time than was possible. 'Hungry Ghosts,' I said— my deadline.

The Qi Gong guy's thumb found a thread at the base of my skull. When he unravelled it, a slice of light flashed across my mind, like the venetian blind slices on the wall of Half Ton's place of concealment.

'Take the low-hanging fruit first,' I said to Foreign Corn.

Inside her neat insideness I saw her wince. What could I

do? It was too late for her to care about Little Frank—though not too late for him to care about his consequence. I saw her measuring her circumstances against mine.

The joker who ran the ferry was called Army. He dressed in paramilitary gear and organised his operation with precision. He had the look of a soldier who could never leave off being one.

I walked carefully along the riverside where kids were horsing about among the rubbish. The camp people had built rickety jetties and fishing platforms. There was a lot of traffic on the river. Maori from way up brought produce down in jet boats and traded it for the stuff you could find in the camps—spare machine parts, wreckers' bits and pieces, drugs, communications equipment. In the middle was Army's ferry operation, running across the river a chain or so from the big old pediments of a blown-up bridge.

Army had cleared a marshalling space on the bank and built a little boarding platform there. His flat-bottom sand barge came thumping across the river on a tangent against the current, a flag flying at the stern and Army at the helm. The flag was a long red pennant with a white cross. Army would reach his landing platform at an angle, the current would swing the deck flush with the platform's edge and he'd tie up and kill the motor. No one ever tried to leave until he'd done this. Then the people who'd been waiting like lambs for his head-jerk would step ashore. He'd stand at the edge of his marshalling area and start taking money from passengers going the other way. Nobody got on the barge until he'd counted up a full quota of passengers. Then they'd all move meekly on to the barge's platform. Army would start up the ancient motor, untie the barge, and move off with his red flag flying. Little Frank found Army impressive.

'What're you up to, Frank?' the Mole wanted to know. His question was the same as my daughter's shadow one. The one she kept asking but not. The text from Half Ton on the Mole's phone had said, 'rom 3 kingdm.' There was a still of Madame Hee hidden in make-up. 'fest hungost.'

We had a date: the Festival of Hungry Ghosts. They'd be doing *The Romance of the Three Kingdoms*. A classic. With that Cao Cao creep.

'How long you need?'

Hungry Ghost deadline.

The Mole was nobody's fool. 'What're you up to, Frank?' He was looking at my elegant apparel. I'd obtained a fur-collared winter coat like Franco Alfano's in the picture with him and Puccini on the white steam yacht called *Cao Cao San*.

'Who wants to know?' He heard the suspicion in my voice and looked offended.

I switched my smile on—not as easy as it used to be. 'Can you keep a secret, Charlie?'

'Not a lot gets out of here,' said the Mole. He didn't know he'd made a joke, so Little Frank didn't laugh.

'I have to get back to Wellington,' whispered Little Frank. I put my finger on Little Frank's famous smile.

'Mum's the word,' said the Mole.

He was right about that, too.

'I'll tell you what else I know.'

I'll tell you what Foreign Corn didn't know. Hours little Frank sat with one finger lifting a slat of the venetian blinds in his porch room at Uncle Geek's. Making light slice the wall. Watching the gate.

'She's not coming, boy.' Geek's beaver smile. He knew something. All those years he knew what Hokkaido would tell her daughter, years later. What Foreign Corn told me. He knew froggie boy's playmate mum went off with a dragon. One of their big guys.

*

In the silence of my room, with its superfluous second glasses and plates, I wiped tears from Little Frank's eyes with a handkerchief in one hand. The other gripped my heavy vengeance the way I'd gripped my cane the day I mowed down the dry hydrangea heads and, along with the birds I could hear again at last, burst into happy song: *How many have I seen die for me.*

Yes, there was much I could regret, including the fact that I hadn't known my daughter's name. But what good would regret do now? Little Frank was still Little Frank, finally. What did she expect him to do? Fold his dry little hydrangea hands over his collapsing lungs and watch the lights dim on the opera whose quarrelsome songs he couldn't even hear any more?

What she knew was what Little Frank didn't know. What Tamar didn't want him to remember after that night in the limo. It might have been driving somewhere. I didn't remember.

'We can put the past behind us.' The Guan Gong mask was rigid, but the sticky-looking, liverish lips inside shone as if artificially moist. 'The present, Frank—what a mess. But, ah—the future!' The siss of refreshing water.

I swallowed from my own bottle in order to moisten the words I had to say next.

'I'm a patient man.'

Inside the cut-out of the choleric red Guan Gong mask, Tamar's lips lifted off his sharp little teeth. 'Patience—yes.' He washed the word down with a sip of the water whose quality you'd get if you did what you were told.

In his room at the Phaedo Peace House, Little Frank put the patient mass of his vengeance aside. He held the handkerchief to his face with both hands. He wept into it for as long as it took to recover from his shame.

Then I said, 'What happened to her?' There was no little mother there to keep froggie boy company with the second plate, knife and glass. 'What did you do to her?'

What did I imagine at the end? The last of Tamar's air

hissing from his raw lips. A sulphurous stink like firecrackers as flames jumped from the windows where Dr Smiles was finished with her final performance. The vengeance of Hungry Ghosts who hadn't been appeased.

The woman slamming down the bowl of egg noodles with fish. Press of bodies, energetic talking.

'Nice suit.' The noodle woman paused. 'Nice smile.' She had one too. Frank was noticed. On the ferry, they stood up to let him sit on the plank. They saw Army looking out for me. 'Got something for you,' she said. Quick fingers smacking dumplings into shape, steam in the early winter air. No one impolitely looking at Little Frank. His lovely smile, his Italian suit, the cane. 'You know what this is?' asked the dumpling woman. I did—old school. The red dragon again, on the wrapper. Dreaming without sleeping.

In the tremendous press of people, already, after so short a time, no one jostled Little Frank. He made his way carefully through the crowds elbowing in around the street vendors selling sticky-rice packets, tubs of hot congee. Someone put a warm rice wrap in his hand.

Qi Gong hand resting on his chest. 'Can't do anything.'

'I know.'

Little Ukrainian church a block back from the ferry, hidden among fading red and gold Chinese ideograms. I rested alone inside the Holy Trinity Ukrainian Orthodox cathedral. Listened to the thick, sliding-out-from-under consonants of men pushing a clapped-out ute backwards into the alley next to it. Church pews, renovated and shiny. Nothing surprised me any more. Not even what I hadn't known and therefore never forgot: my mother the opera singer, the Chinese Opera singer.

I sat in the dim Ukrainian cathedral and pieced it together. I made all the pieces fit. Some of it was logical, and now I could imagine the rest. The opera singer my mother had had the *patients* to become. How many had died for her. The 'new thing'. Gabber had found out. He knew I would too. Knew Franco would finish the opera. The *Quanti ho visto* aria that Smiles was too impatient to wait for on Gabber's *Turandot* recording, back then, in the solarium, with fresh cadaveric resources choppering in to the roof.

'You want me to tell you again? What I know?'
'If it's not too much trouble.' I heard how that sounded. I couldn't stop Little Frank. 'Just ignore the shower-box of emotion in which we're rocking and splashing,' he said.
'I think I can manage that.' My daughter's shadow sentence: 'For how much longer?'
'I'm trying to piece it together.' No use smiling, but Little Frank couldn't stop himself.

My daughter numbered her knowledge on her long fingers again. 'Here's what I know. Your mother left you when she took up with some gangster. You got into competition with the Binh Xuyen. You came to a business agreement with the dragon they call Tamar. That's all I know.' She paused. 'Looks like something went pear shaped, eventually. Shadow sentence: 'No surprises there.'

It was Little Frank's turn. 'And here's what I know.' I lined my pieces up and saw that they fitted into the spaces in Foreign Corn's scheme. They fitted better every time I did it. I watched my daughter's impeccable, professional face close up against what I was able to see and hear clearly now—my little mother, the 'new thing' Chinese Opera singer, fitting inside Foreign Corn's bare story .

'I can only be responsible for your physical well-being,' she said, a bit primly. 'That's what you're paying for.' When she stood up, it usually meant our session was over. This time, Foreign Corn picked up Little Frank's hand and held it. She said what in the past she'd have left as a shadow. 'I'm not responsible for what you can and can't remember, Frank. For whatever sense you make of it all.' She let my hand go. 'Can't do anything about that.' If there was a shadow, it said, 'You're losing it.'

Little Frank ignored that shadow. 'I know,' I said. 'I wasn't running soup kitchens all those years.' My shadow sentence said: 'What did she expect, an apology?'

Her look said that wasn't what she meant. But it was too late, anyway.

What I also knew: I had to move fast.

Sometimes, I liked getting off at Army's Durie Hill landing and walking in careful stages up to where the Dublin Street bridge used to be. The Mole would pick me up there in the house rickshaw. He enjoyed us having a secret phone code. He was thrilled to be helpful.I remembered the kids' playground before it got flooded when the sea levels rose and after the insurgents took out the dam upriver. There used to be big ferro-cement dinosaurs, serpents, whales, octopi, a little railway track, a castle. Now these were mostly under water. I got a kick out of seeing the hoops of some decaying concrete monster break the gluey surface of the Wanganui River. There'd be ducks paddling through the turrets of the toy castle. Shags would be drying their wings on the big guano-splattered spinal plates of a concrete dinosaur, or shitting on the dome of the octopus's head when it wasn't under water.

The Mole said the tide went up at least as far as Upokongaro and Buckthoughts Redoubt. No one went upstream of that unless they'd come from there in the first place. Or unless they wanted to get shot. I was curious about the human resource upriver of the Redoubt.

A lot of travellers pack-horsed in over the Parapara Road. They were heading for the riverside camps around Longacre. I liked to check out the grifters and their merchandise on the bank by the submerged dinosaurs. Mostly, though, I preferred to stay on the north bank and snoop about down past the shambles around Gonville.

One day I'd paid a kid to cart me further below the town where the campers thinned out. There was a stiff offshore breeze. It was cold. A storm the night before had raised the level of the river and muddied the water with eddies. It looked bad—big brown whirlpools, the tide running up against the flood. Wreckage went tumbling along, breaking surface from time to time. Smaller craft were secured and only a few larger boats were out on the river.

The purpose of my recce was the moorings where ocean-going launches could be found. I'd soon need one.

Blowing towards the sea, the cold wind had none of the tang in it that I liked best—the salty smell that blew in over the wetlands. Instead, it brought the Gonville camp stink. This was a mixture of cheap fuel, drains, middens and shit. The path was muddy where the shacks, shelters and old warehouses began to thicken up. There were duckboards over the worst bits. Even so, the water rose through them. As happened after heavy rain, the drainage systems hadn't coped. There was a smell of shitty culvert bottom. The Mole had told me about old people and kids falling into the drains and drowning.

This time of year, new arrivals without clout or people who'd never get it together gathered at the edges of the camps. They had to wade through everyone else's muck. Lots got sick and died when the end of summer made scavenging hard. Plenty more resorted to thievery through the alleys and along the duckboards and up into the town proper as well.

I'd been watching a woman with a white shrieking face trying to persuade a knocked-out horse to negotiate one of the slippery duckwalks that led to higher ground. The horse panicked and shied. Its feet went from under it. Now it was bogged in a ditch to one side of the track. An older boy had joined the woman and they were trying to get the horse to its feet by hauling on a rope attached to its halter. The horse was showing all its teeth in terror. It looked as though the woman and the boy were pulling the front of its face off.

I was getting carted back to the ferry through the shambles when I saw Army coming towards me from the direction of the town. He was wearing marine boots, a quality lightweight snow parka, dark glasses and a knitted hat. If I hadn't known who he was, I'd have taken him for militia. He was banging along the duckboards with the confidence of someone not scared of falling. As we drew level I said, 'What, no ferry?'

'Go home,' he said. He was talking to the kid pushing my cart. And then he said, 'Too much snags in the river. The flood digs them up. You gotta watch your propeller.' He turned the cart around like he was going somewhere. He said, 'What you doing out here, old man?'

'Admiring the lovely scenery,' I said. 'Back along the way I just came.' Something like a laugh jerked the cart forward. 'How about you?' I said.

'You want to see?'

I had the feeling I was going to anyway. It wasn't just my decision that got me out there where winter sickness and flooded dunnies were weeding out the helpless.

One of the last riverside buildings was next to a construction yard depot. The perimeter fence had been yanked down. The only evidence that the area had once been used to store something was the remains of a steel crane gantry on railway tracks. Their sleepers were set in deep concrete that the weeds hadn't broken up. They ran down a ramp to the water. They came out of a solid concrete structure with small, high, glassless windows covered in steel mesh. The landward end of the building was filled with big sliding steel doors. It looked more like a bunker than a boathouse. Army stood side-on to open the personnel door set into the sliding ones. He had a hand-gun in the unfastened holster on his belt. The old wool stores and cool stores down there had mostly collapsed and been scavenged for building materials, though a few of them were being camped in by the dregs of travellers. Their knocked-out vehicles and pack animals were dotted about here and there. In the distance, some men were watching Army as he wheeled me into his bunker. Army didn't seem too worried about getting jumped. He might as well have been carrying a flag that said, Don't even think about it.

He took a flashlight over the other side of the shed. He was tinkering with something. I could make out the dim shape of a large boat. It had high catamaran bows and was shining dully. Then Army yanked life into what sounded like another Chinese tube-well diesel. It was a generator. Next thing, he threw a switch over that side of the shed. Industrial lights glared on the aluminium skin of a big walk-around, ocean-going fishing boat.

The boat was mine. She would be mine. My heart knocked three or four times against my ribcage, as if arriving with an urgent message. A great need like love exhausted the little breath I had to spare.

Little Frank's pirate ship was ten to fifteen metres long. Solid four-metre beam. She had a high deckhouse amidships. Even allowing for the fact that she was up on a cradle, the deckhouse towered above me. The catamaran bows had great flaring strakes back along the hull. The craft was designed to plane at high speed and skip over bar swells.

I sat there in the Gonville kid's hand-cart with my fedora pushed back. This was better than whacking the dead heads off hydrangeas. I imagined coming around Point Jerningham below the Gateways apartments aflutter with cheap underwear. Below the wet markets that replaced the school where Little Frank made the audience of parents stop tittering just by standing up to his full runty height the night his other daughter leapt clear off the side of the end-of-year variety-show stage. Below the discreetly hedged house where he caressed the ripe tomato that Mrs Flitch would soon slice for his lunch. Below the Greek delicatessen where the future husbands of future brides learned from the examples of their future fathers-in-law how to glare at their future sons-in-law. Below the late-sun exposed seat on the lookout where Little Frank had patiently watched changes in the weather for all the years he'd been without imagination. I imagined coming around the Point in this flared craft of Army's. I imagined all this because I could. And because imagining was what would make it happen.

I didn't have to imagine when it would happen: the Festival of Hungry Ghosts. Then, the floating restaurants and the grand corniche of Oriental Bay would be aflame with firecrackers. The paper money, paper cell phones, paper passports and paper kung-fu action figures would be burning their acrid smoke into the air to provide for the restless spirits of the recently dead. The little oil-lamp-lit operas would be squealing away from the backs of flatbed trucks. The *Cao Cao San* would swamp the unwary Mogadishu ferryboats with the wake surging from her deep flared hull.

Then the last of Tamar's breath would squirt hissing from the Guan Gong mask. The windows of Smiles's burning solarium would hurl their hot glass down into the gutted Creepers' yard. Little Frank would hear Madame Hee singing *Quanti ho visto*. 'How many have I seen die for me.'

Army's face was close. He was undoing the top button of my shirt.

'It's okay, mate,' I gasped. 'I'm laughing.'

The hoons who ran these boats over the bar at Raglan used to come screaming in through the swell so fast their sprays would be flying up as high as a two-storey building. They'd be chucking big purple dogfish guttings off the stern platform as they throttled back and grumbled up-harbour.

There was just one time in my life when everything had a kind of golden shine around it. Events moved with lovely slowness and with exciting pace at the same time. I couldn't tell if I was remembering that or imagining it in the future.

'She's a beauty, ay,' said Army.

'Tell you what, skip,' I whispered. 'You could drive this thing straight to town and help yourself. This is a pirate ship if ever I saw one.'

Then I saw Army smile for the first time. There were hunks of silver in there that made his mouth look like an armoury. 'Too right, matua,' he said. 'Any day now. Just need a bit more work first, ay.' His eyes were muddy, like the river. 'Another engine.'

206

He'd pulled me. Me, Little Frank, the vizier of Courtenay Place. That suited me fine. I kept the grin on my face.

'We could talk about that,' said Little Frank.

'Kua ea.'

Another meeting with my daughter, Ruth 'Foreign Corn' O'Sullivan. 'It's not as though anyone's going to come out here and bust you,' I grizzled. 'Besides, I'm paying good money. To the Phaedo.'

Foreign Corn didn't say anything. The shadow of what she wasn't saying went, 'This is my chance to let you go. The same as you did.' I guessed she wasn't saying that out of her consideration for my 'business affairs'. Ten eighty one. She was keeping her eye on that. Then, too, we'd moved on to a kind of parallel track. I sensed her comparing her circumstances with mine. I sensed our paths converging. Behind her functional common sense, doubt was shaking her facts like wakeful light among leaves. What was she on? What could she imagine?

It was time for us to move past a petty family squabble about her father smoking opium in the privacy of his own room. I could feel the tension between us reaching a break-point. I wanted her on my side. I wanted my side to be her side. I wanted her side to be my side, for that matter. I wanted to honour the consequences we'd become. But Little Frank was Little Frank.

Time for us both to come clean.

'It's going fast.' I rationed my words. 'I'm remembering stuff. I'm dreaming. I imagine what's going to happen.' I knocked myself on the chest. 'These aren't getting any better. I don't want to watch the television cricket.' I paused for breath. 'I've got scores to settle.' It wasn't a joke. 'I'm going back, Ruth,' I said. It was the first time I'd used her proper name. 'Your turn,' I whispered.

There were no shadows cast by what she said next. 'This is what I know,' said my daughter. She was managing her father's death and she had that calm professional manner. 'I've already told you everything. I only know because my mother told me. I don't know how she knew. I don't know why she bothered, why it mattered.'

I knew why it mattered to me. What happened all those years ago in the summer at Raglan happened in a life when I knew time was running out at the usual rate, like the big muddy tides that used to empty the estuary. The shallow water would get hot. It would have this great glitter on it out where the wind was ruffling the channel. There'd be the non-stop vibration of cicadas in the hot manuka. Sunlight throwing tree-fern shadows on the ground. The rock oysters tasted of salty sunshine. Love seemed risky, something new you were scared to scratch. There was a kind of despair in the way Hokkaido and I were together. It was always noon, too hot to know that time was shifting at all. We were drifting about on time as still as the high-tide inlet.

And then time flowed on, as it does. That tide went out. Then I became an Expectationer. Maybe I did that because I thought I could stop time. I could dam it. I could take what Tamar was offering—the future! If I could stop time for long enough, I might have enough to get back there. I might find Hokkaido there, in that past dammed up against the future. My little tern, my playmate.

My daughter watched her father, her patient, weep into his handkerchief. How could terrible Little Frank talk like this? Little Frank, whose motto had always been, Only open your mouth after you've checked the change?

When I saw Army's big tin fishing boat lit up there in his shed, I remembered the salt noon sweetness of those stalled tides of love at the same time as I imagined my revenge. I saw that they were the same. Dogfish guttings slithering from the sterns of those pirate boats. They had the same ending. I saw that my playmate mother, who left me under circumstances I hadn't yet grasped, also needed an ending with her little Frank in it. Her froggie boy. How could the patient old man her son had become not love her for what she was? Everything was pointing in the same direction. A match-head of resin from the dragon wrapper made it easier for Little Frank to dream the destination everything was converging to. The Festival of Hungry Ghosts. Which was also when all my borrowed time would flow back into what was left of me and run out, finally, of patience.

'She said she heard your mother went off with some Binh Xuyen guy. Some big shot. A dragon. That then he wouldn't let her come back. I told you this how many times. I don't know if it's true, only that my mother told me.'

The time that would be dammed up in me at the end would include a second-hand kid farting about in the playground at Lyall Bay when Uncle Geek was looking after me. I'd be swinging in my creaky swing by the surf club, watching the surfers and the wave-jumpers out there on the bright water. Years later, Hokkaido and I watched the little coloured surf-sails flying up into the blue sky out there at the Raglan Bar. That would be in there, too. Years and years later I saw a windsurfer slicing through a flock of seagulls on the harbour in Oriental Bay, Wellington, with a backdrop of floating restaurants and the towers of Toyota City, beneath a sky to which the blue seldom came back any more. That was in there. And then it would all flow out, finally, into the future without Little Frank in it. It would all be gone. The smoke told me this. But I knew, anyway.

'She said your mother got involved with some Binh Xuyen dragon. Some big guy. I told you this how many times. He thought she was special.'

'He was right.' This was our litany now.

'He wouldn't let you near her.'

'I stay away from Tamar's business.'

'I didn't say there was a connection with Tamar, but okay. You stay away from Tamar's business. You go on GTX. That's the deal.'

'I forget how to remember. I lose the will to look for her—whatever she was by then.'

'Let it go, Frank. It's just what the drugs do. Check out

the day room. Look at them. See what I mean.'

'Not good enough.' Little Frank was still Little Frank.

It lay all around her, Ruth, the silence of what she wasn't saying, like the darkness in Army's shed before the big lights came on to the boat. My boat. She was measuring me with that inside-herself look.

Then she said it, finally. 'If you want to believe the Binh Xuyen dragon guy who took your mother was Tamar. If you want to believe he thought she was special enough to make into a new thing. If you want to believe the contract was really to keep you away from her.' My daughter's ageless lips were trembling.

Little Frank was still Little Frank. I whispered the end of her sentence for her. 'Nothing you can do about it.'

'It's crazy,' said Foreign Corn. The trembling was momentary. 'You know it is.'

Then there was the official purpose of our meeting. 'It helps,' I said, knowing she didn't believe my smile any more than she believed my tears. 'The smoke does.'

I sat in Army's bunker on an old armchair with a blanket over my shoulders. I liked the speech-defying racket of his lathes and drills. The noise was a kind of silence. It helped me think. When his lips blew steam from a mug of tea, he heard Little Frank whisper about his sailing days on the *Cao Cao San.*

'*Cao Cao San,*' I suggested.

'*Utu,*' he replied.

'You could change it,' I said. There was a certain historical precision in my request.

'Why would I do that?'

'Why would you call a fishing boat *Revenge?*'

Army lifted his cup of tea to his lips and blew on the top of it. A storm was smacking squalls of rain against the steel doors of the shed. It was already winter. My guess was he wanted the boat ready when the weather improved, after the spring gales. I'd sailed back down that wrecker's west coast myself once, years ago. I knew how dark it felt in a five-metre swell trough with an onshore wind. But this was a different craft and a different time.

We were both looking at our cards. Army was measuring my interest in the boat and how close I was to telling him what the interest was. I was wondering how much I could trade for the second engine he needed. Army was wondering how soon he had to tell me why he was calling the boat *Utu*. I was wondering how soon to tell him why I had to change the name to *Cao Cao San*. Because, once the boat was called *Cao Cao San*, it could only have one destination in late spring. That would be non-negotiable.

The Mole researched the engine Army wanted. He said what Army was trying to put together would drive an ocean liner. I didn't quibble. The Mole's eyes lit up like Bengal flares. Too much information.

He downloaded faded sepia pictures, already familiar to Little Frank, of Puccini's white steam-yacht, the *Cao Cao San*. Too much information again. Puccini and his mates strutting about in yachting blazers and peaked caps. Franco Alfano in a fur-collared coat.

'That's right,' I puffed. 'A pleasure cruise.' I let the absurd impossibility hang there.

The Mole knew the kind of sunset cruise Little Frank was really booked on. I borrowed his phone and took a picture of the *Cao Cao San* when Army wasn't watching. I sent it to Half Ton. His reply: 'creepy'. I erased both picture and message.

Gabber used to say that coincidence was the rock concealing the scorpions of bad theology. I missed him.

There was only Night Vision left in the day room and not much of him. I got the Mole to turn off the television and play us the recording of *Turandot* by Giacomo Puccini all the way through.

We sat there in stunned silence, which Giacomo Puccini filled with his argument, by the walls of the City of the Celestial Empire. To the right, the curve of bastions was broken by a high portico covered with sculptured unicorns and phoenixes and with pillars rising from the backs of huge tortoises. Near the portico, a heavy bronze gong hung from two arches. From the bastions, spears impaled the heads of unlucky suitors. To the left, three gigantic gates opened from the walls. In the distance, bathed in golden light, was Peking.

Doubt was Hokkaido's gift of consequence to me many years ago. Now Little Frank needed certainty. I needed to solve the last riddle. I needed to move past the niggle of my daughter's doubt, which was her mother's doubt.

The opera we were listening to slid like a spotlight across the surface of the events I remembered from the beginning of last summer: Little Frank mesmerised by Madame Hee. The riddles. The executioner's toll. And a sensation of familiarity as I followed the libretto with one finger crawling down the Mole's printout.

I felt my doubt retreat from this spotlight that moved across what I knew until everything resembled a stage set. Then we came to the bits polished off by Franco Alfano after Puccini's death. The bits Smiles and Little Frank hadn't listened to that day in the hospital solarium.

'I am different from other mortals,' sang Princess Turandot to Prince Calaf. At that moment I heard my old sphinx Gabber whisper, from the bluish light as his fridge closed with a sigh, 'Listen to this, Frank, effendi, my brother, my sheikh. *I am different from other mortals. My soul is in heaven.*'

Then Calaf kissed her. Their voices cutting across each other in the duet. Franco Alfano handing Turandot her lines across the corpse of Puccini.

'I am not like other mortals.'

Everyone rejoices. The opera ends. With all his strength,

Little Frank smacked his cane down on the cushions of the day-room sofa. The Mole and Night Vision were staring at me like mice mesmerised by a snake.

'What are you up to, Frank?'

Yet another meeting with my daughter. After our fateful excursion.

Little Frank carefully measured the breath needed for his reply. Each word a victory. This needed to go right.

The meeting was taking place in my bedroom, not her office. I was wearing the non-regulation Egyptian cotton pyjamas I'd demanded. There was no photograph of the original Phaedo Peace House with the mismatched couple on the veranda. I'd moved beyond the surveillance of history into a territory where coincidence said everything was going my way. Bad theology or not, Little Frank was the master of his own destiny.

'Whatever you're up to, you're not up to it,' said Ruth. The fumble in her language gave away her anxiety. Hers wasn't a hospice manner, in any case. Still, there was that anxiety about the big reveal. 'Not on your own, anyway.'

'Leave the Mole out of it,' I breathed.

'Charlie.'

'Actually, he's gone off me. He wants me to make him useful.'

'You're an old bastard.' That was when my daughter took my hand. Hers was dry and cool. It was the second time she'd touched me. I knew better than to believe Little Frank was being forgiven. All the same, I couldn't stop the tears. They ran past my moustache into my smile. 'We're in this together now. Whatever this is.' Her factual hand.

The new engine went downriver in Army's ferry barge with a big version of his red pennant flying. Little Frank went with it in a brand-new wheelchair lashed to the rail. Army's crew had come from up-river. I'd never seen them before. They had guns. Their haka as the engine came ashore on the rail-track hoist shook the concrete slipway. The neighbourhood drifters came running to watch.

Back at the Phaedo Peace House, the Mole was sulking.

'You like it?' I released one of my gangsterish smiles and leaned back in my wheelchair, feeling my heart's brine ebb through my body.

My daughter was looking at my fur-collared winter coat with that expression.

I could imagine the sea where the big muddy river ran out. The great flocks of seagulls. Army's boatbuilding shed. I could feel the boat's buck and lurch as the aluminium bows met the first swell beyond the bar. I could imagine myself standing at the wheel with my hat at a jaunty angle.

Charlie Mole lifted me from the wheelchair to my bed. He knew how to prepare my pipe. That was useful.

'Thank you, Charlie.'

He was grateful even for my whisper.

Half Ton Jack's face leaning close to mine in the street outside the cake-shop window with the little pastry cook's rhythmical wooden spoon, glittery bloodshot eyes bulging out of their folds, the huge head with the even wider neck below it, assorted clips and rings disappearing into his fat ears.

The Mole prattling on, making himself useful.

Half Ton's mighty mouth opening. 'Tomorrow they're doing *The Romance of the Three Kingdoms*. With that Cao Cao creep. *The Three Kingdoms*. Like I told you. A classic. With Cao Cao. You should take the time.'

'What do you know about Cao Cao?' I asked the Mole.

Charlie Mole was in coincidence heaven. He was on full

current. He was giving off a smell of hot, useful plastic.

'It's from a classic . . .'

'Classic?'

'. . . classic Chinese novel, *The Romance of the Three Kingdoms*. And Cao, Cao Cao is a bad character. All white face, that's how you know. That he's bad.'

'You don't say.'

Inside Charlie's babble was the ghost of Half Ton's zoo breath, the deep sigh of his voice. The ghost of what Hokkaido told me, what I already knew. The ghost of Hokkaido's voice in what her daughter knew. The ghost of Hokkaido's voice in my dream. The white face of Cao—Cao Cao, a 'fraudulent and suspicious nature'. Charlie couldn't understand why his helpfulness made me angry, why it made me weep.

The sky was full of stars. I still had my eyesight, or someone's eyesight. I was lying on my back looking at the stars through the window of my room in the Phaedo Peace House. The nights were cold. The magnolia had lost its leaves. The sky was brilliant, like last summer the night Half Ton drove in the fraudulent, suspicious moonlight across the plateau from Wellington. I could see the stars up there through the branches of the tree and past the derelict gables of the old mansion next door.

The dark branches were moving against the sky and the stars. There was a breeze out there. I couldn't hear it. A large cloud sailed across the sky, like a big theatre curtain, shutting out the stars. It seemed to have been towing the moon behind it, because a lumpy section of moon had risen into the spaces among the branches. The misshapen moon seemed to have brought cold with it. A chill entered the room where I lay in bed. I was always shivering cold, after that.

Those nights, while Army's crew fine-tuned the second engine in our boat, my dreams were bad. My memories and what I imagined would happen when I got back to the city were colliding. One night I woke up shivering, and the Mole was there, drawing off an ampoule by my bed.

'What the fuck's *that*, Mole?'

'Might help you sleep.'

We had words. But I wanted to sleep and I had to dream. Even if the dreams were bad. I had to imagine. That was how the future would happen.

But now I knew I needed a proper helper.

At first, I wasn't glad about Sam the same way I was glad about the ocean being there. About the *Cao Cao San* rumbling back from her first sea-trial. When Sam was agitated, a vein writhed like a chopped worm in the side of her bony, shaved head. You could almost hear her brain gulping blood. Meanwhile, a sweet smile never left her white face. And Sam's hands—fingers peacefully twined in her lap.

Where did this swamp-brat come from? I saw her pick up a chunk of broken concrete in the same agile turning motion that next had her rotated upward to full height. She smashed the concrete against the big punk's head. That was it. The rest of them didn't hang around. The kid Sam had bashed wasn't moving. He was lying with his face under dirty Gonville water that turned pink. Sam was just easing herself out of the sightlines of the situation. Not running for it or hiding. Just beginning to fade into the twilight where the duckboards buckled between the miserable, bogged shacks.

Her long, skinny body, the dome of her head and the precision of her attack docked straight into Little Frank's recruitment drive. I knew her from the stack of 2000AD comics at the back of Geek's junk shop. Halo Jones, punk mercenary. My first love.

The next time I saw the girl I thought of as Halo there was a cold wind blowing rain and spray over the ruined marina moles. Just as Army was wheeling me inside, I saw the girl's white face in a dark oilskin across from the waste yard in front of Army's shed.

'Someone's casing your place,' I said to him inside. 'That

kid again. I saw her dealing to some opposition the other day, up by the Gonville tip.'

'Or casing you, matua,' said Army. Then he let himself out the other end of the building where the ramp was awash. I heard the sound of the ocean trying to push the river mouth up into the town. The thump of Army's generator dropped under the sound of wind and spray. The fierce mud and salt stink of the stormy delta blew into the shed over the big boat in its cradle. Then Army was gone.

When he came back it was through the front door. He had the girl with him. She stood streaming water from her old oilskin with the hood thrown back off her shaved head. She looked around the interior of the shed at the equipment and the boat. Her expression was calm and pleased. It was the first time I saw this expression. And the agitated worm wriggling in her temple.

'This the one,' said Army, not bothering to make it sound like a question.

'Yes,' I said. 'What's your name, kid?'

'Sam,' she said, in a light, sweet voice. I wanted her to say, Halo, Halo Jones. Her wide, green eyes were recording something above my height. I glanced back to see what it was. There was a version of Army's red pennant, the one with the white cross on it, hanging from a rafter. Then I heard her say, 'Ricky.'

'Make up your mind,' I said. 'Are you a Sam or a Ricky?'

'That's my flag,' said Army. He was staring hard at the girl. 'Rikiriki.'

'Wait on,' I said. 'I'm getting lost here. You two know each other?'

She thought that was a joke. Then she asked, 'Why do you always come down here, mister?'

Army was giving me a look.

'I need a minder.' I mimed Sam's uppercut with the chunk of concrete.

*

217

I lay not dreaming, and looked at the moon.

If you don't pull this together soon, Frank, you'll end up with the tray breakfast on your lap the morning after you can't remember what the moon used to remind you of. Or what it was exactly you were going to do.

Report on memory
My little mother telling me to run around the flat pretending to be a naughty boy while she pretended to be a good mum. That place between her neck and shoulder where I rested my head and, with closed eyes, sipped her peaceful smell of cigarettes and cosmetics. The patient old lady in Chan's who'd sell us kids Double Happy firecrackers and then yell at us later when we tossed them over the fence where she was stacking cabbage crates. The beautiful little woman with citron hair on the muddy estuary there at Raglan, where the big dogfish guttings washed up and filled quickly with the seething mayhem of feasting crabs—Hokkaido, before the veil of laughter dropped down over her face.

'You have to know when it's your turn to laugh,' she used to say. I never figured out what she meant.

When Sam wheeled me to the door of Army's boat shed and banged the combination I'd told her, a breach of trust took place. Little Frank knew this. But I also knew that the next round of discussions with Army had to have a place to start. I knew Army was looking at Sam through the peep-hole. Predictably he didn't open that door. He came around the side from the boat ramp with a sawn-off shotgun.

But there she still was. The craft that would fulfil both our destinies.

'Just about shipshape?' piped Little Frank, reaching up to smack the matt aluminium skin of his vengeance. But this wasn't the time for chitchat. 'Let's get this straight,' said Little Frank in a careful whisper. 'If Sam's with me she's okay. End of story. She can knock on your fucking door any time she wants to.' She sat there looking serenely at the shotgun. 'Next thing,' said Little Frank. 'A trip down to Wellington's a small price to pay for the guts in this thing.'

'Why,' said Army. His gun had more expression.

'If I tell you, you have to keep it to yourself. The same as Sam's going to keep your secret clubhouse knock to herself.'

Just the eyebrows.

I had to believe what I was saying if I wanted Army to.

'Heard of the Binh Xuyen?' I expected Army to say no. But when he slowly put the shotgun down on the floor beside him I took it for a yes. This was surprising in itself. What happened next was more so. 'Some years ago,' I said somewhat fatuously, given my age, 'the Binh Xuyen decided to make a copy of my mother.'

This was why my daughter thought I'd lost it. Timed Out.

Army reached up and took off his woollen hat. His lips began to shake. I thought he must surely be laughing. But no, it seemed he was praying. His eyes were closed. 'Apparently they succeeded,' I said. 'Eventually. With patience.' All at once the ridiculous words sounded real and terrible and I believed them. My belief had something to do with the movements of Army's lips. 'I'm going back down there in this boat,' whispered Little Frank with the last of his breath. 'Those fucking, those fucking bastards.' I closed my eyes to concentrate on getting my lungs full. It was freezing cold in the big shed. So cold that I could feel the spit drying on what must have looked like a smile but wasn't.

'You come up the river first, matua,' said Army's toneless voice. 'Get you cleaned up.' His warmth as he leaned close. 'Then we'll all go around Raukawa together.' His fingers tapped my arm. 'We've got some mahi down there too.'

*

Meetings with my daughter
'Get used to it.' Little Frank does what he has to. 'And a television. Please.'

Life in my otherwise useless living room: Halo Sam's cot replaces the two-seater sofa. I hear her watching television in there. She uses the spare knife, plate and glass. She drinks the fresh juice. She sleeps near the door.

Text from Half Ton
fest hungost rom3 kdoms prog booked hee

A sensation like a wave lifts me over something like a bar of white disturbed water.

Status report on the Phaedo Peace House
No one's watching test cricket on television in the day room any more.

Condition report on Little Frank
Clear, focused, dreaming and imagining together in a space washed pale blue and grey by rain clearing with a latticework of bare dark branches. Swift flights of eager birds resting and darting away again. Patchy hazes and speckles of green, amber, pink at the outer tips of the branches.

Smiling inside my oxygen mask. Rage and hope together in my freezing chest. When Sam lifts the mask aside so I can sip the pipe, the rage and hope converge not in a future but in a real place. Because Little Frank's made up his mind. Solved the riddle. Nothing they can do about it.

When the blue comes back.

Part Three

HUNGRY GHOSTS

I should have known better than to mention my mother's nickname for me. The little crook had it quick as a flash. It could make me angry his smile. When it had as much triumph in it as that.

'Foreign Corn.'

'Don't be corny,' my mother used to say. She meant get real. 'Don't be corny Foreign Corn.'

The tide was running out late in the evening. The days were getting longer pale full moon rising a few weak stars. The girl Sam and I got him down to the river bank below the house. The big ferry guy Army was there with a jet boat and we took him and his wheelchair down the river past the bridge remains to where his *Cao Cao San* boat was waiting below the Gonville camps.

The last time we took him to the river bank below the Phaedo was when we were going up to the Riki. It was incredible that he'd been up there where no one ever went. It was incredible he'd been all around down Gonville where I wouldn't go if you paid me. Stubborn mean fearless—I'd heard about it. Here I was getting on a boat for the first time since I was a kid. I hated them. That squid smell I remembered made me sick. I was getting on it with the same man as last time Frank's yacht all those years ago. When I was just a little child and I met the woman who would be my mother.

Frank went up over the side of his *Cao Cao San* boat in a sling. The oxygen mask was detached for as long as that took. He was smiling. His little white teeth between pink lips under the clipped moustache. The hat he'd insisted on was pushed over one eye by the sling it made him look jaunty. That coat.

'Of course I'm coming you knew that,' I said back to the smile though he hadn't asked.

I began to get sick straight away.

He came in to the Phaedo that first time looking just like what my little mother told me about only in some other institution's white hospital gear. He was out of his mind. This big fat Creep with him made the arrangements. He set up an account and ordered newspapers. He was called Half Ton but we couldn't trace him. There was a very great deal of money transferred from the accounts we checked. I kept checking them. I couldn't find it. He had a system.

Frank spent a couple of months looking out a window without talking and the time after that wandering where no one in their right mind goes. He woke up screaming in the night or else babbling like a child. He scared the other patients away. He was doing crazy stuff handing over his money to some upriver Riki for an engine for this boat. He was raving about the pirates who killed his friends.

The same Binh Xuyen my mother told me about. She said watch out for him called Little Frank he'll bring trouble. That day he heard it from me he just froze. What I knew about his mother leaving him. Time shuttered across his eyes like a venetian blind being reversed is the only way I can describe it. Time opened and shut and changed direction. He walked out. I didn't even know if it was true about his mother going with a Binh Xuyen dragon boss. That's just what my own mother told me.

'Made a wrong turn.' What did that mean? He lost his advantage? He damaged other people? You could never tell.

He never asked for my mother in as many words but that's what he wanted. After all those years. It even sounds stupid to say it. I couldn't believe he didn't know she'd been

224

dead how long? Or if he did know what he'd done to the knowledge? He was looking at me and putting it together his own crazy way but still smiling. No one could really see past it the smile. It drove me crazy.

Abacus Capital Jumps You Up Venture. Why was Frank transacting with those low-level squids? Who was managing his business? That big Creep? I looked at his cash flows. I asked myself why did these go down like power outages? These bites in his reserves? Assets all gone wet. They disappeared somewhere through Abacus Capital. That big Creep. Is this his account manager or what this Half Ton? His minder? Staying under Binh Xuyen radar my guess. But strutting around in broad daylight in Riki territory. Completely out of his mind.

Yes he paid his bills. Someone did. And more.

But you owe me was what I thought. You owe my mother. Run down the Phaedo Peace House all you like but pay it back later. Yes these were unworthy thoughts but what could I do? At least it was a good reason to keep close watch.

The other thing what happened when he saw me in the day room that first time. His curse. Nothing to do with me he said but even so.

It was dark when the boat stopped heaving about so much but whenever I saw the light way back there go behind one of the smoothed-over waves I was sick again. Then the light disappeared for good the boat sped up. The engines roared and the boat rose up on the water. We were going along the lines of the waves with a corkscrewing motion. The moon came and went behind black clouds the sea was like aluminium. No way I could remember when Frank got me off the squid boat when I was a child but something I remembered came and went like moonlight on the dark aluminium water. One of the Riki guys gave me a hot drink tasted of ginger and a handkerchief with something smelled like wintergreen in it. There were six of them on the boat seven with the big ferry guy Army. I knew they were going down the coast to hit FLOW. Charlie told me.

'Please press buzzer to enter,' Frank said to me once with that smile to murder. He meant I was shut. What did he expect me to do? Kiss and hug the man who deserted the woman who decided to be my mother? It was like I woke up to him in the day room his curse like a slap. Why should it start to matter again after my lifetime?

In the morning they brought him into the shelter behind the high deckhouse on a stretcher with a ratchet to sit him up. At first he was facing backwards but he made them turn him round. The girl Sam knew what to do she gave him his vitamin gastrolyte drink in a straw. He pretended it was a cigar and made everyone laugh. He hadn't spoken a word for days he couldn't any more. Even so he made them take him up in the wheelhouse. It took four of those big Riki guys even though I could lift him by myself now. His boat was leaping along the top of the water you had to hang on. The day was windy.

He just came back from the town with opium and showed Charlie how to fix him up. Like he owned the place. 'Old school,' he said. Now try and tell me what he knew about that stuff didn't have him mixed up with Binh Xuyen years ago.

How can I know if I remember correctly? I have the picture in my mind of Frank's sailing boat leaning over going away from my mother and me in the little rubber one. My mother's thin hand on the outboard motor her face not looking back once. I have a mental picture of my new grandfather's Phaedo house on the hill with the old sick people in sunshine and of my grandfather Dr Jack being taken down the hill by police in their car. But I know that my mother told me about these events and perhaps that's what I remember. I remember us coming down country to the new Phaedo Peace House on the river here. This has been my life.

I remember my mother driving the little rubber boat towards the rainy land when we got there and I looked back from the beach his sail boat was far away towards the open sea leaning over. Was he saving me or leaving us at that moment? Then they brought him down again from the wheelhouse. That smile. The girl Sam showed him the dolphins when they swam next to us but I think we were too fast eventually. I could just see the land when the boat was running on the top of a wave. It was like a dark line with a white one under it. This was what he wanted. To go back where he'd come from and 'finish the opera'. He kept saying this playing that music chip in the day room. Terrorising the Deadliners.

I have a memory of going down the side of a dirty rusty boat on a man's back on a ladder but my mother told me about that too. This memory makes me sick. I remember the stink of squid this must be my memory. There are things I can't have any memory of because I only know what she told me but they all feel true the same way. 'Get real.' Nothing she ever said to doubt. What she told me about the Binh Xuyen and Frank making a deal. When I saw him in the day room the first time with that smile that could make you freeze over and the others all scared of him. He was abusing them. I thought he cursed me. I believed he could do all that stuff I heard about. He just got what he wanted. He had Charlie on a leash.

God knows if he really cared who these Riki people were he did the boat deal with. What a joke Frank partnering up with those ones. Pure water pure blood. What they were fighting for genealogy. No immortalised cell lines. Tell me they didn't know who he was. Of course he knew they blew up the bridges and the dam back then. They ran the town. He knew about FLOW. He was a businessman like my mother said. A very rich one from Bellerophon chimera business. From biopiracy. From harvesting. Foreign Corn better 'get real'. 'Don't be corny.' But he went up the river with the Rikis. They took him up. He bought that engine for their boat even if he said it was his boat. He saw what was up there like everyone said another world. I saw it too. But did he really know what was happening? When the girl Sam took his mask off to give him a breeze of fresh air he was always smiling. You couldn't tell.

'Take the low-hanging fruit first.' That smile like he'd enjoy if you argued. He said things like that and then when I was silent I could tell he was guessing what I would say. It was a game. It was a habit. Always the advantage.

He saved my life my mother said even if he did throw us away straight after. She always watched what he was doing because she said don't let him take you by surprise. Always the advantage. He's always up to something. You never know. Low-hanging fruit.

'What would I do in your place?' he asked me. Then he answered the question himself the way he did as if he was reading what I might say from a piece of paper. He made it sound obvious as though I couldn't think about it for myself. He made me so angry. 'I'd believe what Little Frank said,' said Frank, 'is what I'd do. If I were you.' He counted on his fingers. 'That he escaped from a hospital. Because he had his wits not because he'd lost them. That his old friends had been taken out by Binh Xuyen. That the same Binh Xuyen had been fixing him up all these years so he couldn't remember. That he'd sniffed out something at the Chinese Opera down at the Oaks. A "new thing". And don't you forget it.' He gave me that blue-eye smile. 'That's what I'd believe if I were you,' he said and showed the pink tip of his tongue. He shifted the things he carried from hand to hand. The phone the music chip he drove us mad with.

His smile dared me to say he was crazy. Why would I when my mother had warned me to watch out for him this was his kind of trouble?

'That there was a "new thing" out there they didn't want Little Frank to know. If I was you I'd believe that. A. New. Thing.' He talked as if I was an idiot his daughter. 'Foreign Corn.' Hand to hand to hand. Over and over. 'Believe it.'

I didn't say I'm not you but I believed some of it just the same. It was what I heard. The rest was just him losing it. I never said that but he saw me thinking it. Out of his mind. Timing Out. I'd seen it before how many thousands of times. But this time I couldn't let it go.

The weather was clear later with the waves flattening out I was feeling better. The girl Sam never left him. They played a silent word game he made 'Halo' with his little mouth she made 'Hello' back over and over smiling. She never left him. This is what he did to people even when he couldn't talk. He wanted to face the way the boat was going and she tied his hat on with a string under his chin. You could see he knew how crazy it looked. She kept his oxygen going measuring the time he went without and I didn't have to tell her anything.

The only one time I took him out myself was when he began to stop talking. What does that say? He used to tap the side of his nose above his moustache and I knew that what he meant was 'It's about consciousness.' Tapping his nose. 'You think this is bullshit?' Tapping his nose. 'You think I'd waste my time?' The way he said 'time'. The smile stretching across and going thin. Stretching time thin.

The other things he said. His smile pretended they were jokes but they made me angry I stopped talking then later I had to figure why they hurt.

'The shower-box of emotion in which we're rocking and splashing.'

'No point being scared to death.'

'The scorpions of bad theology.'

'I wasn't running soup kitchens all those years.'

'You have to know whose turn it is to laugh.'

'Get real.' My mother used to say that. I told him. 'Get real.' The woman he called Hokkaido.

*

The one time I took him out. When he stopped talking.

I didn't know he'd hired the girl Sam he called Halo but I saw her slinking on a parallel through the old arcades on the opposite side of the street. She was more like a ray of light than a shadow. She was watching us from just behind that was obvious. Sometimes I wouldn't see her then there she'd be again.

I was pushing Frank along from the ferry in his new wheelchair. We were going to 'get noodles'. I knew what that meant. There were big crowds down by the jetties. Some kind of salvage was coming ashore. Riverboats were pushing for space among the fishing platforms. These pale shapes were being passed up on the bank. They were frozen lamb carcasses. Not frozen any more by the look of it. They were in milky-coloured plastic hundreds of them. People were paying money or bartering taking them away in rickshaws and carts. I could see the buzz of it made Frank happy. It was the Rikis distributing the meat who else? A highjack. Frozen lamb.

What was strange. I could never be sure what time he was in. What was he enjoying and smiling about there with the lamb carcasses? A memory? What he was looking at combined with a memory? What he was looking at all by itself? Some kind of future? This was different from Timing Out the thousands I'd seen. It was like he was conscious even when he was lost. He just went with it.

Then something terrible happened to his smile. 'Glabber bladder gabber.' He said something like that over and over. He fell forward out of the wheelchair as if he'd pushed himself. He was on his knees in the crowd holding himself up with his fancy cane. He was looking down into his hat on the ground in front of him.

Then the girl Sam was there she just picked him up. 'Riki's,' she said and began to push the chair fast. I followed with his hat I couldn't stop her. This one would kill me quickly. She already knew the way to the boat shed I'd only heard about.

'I have to finish the opera.' What he said all the time taunting me.

As though he did believe he was some Italian composer called Franco Alfano. That fur collar coat. Other times he said that and smiled the way he cut the meaning in half. Taunting me. His smile gave you half the meaning and he kept half for himself. But when he was the composer the meanings he was dealing with all rushed towards him at the same time. I saw he couldn't tell one from the other. I've seen this how many times? Timing Out. They don't know where they are. When they are more like. Only Frank made it happen. He went there. He made himself.

'I have to finish the opera!'

'When the blue comes back!'

The words he said. The words his smile didn't say.

'But ah—the future!'

The words he seemed to be quoting.

'"The heart and the mind what an enigma,"' he said once. He said, 'Charlie Chaplin *Limelight*.' Then he said, 'Mack,' and began to cry. He went on crying when he said, '"You can make a fresh start with your final breath," Berthold Brecht.'

He said, 'Finish what you start.' He didn't cry when he added, 'Uncle Geek always said that.' He smiled that sweet smile I couldn't get past. 'He was right.' The smile waited for me to ask why Uncle Geek was right but I didn't. Who Uncle Geek was. Why you had to finish what you started. Something in me woke up that day I heard his curse in the day room. Now we were going somewhere together. We were finishing something together. What I hid from him my father. My question. How could it still matter after my lifetime? What he was?

At the boat shed that day Frank fell over it was the same big Riki that was driving the *Cao Cao San* now. The ferry guy Army. He helped us get Frank in the shed after the frozen lamb thing. So this was the boat he was taunting me about. Where the money was going. Those Abacus squid Jump Ups. The big fat Creep Half Ton. What they were up to.

'He's dying,' said the big Riki guy. 'Who are you?' He was talking to me not the girl Sam. He knew her. Frank's face the same cold aluminium colour as the boat.

'His daughter,' I said. I heard the words come out of my mouth. I was breathless from the fast walk but then from saying the words also. When I said, 'And you are?' the words echoed in my head what I'd said first had gone hard there my voice was hitting up against it. 'His daughter.' A generator was banging in the shed over and over the same sound. 'His daughter.' It went on and on banging then the big guy said, 'Army.' He was looking at me. He could see what I was an Expectationer the Rikis were against that. They were at war with that. He was looking at my Asian eyes. 'Army. That's what they call me.'

When I went to check on Frank in his wheelchair Army said, 'The girl can do it.' Sam had an oxygen mask on my father's face. *My father's face.* What else didn't I know about? Then Army said, 'He tell you about this.' It was a question. There were two little dots of pink in my father's cheeks now. When his eyes opened they were the same little blue ones. They looked straight at the girl Sam. She was nodding at him she was mouthing 'Hello.' She was nodding yes. Yes hello. My father's smile lifting his pink dot cheeks under the mask.

'Did he.'

My father's blue eyes had closed again. The girl Sam knew where there was a blanket as well. Army's face very close to mine. His eyes were red he smelled of metal. 'Yes he told me about the boat,' I said. 'My father did.' I tried saying the words again. It got easier. My father. His daughter.

'Got to get him up the river then,' said the big Riki guy called Army. 'Your father. Before we go. Clean him up. Not long.'

I was listening to him say, 'Your father' and didn't ask him, 'Go where?' I knew what 'Not long' meant.

*

That last session we had. My father and his daughter. Shifting those things from hand to hand. What Frank told me the last time we were talking before the lamb carcasses. How he was losing it. As if I didn't know. After that he stopped talking altogether.

'It's like I fall asleep Ruth,' he told me. It was during one of our sessions the last one. I saw him slip past our conversation into a silence. He'd started calling me Ruth. It was a trick. 'Words are the poison in a song'—I remembered from a Bei Dao poem. He was trying to get me to talk about what I remembered coming down the side of the rusty squidder but I wouldn't reach back where he wanted me to. Where I came from. What did I have? The squid stink that made me sick before that the smell of a loud city filled with dirty water. I held this inside I made my silence stand between me and my father. I hid my question there. Why should I finish what he started? He was hiding something too. When this happened his eyes didn't close but they stopped looking at me. Stopped seeing me. No smile. He slipped away somewhere. 'I had this dream Ruth. Foreign Corn Ruth.' He should have been smiling again he always did when he said my name like that but he wasn't. 'I dreamed I was with my mates down by Chan's greengrocer in Lyall Bay.' He held the phone that music stick he was trembling. 'Jason from Samoa.' The little tongue tip quickly wetting his lips. He held his arms out measuring a space with his hands. One with the phone and music stick in it. He was dressed to go out in the fur collar Italian coat. The sleeves were too loose on his little wrists they rode up his arms when he spread his hands apart. 'It was a long time ago,' he said as though he was scared of a memory coming all that way across the gap between his hands. The little tongue tip. 'He was a big kid that Jason was,' said Frank losing his breath. 'He used to chuck Double Happy crackers into Chan's yard.' The tongue tip. 'He could run faster than the rest of us.' The hands measuring how far Jason ran? No. Measuring time. 'How could it be so long ago when?'

233

He ran out of breath then couldn't keep his arms stretched out any longer. I saw him understand what was happening. Time closing up.

'Double Happys,' he puffed. Past and present closing up. Soon they'd meet and that would be that. Game over. He wiped the little tears away with his fussy ironed handkerchief. 'Christ all fucking mighty,' he whispered one hand on his little panting pigeon chest. Usually he didn't swear. 'Good night nurse.' This was a joke. 'No time to lose,' he said making another joke this time he did get that smile organised those blue forget-me-not eyes came back to life. 'The dragons,' he said. 'Those bastards.' It was all Timing Out rubbish. 'Finish what you start.' The forget-me-not tears running into his smile. I couldn't believe he'd finally lost the plot. Little Frank. That my mother told me watch out for. You watch out for Little Frank. Because one day. Your father. What I knew now he made it happen. Whatever he wanted.

What I saw now all those years he was in the business my father Little Frank. Bellerophon chimera organs blood products pharmaceuticals. Then some deal with Binh Xuyen. All those years making people Expect. Like him like me Expectationers but never my mother he called Hokkaido. All those years getting rich making Deadliners and all those years at the Phaedo Peace House they came to Time Out. All those years my mother helping them get out of what Frank had put them in. All those years two businesses a perfect fit just like she said her and Frank. Small people a perfect fit in that yacht I saw its sail leaning over going away against the grey sea. That day my mother told me he saved me and left us. He was in the business of making them she was in the business of helping them get out. What he made she unmade at the Phaedo Peace House. It was a shape a meaning. It had been my life. I had to see how it ended.

'Of course I'm coming. You knew that.'

*

234

It was getting dark again when Frank's boat went behind the island called Kapiti. All day he'd stayed out under a blanket his hat tied on looking up at the blue sky. A red sunset over the lumpy sea horizon. The distant mountains further south lit up a pile of hot coals. I knew enough to see Frank was thinking dragons. Looking in that direction his secret expression. He lifted the mask off his face made an exploding shape with his mouth. Bang! Boom. Pouff! Then we went in under the cold shadow of the island. The sea was the colour of the aluminium boat. We were going along slowly inside our own shadow under the shadow of the island. The girl Sam and my father were doing that staring at each other thing again. She was nodding and she put her fingers around his neck. She kept them there while they nodded at each other. Yes yes yes. Hello. Halo. She gave him a little shake. They had this secret thing going. The light faded off the ranges on the mainland but my father's teeth were still showing a little white bite-line under his neat white moustache. His nippy white teeth above the girl Sam's long fingers around his neck. Nodding and nodding. 'Hello.' He could hardly move but he still looked dangerous like a dapper rat. The girl Sam's smooth head pale in the dim light from the wheelhouse. There was a vein in the side of it close to her ear. I'd seen a pulse there but now it was too dark. Whatever plan they'd schemed involved where Frank's *Cao Cao San* boat was going and the people he would find when he got there. The dragon Tamar that he believed took his mother. 'Nothing you can do about it' was what he said. I was going to be there. Because he owed me. Because this was where it all ended.

There was a light blinking on and off on the end of the jetty where the island flattened out. The *Cao Cao San* going forward slowly. The hidden thud of its engine was like the squidder Frank took me off the day I met the woman who would be my little mother. Sometimes the squid stink of it came back I couldn't stop it. When they turned the engine off I heard water smacking the side of the boat a bird in the bush that made a scraping noise and a whistle. The big Riki guy Army held his hand out over us meaning keep quiet. I was feeling sick again remembering the squid stink. The big Riki Army went over the side of the boat. He pressed his nose against men on the jetty. One with a gun over his shoulder. Army walked along the jetty to the beach. He bent down there stirred the water with his hand the same as he did that time up the river at the Riki place. The bird scraped and whistled then it stopped. I was feeling sick remembering the squidder but that was long ago like the gap Frank made with his little mauve hands. We're both old I thought how strange we've decided to end it together. How strange. So old yet Frank still needing to find his mother who left him. What difference did it make. My father who left me.

They lowered Frank down the side in a sling sitting in the girl Sam's lap she had her arms wrapped around his little chest. The girl he called Halo when he could still talk. There was a crane like fishing boats have. He did a wave as he went over then his hand dropped. Not much strength left. They carried him up the dark jetty. He was holding his oxygen tank on his chest. It was like that time we went up the river to the Rikis.

'Where's Gabber's?' was what he said almost the last thing that time back in the boat shed after he fell out of his wheelchair at the lamb carcasses on the river bank. Our only excursion going to 'get noodles'. He made a little squeaky sound I couldn't tell if he was trying to or if it was his wheezy chest. 'Where's Gabber's?'

'His music,' said the girl. He was trying to sing. He had this recording on a memory stick these days he carried it on a string around his neck. She pulled it up out of his shirt and put it in his hand. He liked to hold it. It was what he wanted us to play the day not long after when they came with the jet boat to take him up the river to the Rikis. We got him into the jet boat down the bottom of the slope below the Phaedo Peace House. The girl put ear phones in for him he lay back with that little grin while the jet boat sped up the river. The big Army guy was there and another one driving the boat.

Only when he said, 'Where's Gabber's?' back then in the boat shed that time after the lamb carcasses it came out wrong. I worked it out later. Darkness fell on his speech. Like the bird in the dark bush he did one last scraping whistle of song then he stopped. Whatever was going to happen was already going to happen because he'd made his plans. It was all going to finish. His plans fitting into the space between his past and the present. Between his hands. The space getting smaller and shorter every day it would close up when the last thing he wanted to do was done. Then the space between his hands would be gone he could fold them together and be still. He could clap then stop listening to the music. He could clap because his opera was finished.

That time he made Charlie play his music in the day room the time he completely lost it. Beating on the sofa with his cane. Waving his arms around. 'How many!' The one he called Night Vision was pretending to have a drink through his plastic straw you could see his drink bottle was empty his hand was shaking. 'How many have I seen die for me!' Charlie that he called the Mole was making smoke-time signs at me. 'I am not like other mortals!' This is my father said the voice inside me the one that made me want to get to the end of it. Made me want it to end. The poison words. But this was my father. I was old like him why should I care?

'I am different from other mortals!' yelled my father. 'Hear that?' He kept playing that thing in the day room of the Phaedo over and over the last Act. He frightened everyone away. What could I do? There was this voice inside me that argued with me saying he's your father. That made me go quiet. My silence made him taunt me. 'Take the low-hanging fruit first!' *He saved me.* I didn't know what that meant. I didn't know what believing that meant.

But he lay back calmly smiling listening to the music in the jet boat the day the Rikis took us up the river. It was a few days after he fell over by the frozen lambs. The big Riki

Army's block-of-wood voice: 'All he ever does ay he goes on and on about when he was a kid. On and on mate.' He was talking to me but it was the girl Sam who shouted an answer over the noise of the jet boat.

'He knows what he's doing.'

'On and on mate. All the same.'

Back that day Frank fell out of his wheelchair by the frozen lambs I heard the big guy Army say to the girl Sam in the boat shed, 'No worries. We can go up the river first. Get him fixed up. Clean him up. We can go up to the Riki. We can take him up there. He's got utu with those Binh Xuyens. Well so do we. Their abominations.'

Army was talking to her not me but what he said was for my benefit too. I never heard him say that much again except that time we went up the river to the Rikis he stood up on the platform by the flagpole and talked to the people there. I didn't know what he was saying it was Maori.

You wouldn't notice it was spring down by Gonville where the boat shed was no cherries and peaches starting to blossom but plenty up the river where we went that day the river smacking against the jet boat. The poplars by the old pa sites were green the willows green and orange. Purple buddleia along the river. I remembered smacking across the water in the yellow rubber boat with my little mother.

The little old dying man my father was propped up in the jet boat cockpit his cheeks shiny with cologne and wind. At Upokongaro two jet boats came out they had the red Riki flags. We sped up through fast water in a gorge and came out to cherry orchards in blossom the green of cleared country. I was old and not old the same as my father before he came to the Phaedo Peace House to find my little mother. Now he was going back into spring but I didn't know where I was going yet.

At Hiruharama they had a boom across the river there was a Riki flagpole on the bank. Two women came back along the landing with Army they were looking down at Frank.

'This him?' said one of them. Her lips were dark with that tattoo.

'This the one,' said Army.

My father trying to look dignified I could tell. Sweat ran from under his hat into his eye he had one shut. Mud smell under the jetty and the smell of Frank's piss. We cleaned him up changed his diaper and went on once they'd raised the boom.

No way I could feel sorry for him the man who'd sailed away from us that sail leaning over towards the open sea all those years ago. My father not my father. My father for a few hours between the squid stink and the yellow boat smacking across the waves towards the rainy hills my little mother's eyes only blinking at the spray. My father for as long as that took. My father not my father in that memory.

'Taste the unnecessary tears,' and another Bei Dao poem, 'Who believes in the mask's weeping?'

'Words are the poison in a song,' I said to him more than once when he tried to make me sorry for him. Weeping into his little moustache. I said, 'Bei Dao.' He didn't know what I was talking about. He looked at me then went on telling me his sad story but his voice had changed. He was giving me half the meaning and keeping the rest back.

'Yes. And then what happened?' I asked my father as if I was there to help him with his sadness when I just wanted it to end. Wanted him to stop wasting his time on whatever was biting his reserves like a shark. On that fat Creep his Riki boat this craziness. Wanted my own unworthy thoughts to end.

'This him?'

'This the one.'

What everybody knew about the Rikis what they were fighting for. Pure blood pure water. No immortalised cell line banks no chimeras. But here came this little old crook rich from dealings with Binh Xuyen. From harvesting. From Expectations from Bellerophon chimeras.

'This the one? Going up to Maraekowhai?'

'This the one.'
Get real. Don't be corny.

We went up the Kapiti Island jetty in the dark. Owls hooting in the bush after they turned the big house lights off. I heard the girl Sam looking after my father during the night. In the morning early they locked us in the house. Stuff being taken down the jetty the whine of the crane. The smell of the squidder was inside me. Now it was coming out again like a poisonous leak it was leaking out like time. They said prayers like up at the Riki then we went back on the *Cao Cao San*. The big Army guy stirred the water again by the beach like the night before. Threw some over his head. There were six more on board my father's boat. No one talking. They'd loaded fishing gear up on the deck where it could be seen some orange buoys. They kept us down below out of sight. Why should I still care? Then I thought let him finish what he started I'll be there at the end of it.

Water flew past the boat's windows where Frank lay with his headphones on getting closer to what I'd seen when my mother took me there. Oriental Bay the Festival of Hungry Ghosts. Mee hoon stalls popiah laksa steamboat concessions and the fireworks and dragon boats. The madness of the Seventh Moon crashing cymbals of the street opera. She was old my little mother that time and she died soon after.

'Changed my mind,' she said then. 'Better off without him. You too.' Did she tell me everything she found out? We came back home to the Phaedo Peace House by the river.

That day we went up the river to the Rikis he had the same childish look on his face. The water flying past. My guess he was thinking about board riders the way he often talked. Years ago with my mother later. I couldn't think of her in his life. I didn't want to see him smiling about that as if she was his. With my mother all those years ago when they had

240

that boat the one that leaned over going away. That little sail going out into the grey sea.

Pure water pure blood nobody else can own it. How could my father be the one? 'Better off without him. You too.' The jet boat's wash pushed us against a ramp of tractor tyres in a bend of the river. Many singing birds. A big paddock of thistles. Down river dark lines of hills standing behind each other fading into mist and the river booming in its gorge below. A line of buildings on the rim of the thistle paddock a satellite dish on the ridge.

'Aukati.' Army drew a line across the air where we were. This was the border. This was as far.

Then I had a different thought. I sat there in the boat. It was another shock like my father's curse in the day room. They were lifting my father not my father out of the jet boat. I thought this is the line you cross over and you're dead. You can die. That's what time it is. The girl Sam was helping she was holding his oxygen. 'Clean him up.' I wanted to stop them.

'Low-hanging fruit.'

'Please press buzzer to enter.'

'I have to finish the opera!'

'But ah—the future!'

'You can make a fresh start with your final breath.'

I sat in the jet boat watching him go. Yes that's where he was going. Then I climbed out too and followed. Wide awake clear mind. I thought yes I'm crossing the line. Yes I'm going too. I'm going with him. That's when I decided. Time to finish it. They were over there across the thistles there was a track. They had my father on a stretcher they kept going to the buildings with the setting sun behind.

At one end of the field was a tall pole with four arms and another on the eastern side the sun going down behind the four-arm one. A flagpole near the buildings with a long red pennant flag snapping in the wind.

The girl Sam fingernailing prickles from her trousers. 'There you go Frank,' she said. 'The big Riki.' He was holding her other hand. I thought do you know what time it is? This is when it starts to be over for you Frank. I'm going with you. I'll be there when you finish your opera.

That night Army talked to the people who came. There was a video screen dragged there by a tractor a satellite link with cities crowds of people the FLOW signage. Hundreds of people moving around the Riki flagpole my father being jogged around the pole on his stretcher. Afterwards he slept peacefully all night without anger. I lay awake on one side listening to the girl Sam sleeping on the other. Four of my father's breaths to every one of hers. Little sipping breaths in the mask. The bush was full of owls. In the morning they washed my father in the river we went back down through the gorge. A small red Riki flag around the crown of Frank's hat. We went down river through the blossom trees to the Phaedo Peace House. Frank shook his head no more smoke. He lay and looked out his window. Some days later we went on down the river to the *Cao Cao San*.

'Tutangata Kino,' was what Army said back at the bank below the thistle field. The dragon of the river. Get him on side. Stirring the water there with his hand.

Get him on side before what? The Seventh Moon the Festival of Hungry Ghosts where I was going with my father. How our situations compared.

It was starting to be dark again the third night away from the Phaedo Peace House when we came to the Wellington harbour entrance. Down below the Riki guys assembling weapons not talking to us. The *Cao Cao San* sank down in the water going slow. A moaning noise we went past a buoy with a light. Through the windows I saw strings of lights along the coast. Frank was having his time with no oxygen mask. Eyes shut that smile not a smile. Two weeks now without real food. Hard to tell if he was smiling or if it was just his teeth. The girl Sam helped him with his gastrolyte drink. Then something happened. His hand touched mine. It crept across his blanket and there his little fingers were creeping on the back of my hand. His mouth his teeth made a shape. His tongue tip wetting the shapes of some words.

'Thank you Ruth.' Was that what he said or what I wanted him to say? What did it matter in the end. Both of us so old. My father not my father his daughter not his daughter. How our situations compared. Both of us finishing now finishing the opera. His mother the opera singer was what he believed. My father the terrible Little Frank my mother told me. How he saved me and left us.

'It doesn't matter what I believe,' I said to the little mauve hand chilly on mine. 'It doesn't matter any more what you believe what I believe. No time left now Little Frank.'

There was strength left in his hand a closing. The little white teeth maybe that smile. He was making a sign upwards with his chin. Take me up. Up there.

'Yes,' I said to the big Army guy. 'Now he has to. Now he has to come up. You have to bring him up.'

First thing we saw the lasers in the sky above the casino. Then the sounds of fireworks the sky filling with showering dragon shapes with trees of fire like spring blossom. Red flares and skyrockets rising above the headland then we came around the point into the inner harbour. All around it coloured lights the sky full of falling fire. Lights and smoke around the rim of the harbour by the sea walls the floating restaurants lit up some with lasers some with tethered balloons like dragons. The buildings up the hillsides were all lit the roar and clatter of people came over the water. Tinny cheap echoes of flatbed truck operas. The harbour full of speeding boats with strings of lights. The *Cao Cao San* cut carefully slowly through this. He was watching with those blue forget-me-not eyes wide awake now he was smiling sure enough. The others were all below they put the weapons in sports bags.

I came here once with my little mother before she died. At the time of the Seventh Moon. I never believed any of that stuff nor did she. He's here somewhere that Little Frank your father only he's not really you know that. You watch out said my mother who wasn't really either.

243

'Changed my mind,' she said. 'Better off without him. You too.'

Why should I believe anything? Why should I believe that rubbish the Riki tied around my father's hat the Tutangata Kino water dragon in the wake behind the *Cao Cao San* with lights on it? What I believed was what I saw and heard. 'Those smells making you remember again,' like Bei Dao says.

'Taste the unnecessary tears.'

'Who believes in the mask's weeping?'

'Words are the poison in a song.'

Yes all that and my father's not my father's smile that gave me half his meaning and kept half. That kept the half of what he was doing when he took me off the squidder back before I could tell the difference between remembering and what my little mother not my mother told me.

What I believed when I saw what that cruel little smiling Frank did to Charlie the Mole to Night Vision back at the Phaedo Peace House. I saw it how he terrified them. Transacting with those Abacus Capital Jump You Up squids. I saw that in his accounts. Cunning little smiling Frank. That Aukati line we crossed at Maraekowhai the stretcher with Frank's hat showing on it that fur collar coat going towards the setting sun behind the pole with four arms. I was going with him I made that decision. To the Festival of Hungry Ghosts the moment when his time would close that gap he made to measure. When his hands would close like the girl Halo Sam's did when she did that thing with his neck. Nodding and smiling. Hello hello. When that happened. Comparing our situations. Ending it.

The harbour was full of noise and light but dark by the broken down terminal where the breakwater mole was built up across the front of the marina. On the inside of the breakwater hundreds of small boats some with people living some ferries. That stink of shit generators oil lamps. The backwater at the top of the terminal filthy with rubbish pushed up there by the waves. Wharf timbers leaning crooked and the rusty sides of fishing boats we slid past. I saw *Atlantic Elizabeth* in white on red steel scraped back to rust. *Santa Monica Rarotonga* rusty and white on old blue paint and a gap with water running out that we went past so close I saw torn oily rope and an empty tin on its side. *ZKU2041* half scraped off to metal and a glimpse across the deck with green nets piled up.

'Those smells making you remember again,' Bei Dao.

A bow rope frayed knotted to a yellow bollard like a hump dwarf. The rails filthy with rust and that stink I knew. *Baldur* there freshly painted with a squirt of shit across the middle of the word. A giant scrape below *Baldur* like a collision. These ghosts slid past the dim lights of *Cao Cao San*. *ZMBD* black letters and another hole in the side of the boat with shit dribbling. The squidder that stink a gantry rigged with glaring green lights. We slid past. Back in the dark the crazy sounds from the crowded side of the breakwater. There were kids over there babies crying boat people. White painted numbers measuring off down the front of a red boat with splashes of white paint spilled down it. *3M 8642 2M 8642*. Measuring off the gap between Frank's hands closing under the weight of what was going to happen. A squid stink of time leaking out of the gap. Something like a torn white wetsuit hanging off a rope stretched over to the dark wharf like a pale ghost. Men smoking at the rail of a boat with that squid stink their cigarettes in the dark their voices between the sounds of firecrackers. Fires where people lived in shelters leaned against the old wharf buildings.

Why would I want to remember anything before my little mother? Before my father's sail leaning to the grey sea? Before Dr Jack my grandfather's deep chest voice against my cheek? Frank's curse in the day room my father that my mother said look out for him. Better off without him. Too late now.

'Finish what you start.'

'Those smells making you remember again.'

*

The Creeps were there the fat freak Half Ton waiting in the dark by the wharf gates. All the *Cao Cao San* lights were off. Little fires burning along the wharf under the broken eaves of the terminal people living there in sheet plastic shelters. A little park with trees stripped for firewood above the flood line where the breakwater met the land. The bars of an old security gate were twisted back there and the Creeps pushed Frank through into the park and set him down. I saw the Rikis cross the wharf the other way with those sports bags heading for FLOW. Many others there meeting them from the broken down wharf sheds. Inland from the old terminal the dark flooded wetland with city lights around it shining on the canals and swamp. Why would I want to remember anything like that? The city built on water the thousand lights the smell of fish and shit. All that stuff back before my little mother held me in her arms after Frank took me off the squidder. The Half Ton Creep was holding my father in his arms like a little child and crying on him. Frank's hat fell off his little arms hung down like a doll in that foolish fur collar opera coat. Yes I remember the canal stink the thousand lights the smell of fish. I don't remember anyone held me like that before my little mother. Her arms grabbed me off the squidder's back when the boat heaved up that's what I remember. She held me when I was sick that squid smell coming out of me.

'You hang on there Little Frank when the blue comes back okay,' the big Creep rocking him like a tiny baby. 'Hungry Ghost time now Frank.' His voice like a drum beat. 'Yes yes Little Frank Hungry Ghost time now. Hungry Ghost time now. When the blue comes back.' Like a lullabye. 'Just like you said Frank. When the blue comes back.'

There was a crowd of Creeps there. We set off across the swamp boardwalks. Some went the way the Rikis took. All around us the racket of the Seventh Moon of Hungry Ghosts. Like a war the sky lighting up everywhere.

*

The first time he saw me come into the day room at the Phaedo Peace House I watched something like cold concrete fill up his veins. Because I wasn't my little mother he'd hoped for. Who he thought he could come back to. That little smile like he was holding something in his teeth until it stopped moving. Just clenched on it. He was walking around with a phone and that memory stick with music. That piece of paper folded with the big Creep's text copied out. First time in months after looking out his window not speaking.

The next time we met he saw I knew something about his mother who left him. I watched time shutter down in his eyes. There were memories coming back in there somewhere but he didn't know what they were. After that he was always trying to make me talk.

'Take the low-hanging fruit first.'

I watched what happened to his face. The cold concrete in his veins time shuttering down his eyes memories he didn't know they were. When I told him what my mother told me. His mother leaving him for a Binh Xuyen dragon guy. His deal with Binh Xuyen. He just left the room. 'Have to finish the opera.' His crazy piecing everything together.

'Made a wrong turn.'

'Something new out there.'

'You have to know whose turn it is to laugh.'

'Get real.'

'Foreign Corn.'

The racket of the Festival of Hungry Ghosts was all around us but at a distance where we waited on the far side of the swamp for the big Half Ton Creep to do the next thing.

'But ah—the future!' What Frank used to say. That smile I couldn't talk to.

What the big Army Riki guy said back at the boat shed that time Frank fell out of his wheelchair by the frozen lambs. Why should I believe any of it this craziness. But Frank couldn't talk any more. 'The red one that's the Riki. When there's trouble brewing we use that one.'

The big Creep put Frank's red Riki hat back on his

head. 'We use that one.' Hungry Ghosts talking. When the transport arrived we loaded him in while explosions shook the windows.

Sometimes back then at the Phaedo Peace House he would lean forward when he talked sometimes he sat back and made a space for me to fill up but I wouldn't. His long stories to make me sorry for him but his smile that mocked me. His tears I didn't believe. The half he kept back.

'My mother put paua shells over my ears. I heard video waves. I'd sneak down the back of Geek's place. The pirate ship video game. My mother would find me asleep there. Her neck had a soft part where it went into her shoulder. The rest was thin and hard. I'd put my face in the soft part when we were on the bus going home. It was getting dark and I could hear video game waves down the end of our street.'

'We're running out of time Frank.'

'I couldn't tell where I stopped and she began.'

I watched the predictable tear run out of my father's forget-me-not blue eye into his fussy little moustache. 'Is this going anywhere Frank?'

'I lived more and more at Geek's place which video games filled with the sound of the sea at Lyall Bay. Until the day my mother didn't come to pick me up at all.' He imitated a little boy voice and the voice of his uncle. '*Where did Mum go, Uncle Geek? I dunno, son, but I bet it was a long way from you.*'

Then his tears stopped and I saw the other Little Frank the one that terrorised my patients. 'Go on.' As if I could stop him.

'What kept me to my purpose.' Little Frank sitting forward the blue eyes like little acetylene torches. The same stuff over and over session after session. '*I remember his giant hands holding the tiny platinum spoon without difficulty working it into the flesh of the pears. I remember the murdered planet stretching all about us.*'

He remembered these comics the video games his mother. He made himself remember everything. Everything hurt him. Then there was what he couldn't remember because he didn't know it. His mother leaving him for the Binh Xuyen dragon. I told him what I knew. 'I was General Cannibal.' That smile to murder. 'My intergalactic cabin cruiser had free lunch drive.' He was a hundred and twenty years old about to fold his hands over the moment his time ran out. No more expectations. 'My tusk bit Halo's shoulder. I was going to reduce a planet to rubble.' He was in a story he was telling himself one he could remember now as though it was happening to him.

'Get real.'

He gave me that look as if to say what do you think this is?

'Why are you telling me this? Don't you think it's a bit late?'

He sat forward in his chair. 'Out at the Raglan Bar Hokkaido and I watched the windsurfers flying into the air above the breakers. I remember this morning because we were a perfect match your mother and I. We ate the same little amounts. We drank the same little amounts. I loved her,' said my father not my father. He was dry and cool talking one hand holding his phone and that memory stick with the opera music to make him calm. 'I remember this early summer morning of my life with Hokkaido which I thought was perfect and deserved to go on for ever because it was about to change for ever.' Then he did those voices again. '*Where did mum go Uncle Geek? I dunno son but I bet it was a long way from you.*'

Comparing our situations. I looked back there he was his boat leaning over out there a little white sail against the grey sea the grey sky. Where you couldn't see where one started the other stopped. And never saw him again for what? More than a hundred years.

'Don't expect anything from Little Frank,' was what my little mother said that he called Hokkaido. Whenever he said her name he made his beautiful little mouth his smile round and soft around the word of her name as if he was blowing a kiss maybe a kiss goodbye.

They lifted Frank out of the transport in a yard next to the big hospital chimneys. Stink of doused fire in the blackened yard. Smell of old hospital stuff on the stairs like disinfectant drain water bad breath of broken aircon. Frank riding on Half Ton's back like a little child his hat with the red band. The girl Sam there always just behind with his oxygen. Big explosions out there in the city the red light of fires through the dirty windows. The light from a helicopter choppering to the roof. I saw my father's teeth when he turned his head that way. He was making a biting movement maybe it was his breathing without oxygen maybe he was making the shapes of words. Wolfish and ready still that look aside when we went past a security guard lying in blood on the green floor of a corridor. Frank's plans. Gunfire somewhere at the other side of the hospital.

She was there the doctor in a room with a fountain and green plants a big picture window. The Creeps had her sitting in a chair her face lit by real fire not fireworks from across the city FLOW my guess the Rikis with their sports bags. Sirens and explosions helicopters out there and in here my father's teeth to bite hidden in his mask now. The girl Sam holding it.

The doctor looking at him. 'My my Frank.' A mannish voice a kind of hiss. 'A bit the worse for wear my dear.'

I thought he was nodding my father. Yes yes yes. Hello. He moved the mask aside himself. That smile not a smile. His mouth making a shape a word. Tamar.

'Tamar.' The Creep Half Ton said it voice like a big engine. He was making the word the shape of my father's mouth that biting smile. Tamar. That smile stretched thin his head with the Riki flag hat nodding. Yes yes yes. Halo. Looking at the girl Halo Sam nodding that smile.

'Tamar,' her voice sweet and clear. 'Hello.'

'You too big man,' said the doctor. 'My my.' She was looking at Half Ton. 'And who's the child?' The girl Sam didn't answer she stepped behind the doctor she was watching Little Frank.

What I knew my mother told me. Tamar was a dragon title it got passed on. Tamar the dragon that took his mother the one Frank made his deal with in his mind the same.

'Who'd have thought it. Little Frank.' The hissing doctor Tamar not trying to move. 'There's just no stopping you Frank is there.'

Another shape of words on my father's little mouth under his moustache. That nodding that smile. A silent shape with 'Ah' in it opening his little wolf rat mouth wide around it. 'Ah.' And again, 'Ah.'

'But ah—the future!' Half Ton reading my father's little mouth not watching the girl Sam behind the dragon Tamar. Watching Frank that nodding smile when she moved so fast the girl I almost didn't see it the doctor's head snapped sideways. Her fingers around the doctor's neck. Siss out of breath. My father Frank and the girl nodding at each other nodding the way they did their routine. The girl's long fingers around the doctor's neck. That vein like a beating worm in the girl's head. The doctor's eyes were red lit up by fire outside the big window then they shut her tongue came out the wet colour of liver. That dead squid shit smell there it was again. Time leaking out the doctor's time this time. What Frank knew this time.

'Tamar.' My father's silent smile that word shape peaceful now before the oxygen mask went on again. His eyes closed and peaceful now. Worked everything out at last. *Peaced* it together his joke. Like my little mother said watch out for Frank for Little Frank. You never know. Finish what you start.

*

251

Always trying to get me to talk at the Phaedo Peace House back when we had our meetings. I couldn't get my own words past Frank's smile that gave half of what he meant and kept half back his words the poison in a song. His words all gone now time leaking out the gap closing up almost shut now.

'Get real Frank.' When I said that to him those times back at the Peace House I heard an echo my mother saying it to me. 'Don't be corny.' His crazy piecing together that broke the doctor's neck he thought was Tamar. That killed the dragon. Yes he was crazy but he got what he wanted the dragon Tamar's breath hissing out for the last time.

Helicopters with search lights over there on the other side of the city. Stink of burning in the hospital yard lit up now by fire. Hungry Ghost fireworks or explosions I couldn't tell the difference.

Now what?

'The Chinese Opera.'

Where we were going. Little Frank's plan.

In the yard below the burning hospital I watched the girl Halo Sam say goodbye to my father. She lifted him against her. His little arms hung down in the opera fur collar coat his Riki hat fell off. Halo hello. Frank's little smile. She was gone running aslant the yard into the dark. The transport stopped at the edge of a market people running with looted goods. Frank on a trolley we went through the market. Outside the Chinese Opera bodies on the pavement the gold crimson façade pocked with bullet holes. Half Ton's people wheeled him in my father Little Frank through the dragon entrance.

'See she's here. Madame Hee. Like I promised.' Half Ton carried him down past scarlet drapes to where the Chinese Opera singer waited with flickering oil lamps waxy sheen of greasepaint her brocade sleeves spread across a sofa. 'Like I promised Little Frank.'

*

What could I tell him that he needed to hear then? What did I know that he didn't? It was too late for any more words between us. Now it was finishing. We went in with Half Ton through the big red and gold dragon entrance of the Chinese Opera. There he lay a little husk in his fur collar opera coat with that hat the red Riki band around it. No oxygen mask on his face now pink and papery cheeked almost nothing left but that smile. How he knew everything and damaged everyone. My father not my father Little Frank's eyes clear and blue as usual never leaving the face of the painted singer who held his head the only part of him with any weight left in it. Cradled his little head on the curve where her neck joined her shoulder. He looked like a little boy my father and he looked like a terrible old man I couldn't see where one stopped and the other began. What was the sky what was the sea. What was the sea and what was video game waves he used to say to make me sorry for him.

The opera singer's face was white and red like a mask but the lips that were making the shapes and sounds of the Italian language were exquisite like Little Frank's. The rims of these lips were fine a coo of courtesy and bliss. Words the poison in a song but now how sweet like Little Frank's that smile. Little Frank was smiling now his time running out his sweet smile all that was left of him. Then the little blue forget-me-not eyes closed I stopped my sob with a towel scented with Madame Hee's make-up the old smell of the Chinese Opera.

But he was still smiling my little father his smile the silent half of what his mother's lips were singing in the painted pink and white face of Madame Hee. This was true at the moment Little Frank's time ran out. Little Frank's mother that Tamar stole from him that left him to learn his junk shop vengeance singing the words they both knew they were singing together. *Quanti ho visto morire per me! How many have I seen die for me.* The reward for his patience my father not my father finished the opera. So it finished.

Madame Hee moved her fastidious sleeves aside. 'So this is the one,' no expression on her painted face. Little Frank lay on the sofa his fur collar framing that smile. The oil lamps flickered as she passed them on her way out.

Little Frank rest in peace. My father not my father. May the things that happened to you in your life pass away with you. May your consequences like you always said with that smile may these also reach their deadline one day. Time Out some time and end their schedules.